MESSAGE FROM A KILLER

I stepped closer to my hotel-room door. The flower arrangement was more wide than tall, and it spread in front of the kick plate. My eyes had stopped watering, and I paused some twelve feet from the door. The colors were a jumble of greens, golds, and tans. But no cut flower I knew, even a fresh one, shimmered quite like that.

Plus, the arrangement seemed jagged, much too jagged for a professional bouquet. I crept a foot or two closer. Was that a feather sticking out from the top? It *was* a feather, although that didn't make much sense.

I froze. My eyesight had cleared. It wasn't an arrangement of blooms and bulbs, leaves and stems. It was fabric, poking out from a greasy paper grocery sack. It had been left on the ground where I'd be sure to find it.

I forced myself to walk the last few feet to the door. I bent to pluck the feather from the sack. It was a quill, of all things. A pheasant quill, with barbs ripped out at random spots. A quill like the one used in Ivy's Victorian hat.

My fingers released the feather, and it twirled to the floor. Whoever destroyed Ivy's hat must have been angry, because the cuts were jagged, unplanned. They must have found the hat on the front porch, where I'd forgotten it once Lance arrived.

Why would someone destroy her beautiful hat like that? Even smashed, the hat was exquisite and obviously expensive. Now it sat in a ripped grocery sack, a jumble of tulle, ribbon and felt, topped with a bedraggled pheasant quill.

It was a message, obviously. Someone wanted to frighten me. I'd been holding my breath for the past few moments, which I slowly exhaled. If that was the person's goal, they'd accomplished their mission . . .

Murder at Morningside

A Missy DuBois Mystery

Sandra Bretting

LYRICAL UNDERGROUND
Kensington Publishing Corp.
www.kensingtonbooks.com

LYRICAL UNDERGROUND BOOKS are published by

Kensington Publishing Corp.
119 West 40th Street
New York, NY 10018

All Kensington titles, imprints, and distributed lines are available at special quantity discounts for bulk purchases for sales promotion, premiums, fund-raising, educational, or institutional use.

Special book excerpts or customized printings can also be created to fit specific needs. For details, write or phone the office of the Kensington Sales Manager: Kensington Publishing Corp., 119 West 40th Street, New York, NY 10018. Attn. Sales Department. Phone: 1-800-221-2647.

First Electronic Edition: May 2016
eISBN-13: 978-1-60183-713-4
eISBN-10: 1-60183-713-5

First Print Edition: May 2016
ISBN-13: 978-1-60183-714-1
ISBN-10: 1-60183-714-3

Printed in the United States of America

For my daughters, Brooke and Dana. Because once upon a time we sat on your bunk beds and made up stories about a beautiful princess who lived in a faraway kingdom. Thank you for that memory.

Chapter 1

Time rewound with each footfall as I began to climb the grand outer staircase at Morningside Plantation. The limestone steps, burdened with the history of five generations, heaved their way toward heaven.

At the top lay a wide-plank veranda supported by columns painted pure white, like the clouds. By the time I took a third step, the digital camera in my right hand began to dissolve into the sterling-silver handle of a lady's parasol. The visitors' guide in my left hand magically transformed into a ballroom dance card bound by a satin cord.

Another step and the Mississippi River came into view as it flowed to the Gulf, languid as a waltz and the color of sweet tea. Could that be a whistle from a steamboat ferrying passengers past the plantation? If so, a turn and a wave wouldn't be out of the question once I reached the top of the stairs, and good manners would dictate it.

I was about to do that when I realized the whistle was only my friend's cell and not a Mississippi riverboat. "Ambrose! Turn that thing off. Honestly."

"Sorry." He shrugged. "I always forget you were Scarlett O'Hara in a past life."

The mood was broken, though, and the sterling silver in my hand returned to plastic, while the linen dance card hardened to a glossy brochure. Ambrose patiently waited while I finished climbing the stairs.

Whenever we're out and about somewhere new, my best friend likes to go all out. Today he wore a striped bow tie and seersucker jacket from Brooks Brothers. Never let it be said Southern men didn't know how to dress. Of course, as a wedding-gown designer, he had more fashion sense than most, and his favorite motto was one could never be too rich or too fabulous, even though we both had more fabulous than money at this point.

"It's almost time for the tour," Ambrose said.

I wasn't ready to release the fantasy, though. "Isn't it magnificent?" The veranda wound around the entire first floor, broad enough for a dozen wooden rocking chairs, most of which faced east. Black storm shutters framed the windows, like dark lapels on a white dinner jacket, and they matched an enormous front door with beveled glass. Suddenly the door swung open, as if to welcome its lost owners home.

"Welcome to Morningside Plantation." A girl, probably a coed at nearby Louisiana State, appeared. "My name's Beatrice, and I'll be leading the four-thirty tour." Her pleated skirt and starched collar were almost enough to make me cry with happiness, though I refrained. "Looks like you're my only guests today. Feel free to pretend you're staying here in the spring of eighteen hundred and fifty-five. By the way, I love your hat. Blue is my favorite color."

It was lapis, but no need to nitpick. Obviously she had a good head on her shoulders. "Thank you. I made it."

The girl ushered us through the foyer and into a glittery ballroom. Every curtain, the ceiling and the floors, not one but two fireplace mantels, all of it had been gilded to within an inch of its life. A parade of professional-looking wedding portraits marched along the mantels.

"May I have your tour tickets, please?" Beatrice asked.

"I was told the tour was included with our reservation." Not that I wanted to speak for Ambrose, but I'd been the one to book our stay at the plantation. As soon as the bride asked him to design a custom gown and then turned around and asked me to create a one-of-a-kind veil, I called up to reserve our rooms for the weekend.

"You're staying at the plantation?" Beatrice waved her hand. "Then you're right. It's all included." She drew closer, as if she wanted to share an important secret with me. "After the tour, I hope you'll peek around. There are nooks and crannies everywhere. Some people even say the mansion's haunted." She smiled slyly before resuming her tour-guide pose. "This ballroom was painted pure gold on the orders of Horace Andrews. Even though the Victorians loved their color, he didn't want a bunch of bright colors to distract from his daughters' beauty."

I must have looked a tad incredulous, because she rushed on. "That's what they say, anyway."

"Is that the lady of the house?" I pointed to an oil painting above one of the mantels, which showed a gloved woman in a silk bodice who looked to be about my age. Or, as I liked to say, on the north side of thirty. She even had the same auburn hair and emerald eyes.

"Yes, that's Mrs. Andrews. She had twelve children before she died."

Before Beatrice could say more, the front door flew open and in stomped an elderly gentleman. He was on the verge of a good, old-fashioned hissy fit.

"Y'all don't deserve a say in this wedding!" he said to a young woman who'd slunk in behind him.

The girl looked to be the right age for his daughter. She wore flip-flops and a wrinkled peasant blouse, and she buried her head in her hands. Well, that lifted the blouse an inch or two and exposed her bare stomach.

Lorda mercy. It seemed the girl and her fiancé must have eaten supper before they said grace, as we said here in the South, because an unmistakable bump appeared under her top. She looked to be about four months along, give or take a few weeks, and I could see why her daddy wasn't too happy with her right about now.

After a piece, she lifted her chin and glared at him. "I hate you!" Her voice rippled as cold as the river water that ran nearby. "I wish you were dead." She stalked away.

I fully expected the man to cringe, or at least follow her. Instead, he merely glanced our way and shrugged. After a minute, he pivoted on the spectacle he'd caused and casually strolled away, leaving a bit of frost in the air.

"Oh, my. Why don't we continue?" Beatrice said.

Poor Beatrice. She obviously wanted to divert our attention elsewhere. It couldn't have been every day one of her hotel guests wished another guest was dead. She hustled us farther into the ballroom, as if nothing had happened, all the while explaining the history of Morningside Plantation.

Turned out one of the grandest plantations in the South almost didn't make it through the Civil War. If it hadn't been for some Union soldiers who couldn't bear to see it destroyed, the mansion might have been shelled like its neighbors. All I could think of was hallelujah for chivalry and those cavalrymen's romantic natures.

"As I mentioned, the Andrewses had twelve children. One of them, Jeremiah, died in the war. Some of the maids swear they've seen a soldier patrolling the halls after dark."

Now, I've read my share of stories about ghosts—mostly in the *National Enquirer* at the Food Faire—but they always haunted musty graveyards or neglected attics and not elegant ballrooms painted pure gold. "But this place is much too pretty to be haunted."

"The house used to be a plantation with a bunkhouse for slaves. Think about it . . . there are probably hundreds of restless spirits here."

First deceased Confederate soldiers and now wandering ghosts. It was all becoming a bit much. "We'll be sure and let you know if we have any visitors tonight. Won't we, Ambrose?"

Before my friend could reenter the conversation, though, someone else's cell rang.

"I'm sorry." Beatrice reached into a pocket and pulled hers out. "Looks like it's the front desk. Do you mind if I let you explore this room on your own for a few minutes? It's not what we usually do, but this shouldn't take long."

I covered my joy with a quick nod. "Of course not. We don't mind at all. Take your time. We'll be fine until you get back."

She hustled away and quietly shut the door behind her.

Gracious light! If she believes we'll actually stay in one place, she is one brick shy of a load.

I quickly grabbed hold of Ambrose's arm. "C'mon, Bo. Follow me." I counted to three and then opened the door and stepped into the hall. Ever since we'd walked through the front door, there was one other room I'd been dying to see. It'd called to me from the foyer. Only, I couldn't do much more than peek at it through the doorway until now. The coast was clear. I tiptoed down the hall with Ambrose in tow, until it appeared.

The dining room. Dripping in yellow paint with matching curtains, it looked like a pat of melted butter. A gleaming mahogany table had been set for fourteen with bone china, crystal stemware, and delicate bowls for washing one's fingers. Had a room ever looked so magnificent?

I pulled a mahogany chair away from the table and delicately perched on its silk cushion.

"Missy!" Ambrose frowned at me, though he probably wished he'd thought of it first.

"I'm not hurting anything." Lord knows the chair had lasted more than a hundred and fifty years, and it surely would last another hundred or so whether I enjoyed it or not. It was meant to be sat on. But much as I hated to admit it, the carved chair-back did *not* feel good against my spine, and I rose again. "You wouldn't like it. Hard as nails."

I moved past the offending chair to a pair of windows. With elaborate gilt cornices and silk tassel tiebacks, they looked like something from an old-fashioned movie theater. Couldn't help but notice the picture-perfect May weather outside. Almost nice enough to compete with the gorgeousness inside.

I was about to mention it to Ambrose when something caught my ear. A low voice, quick with anger, its fierceness surprising. Whatever could someone possibly find to argue about in such a glorious place? The curtain sheers lifted easily enough and there was Beatrice, with her back to an azalea bush and her cell to her ear.

"I told you no." For someone who was supposedly dealing with the front desk, she sounded awfully mad. "Don't call me until after the wedding. You know what you have to do."

Ambrose quickly joined me by the window. "Well, well. What have we here?"

"Sounds like this place has more drama than wandering ghosts." All I could think of was hallelujah . . . and pass the finger food.

Chapter 2

A warm glow prodded me awake the next morning as sunshine seeped through the curtain sheers in my room. What a fantastic way to be wakened, watching everything lighten from rose to cotton candy to baby-girl pink, with nothing better to do than sit back and enjoy the show.

Time for my wake-up call to Ambrose. Normally he was up long before I was, and he'd have finished the *Times-Picayune* by the time I called. The scenery must have slowed him down, though, because he didn't answer when I dialed his room, or maybe he'd already left for the morning. Either way, I gave up after five rings.

I gathered my things and walked into the bathroom. A claw-footed bathtub sat next to a marble double sink. Once I figured out how to use the bath's handheld sprayer, after spritzing the sink, I came to like it. Easier to wash shampoo from my long hair and twice as quick.

Someone knocked on the door to my room as I stepped out of the tub.

"Hey, Missy. You up yet?" It was Ambrose, of course.

"Give me a minute," I yelled. Guess he'd had time for the paper and a morning stroll. Luckily for him, I can put on my face and fix my hair in fifteen minutes flat. I grabbed a towel and stepped into the bedroom. "Do you mind if we walk around a bit before breakfast?" I asked, as I towel-dried my hair. There was a good chance he might say no. He'd already been out and about, and Ambrose wasn't charitable about much else getting in the way when it came to his stomach.

"Would you like that? Well then, that's what we'll do."

It warmed my heart he could put my happiness above his appetite. "You're the best!"

We walked down the hall a short while later. Ambrose had convinced me the night before to wear my mint-green shorts that matched his, so we looked like two juleps walking down the hall. That was the wonderful thing about having a fashion designer for a best friend. Tons of fashion advice worth its weight in gold lamé.

No sooner had we walked down the stairs and reached the landing when someone rushed past.

"Lorda mercy!" I said.

The girl stopped and turned, her face flushed to high heavens. "I'm so sorry. Excuse me."

It was Beatrice, our tour guide from the day before, wearing a felt hat called a *cloche* from the Roaring Twenties and a beaded dress to match. Whatever could Beatrice be doing running around the hall looking like an old-time flapper?

"Beatrice, is that you?"

She finally slowed and took a deep breath. "Yes. Sorry if I startled you. I'm very late."

I tried not to stare, but her hat was terribly intriguing. Lace embellished the felt and a petersham ribbon decorated its side. The milliner had done a bang-up job of balancing the ribbon against the angle of the brim, something I knew a thing or two about.

So many people took a fancy to the hats I whipped up for Derby parties and whatnot while I was a student at Vanderbilt that I decided to open a hat shop right here on the Great River Road. And not just any hats. My specialty was designing custom veils and fascinators for brides, who were a sight more difficult to manage than your average customer. Bless their hearts. Part of me always wished I'd majored in psychology at Vanderbilt and not fashion design.

After a few years in Tennessee, I shipped my grandma's chifforobe to Bleu Bayou and scouted for a storefront. Before long, Crowning Glory opened next door to Ambrose's Allure Couture, and the rest, as they say, was history.

"Are you giving another tour?" I asked.

"It's not a tour." Beatrice laid her hand against her heart. "I need to open the tearoom for our hat competition. Those ladies don't like to be kept waiting."

Glory be! I'd stumbled upon a hatbox full of potential clients. The good Lord did work in mysterious ways. "You don't say."

Of course, sometimes a hotel placed a limit on the number of people who could participate, so I could be setting myself up for a big dose of disappointment. "I don't suppose you have room for one more, do you?"

"I'll have to check. We stopped taking reservations yesterday, and I'm not sure how many the front desk got. All I know is I'd better be done with the tearoom by eleven or I'll be in big trouble." Her eyes narrowed a smidge. "I'm not even supposed to be here today."

"Then why are you working?"

"I need the money. You know how it is."

I gave a heavy sigh. "Do I ever. On the plus side, that hat of yours is amazing." And that was the God-honest truth. The black felt didn't look out of place, even in daylight, and it suited her dark hair and almond-colored eyes. Of course, the milliner did pick out the easiest fabric to work with when she chose felt, which was ten times easier to block than straw or fabric, but I couldn't fault her for that.

"Thank you." Her frown disappeared. "I guess the wedding this weekend has me flustered. Everything has to be perfect."

"Are you a friend of the bride?" Ambrose asked.

"I wouldn't say that." In fact, she didn't seem to want to say much more, because her eyes darted past us as if looking for a way out of the conversation.

"Then you must be a friend of the groom," I said.

"It's complicated. Let's just say I don't think there should be a wedding. I've got to go now or I'll be really late. Mr. Solomon told me to be done with the room by eleven." She turned away and hustled past us as quick as anything.

"Did that seem strange to you?" Ambrose asked, once she disappeared.

"Sounds like she doesn't agree with the wedding." Or the bride. "Though I can't imagine why." At least we had complimented her hat. "C'mon, Bo. Let's get some eggs in you before you faint." We headed for the restaurant, which was located at the south end of the property.

After a few minutes, Ambrose reached for my arm. "Wait a minute. You know you should go to the hat competition. There's no telling how many new customers you could get."

Sweet of him to say, what with his empty stomach and all. "Of course, you're right. It *would* be fun to look around." I'd entered a few hat contests in my day, and both times I'd won the grand prize and a handful of new clients. "Do you think I have time?"

"You won't know until you try. I'll check with the front desk while you go and get fixed up. How about that lapis one you wore yesterday?"

Only my Bo would know the difference between lapis and plain ol' blue. "I brought even nicer ones." In fact, my parabuntal straw would be perfect. And it matched my spring shift with wildflowers that bloomed across the front. "You sure you don't mind?"

"Not at all. You hop upstairs, and I'll go put you on the list."

"Thanks. You're the best." Quickly, I pecked him on the cheek and hurried away as I planned the whole thing out in my head. Straw hat, spring dress, Chanel Rouge lipstick. People normally went all out for these things, so maybe I'd add white gloves and sass it up as someone on her way to a garden party. I'd completed the outfit in my mind when voices sounded from somewhere down the hall.

"You can't go through with this!" It sounded like Beatrice again, and she seemed ready to spit nails. What was it about this place that made people yell so at each other?

"Trust me." A man's voice. "I know what I'm doing."

When I rounded the corner, I almost collided with Beatrice and a man who looked like a cover model straight out of New York City. Like one of the models in a Ralph Lauren ad, with teeth as shiny as my grandma's pearl necklace and just as straight. Gorgeous. He was simply gorgeous. But handsome or not, the stranger glared at me as if I'd waltzed into his photo shoot by accident.

"I'm sorry—" I said.

"Do you mind? This is private." He spit the words between the pearly teeth.

Reluctantly, I began to back away. Beatrice must have been really upset because the cloche lay on the ground, where it puddled like an ink stain. I would have scooped it up for her, since felt crushed so easily, but this didn't seem like the time, nor the place. In fact, I would have loved to sink into the carpet and reappear as a housefly on the plantation's wallpaper. Maybe then I could figure out why the Ralph Lauren model had stopped yelling at Beatrice and now cupped her chin so lovingly in the palm of his hand.

Utterly confused, I turned away from them and almost got lost on the way to my room. The way that man cut his eyes at me! As if I'd purposefully eavesdropped. Which couldn't have been further from the truth, since I knew better than to make eye contact with them if I wanted to overhear something juicy. Not that I had any experience with that sort of thing.

No use spending all morning worrying about other people's problems. I made it to my room again and pulled the key from my pocket.

Once inside, I flung open the closet door and pulled out my Sunday-go-t'-meetin' spring dress. Then I slipped out of my shorts and top, slid into the dress, and dislodged the hatbox from its place on the shelf. This one had given me fits and starts when I steamed it onto the form, since the brim was a foot and a half around, but it played up my green eyes nicely.

I quickly stabbed a couple of hat pins under the brim, drew on a slash of Chanel lipstick, and scooted out the door. This time, if I ran into Beatrice and that male model, I might pretend to divert my attention elsewhere and overhear some juicy snatches they might throw my way.

By the time I arrived at the tearoom, the two had disappeared. The room buzzed with conversation, and I paused on the threshold to work up my courage. *Oh, my.* Women and girls wearing hats, just like me, filled the place. They were at oval tables set for five and passed delicate trays back and forth. I scanned the competition and noticed that most people had chosen conservative trilbies, tiny fascinators, and even a beret or two. No one was brave enough to wear something oversized, which would work in my favor.

The din softly faded as people seemed to notice my arrival. It reminded me of all the times I floated into a Derby party, little whispers coming from under the hats. I squared my shoulders and did my best catwalk strut into the tearoom to a spot at the first table. After a second, the conversations around me resumed, which was just as well, and I finally exhaled.

"What an interesting hat!" A lady across the way leaned over the table. "Most people wouldn't be able to carry off a brim that big."

Here in the South there's a fine line between a true compliment and a backhanded one, and since I couldn't quite tell the stranger's intentions, I decided to play it safe.

"Why, thank you. It's my own creation. And yours is interesting too." It looked expensive, with curled quills that fanned out in all directions, with not a stitch to be seen. She must have found a very good milliner in her hometown. "Love the pheasant quills."

"Thank you, kindly."

Truth be told, it was a beautiful re-creation of a Victorian-era hat, and she wore a high-buttoned silk blouse to boot. This one was going to be tough to beat.

"However did you pack that?" I asked. "Feathers do tend to get crushed."

"Isn't that the truth."

Since I still couldn't decipher my tablemate's intentions, I reached for a porcelain teacup, in lieu of saying more. Flowered pots sat on every table, along with sugar cubes, stir sticks, and tea bags. Mostly Earl Greys, with a few Bigelows thrown in for good measure.

"Luckily, I didn't have to travel very far." Then she poured hot water into her cup and began to steep a tea bag in it. "My stepdaughter, Trinity, is getting married here tonight."

"What a coincidence! Her wedding planner hired me to make the veil." Thank goodness I'd been civil to her, since she'd be the one to pay the 1200 dollars for a custom creation of Alençon lace. "I'm Missy DuBois. The planner hired my shop to do the bridesmaids' hats too."

"But of course. Ivy Solomon. Charmed, I'm sure." She glanced at a diamond watch on her wrist and frowned. "Trinity should have been here by now. She promised she'd come down and keep me company."

"Really? I'd have thought the bride would have a million other things to do, what with the ceremony and all."

"Oh, no. The wedding planner took care of everything. Which didn't leave any room for me, I'm afraid."

What a shame. To be the stepmother of the bride and have nothing to show for it on a big day like today. "That's too bad. I'd think she'd want your opinion on everything."

Well, that did the trick. Ivy stood and scooted over to an empty spot beside me, her tea cooling in her cup. Apparently she wasn't standoffish. At least not when she liked which way the conversation was going.

"It's enough to make me cry," she said. "Here she went and spent all that money on a 'professional' when I could have told her just as well what courses to serve."

I offered her my hand. "Nice to finally meet you."

"Likewise." She placed her palm in mine. "Now, where did you say you're from?"

I hadn't, but that was neither here nor there. "Bleu Bayou. Down the road a piece."

Her eyes widened. "Why, my whole family's from Bleu Bayou. The Girards. Have you met them yet?"

"Met them? The very first person who welcomed me to town was Maribelle Girard, right around Christmastime. Couldn't have been nicer to me."

For the next few minutes, Ivy Solomon and I talked about her family and mine, the things we liked and disliked about wedding planners, and all the ways in which a good hat could make anything better. By the time Beatrice finished working the room and stepped up to the podium, we were thicker than thieves and laughing like a pair of wild hyenas.

We stopped when Beatrice began to speak.

"We're going to start in a few minutes," she said into the microphone. She'd apparently pulled herself together after the spat in the hall and placed the cloche back on her head, where it belonged. "First prize is a weekend in Charleston, so good luck to everyone."

Not knowing what to expect, I glanced around the room at the others. Two dozen women sat at tables like mine, sipping from porcelain cups and nibbling on Walker shortbreads. Some wore parabuntal straws, the tightly-woven ones that were impossible to block, while others had on felt cloches, like Beatrice.

"Wherever can Trinity be?" Ivy glanced at her watch again. "She's not perfect, but she *is* punctual. Something must be wrong."

"She'll be here, I'm sure. Cookie?" I passed her the plate of shortbreads in an attempt to take her mind off her troubles.

"You don't understand." Ivy didn't even glance at the platter. "Ever since Trinity was little, I could set my clock by her. Ballet lessons, art classes, piano recitals . . . I can't tell you how many times I had to wait in the car with her because we were too early for something or other. I'd better go see what's keeping her."

"But you'll miss the competition." I lowered the plate only when it became obvious Ivy had no interest in anything but finding her stepdaughter.

"How is everyone this morning?" Beatrice approached our table, looking as sunny as the skies outside. "What beautiful hats! We'll have to take your picture for our web site. Promise you won't leave before we can do that."

Quickly, Ivy reached out and grabbed Beatrice's wrist. "We can't start yet. My stepdaughter isn't here."

Beatrice glanced at me helplessly as the skin above her wrist blanched white.

"I'm sure it's nothing," I said. "She probably overslept, what with all the excitement."

"But this isn't like her. I can't understand what's taking her so long."

"What if I go check?" Beatrice managed to dislodge her wrist from Ivy's grasp. "We're not going to start for a few minutes. I can run upstairs. It'll only take me a second."

"Would you?" Ivy asked. "She's in room two-fifteen. She's a light sleeper, so you won't have to knock very hard. Tell her I'm waiting."

"Yes, ma'am." Beatrice turned to leave, rubbing her wrist.

Now that everything was under control, I relaxed a bit. "Tell me about the wedding." Anything to take her mind off her absent stepdaughter.

"First of all, the designer who made her gown told Trinity she should put the bridesmaids in black. Can you imagine? He said it's quite popular on the East Coast. I had to put my foot down on that one. Why would the bridesmaids wear black for a spring wedding?"

I tried not to smile. She had no way of knowing Ambrose and I were friends. "Hmm. What did he say when you told him no?"

"I imagine he took offense. That's the one good thing about hiring a wedding planner. She had to be the one to say that, not me."

We chatted a bit more about the wedding colors—peach and cream won out—the flowers, the dance music, and whatnot. Turned out Mr. Solomon hired the Baton Rouge Symphony Orchestra to play "Here Comes the Bride" on the front lawn. Between that and a fireworks display set to explode at midnight, I got the feeling the bride could have bought a house in Bleu Bayou for the cost of this wedding.

Just then Beatrice dashed into the tearoom and made a beeline for our table.

"She's gone."

Since the girl seemed to have a flair for melodrama, I didn't get too worked up. "Slow down. What do you mean, she's gone? Maybe she took a walk to get some fresh air."

Beatrice shook her head. "The maid told me no one used her room last night. Said she left chocolates on the pillow, and they haven't been touched."

I glanced at Ivy. While I did *not* want to be indelicate, there was one obvious explanation. "Could she be with her fiancé?" Odds were good she spent the night in his room if hers looked untouched.

"I was talking with him earlier in the hall," Beatrice said. "He hasn't seen her. Not since last night."

Well, now. The handsome stranger whose eyes blazed like hellfire must have been the missing girl's fiancé. If only the mansion's walls could talk, I'd get an earful and then some.

"Wherever could she be?" Ivy asked. "This isn't like her."

Of course, Trinity Solomon wouldn't be the first bride to up and run. But someone with a handsome catch like that, and carrying his offspring, no less, wasn't likely to hightail it out of town. "She's probably with her bridesmaids. You know, having fun while she still can." That made perfect sense to me, and it seemed to calm Ivy down.

But only until Beatrice pointed to the opposite corner of the room.

Ivy and I turned at the same time. Five girls lounged around a table, wearing the peach-colored sunbonnets I'd designed. I hadn't noticed them with all the fuss.

"The tall one told me they figured they might as well come here and get some use out of their wedding clothes," Beatrice said. "At least the hats."

Ivy and I both stared at the table. Sure enough, the girls took turns splashing water into each other's glasses with lots of giggles all around.

"I'm going to find her," Ivy finally said.

Maybe it was my Christian upbringing, but I couldn't bear to let her go alone. "I'll go with you."

"Oh, no. You'll miss the competition. I can't let you do that."

I tried to sound nonchalant. "It's not that important to me." It'd be a shame to walk away now, but my new friend was about to panic.

Beatrice cleared her throat next to us. "I'm afraid I have to start the contest."

"Of course," I said. "You go right ahead. We'll slip out the back door."

As Ivy and I left the room, I glanced back at the party of bridesmaids, who didn't seem to have a care in the world. One by one, they stacked packages of Earl Grey into a tower and then poked at it with a stir stick until the thing came tumbling down, which made them all squeal with laughter.

Even though Mr. Solomon had broken the bank for this wedding, it looked like the bridesmaids didn't notice the bride was gone. The squeals faded as Ivy and I made our way down the hall. She linked her arm in mine, which seemed to give her strength; though it made navigating the path a bit tricky.

Since no one had seen the missing girl *inside* the mansion, our best option was to explore the grounds. From what I remembered of our tour the day before, a pool and Jacuzzi lay on the south side, as well as a day spa. That was probably where I'd have gone on the morning of my wedding if I wanted to find a little peace and quiet.

We walked past a garden with a boxwood hedge first and then a brick fence that wrapped around the pool and hot tub. No one else was on the path.

The iron gate to the pool stood open. The pool was nice and broad, with more than enough room for a healthy workout. Problem was, the only people in the pool were a mother and her two small children.

Ivy glanced at me, crestfallen. "She's not here, either."

"Don't be too hasty." I'd seen a blur by the hot tub and thought maybe Trinity could be relaxing there instead. Even though a girl in her condition shouldn't submerge herself in scalding water, she might have decided to sunbathe there.

We ducked past the woman and her kids and then headed for the hot tub. No luck. Someone was lounging there, all right, but she'd tossed a chef's coat over one of the folding chairs.

"Hello," I said.

The stranger next to the hot tub held a copy of *Gourmet*. Lo and behold, an inked serpent crept around her collarbone, slithered under both ears and ended just shy of her chin. The whole thing looked like frothy swirls on parchment, which would have been beautiful if the artist had drawn it on a piece of paper instead of the poor girl's neck.

She scrunched up her nose. She'd dyed the tips of her short blond hair red, like a book of matches set on fire. "Hello."

"Have you seen anyone come by?" I asked.

"Mmm. Don't think so." She tossed the magazine onto a tempered glass table, where it landed next to an open bottle of Coppertone.

"I'm Missy DuBois and this here is Ivy Solomon."

"I'm Cat Antoine, the head chef."

Which was all well and good, but we still had a bride to find. "Have you seen anyone come by this morning, Cat?"

The girl stared at Ivy. "I know you. You're married to the guy who owned that refinery my dad used to work at."

"Excuse me?" Ivy seemed a little flustered to be recognized. "We're looking for someone—"

"That's it. I recognize you from the newspaper stories." The two of them seemed to be having parallel conversations with neither one paying much attention to what the other said.

"—my stepdaughter is never late, you see."

I *had* to intervene. "We're kind of in a hurry. Do you know if the spa's open?"

"Should be," Cat said. "I've never used it, even though I live right there." She gestured to a building behind the pool that looked exactly like the main house, only smaller. The employees' housing, apparently.

"We should probably try the spa next."

Who wouldn't want a massage on the morning of her wedding? I was about to say good-bye to Cat when a high-pitched scream rent the air.

Mutely, we all turned toward the mansion. Ivy reached out and gripped my arm like she'd done with Beatrice earlier.

"Ow!" Instinctively, I pulled away. Mauling me wasn't going to help anyone. "My goodness." I started toward the pool gate and Ivy followed, our heels tap dancing on the deck.

Someone had screamed near the main house. I was sure of it. Near the back, if I had to guess. We hurried there. A flurry of activity met us. A man wearing a tool belt blocked the mansion's back door, waving people away with a pair of garden clippers and shouting at everyone to stay back.

One of the waiters was there too, judging by a black apron he wore around his waist. He tried to comfort a shrieking woman in a maid's uniform, but her cries only amplified the chaos. By this time, several guests had joined the melee.

Ambrose was nowhere to be seen. That made my heart race, and I made a beeline over to the waiter and the distraught housekeeper.

"What is it?" Although I suspected a kitchen fire, there was no smoke or flames.

The waiter had his hands full with the crying woman and didn't answer. I moved on to the gardener, who was doing his best to keep everyone at bay.

"You, there!" I hoped he could hear me above the hubbub. "What's going on?"

The man stopped waving long enough to fix his pale aqua eyes on me. "Find da manager, quick."

"Why? What's going on?"

"Da maid found a body in dere. Women's batroom."

Ivy gasped behind me. It couldn't be, could it? I turned to gauge her reaction. She silently swooned, like an old-fashioned paper doll cut free of its pattern, and fell to the ground.

Chapter 3

Paramedics maneuvered the stretcher slowly—too slowly—out a side door and down the path. Ambrose had emerged from the main house safe and sound, and I was so happy I threw my arms around his neck to hug him for all I was worth.

We had to wait on the lawn until a Louisiana state trooper arrived to cordon off the area. A second officer accompanied him, and he gestured for Ivy to follow him into the house.

My heart hurt for her. Who could have guessed the morning would turn out so? Once she disappeared into the house, a man with a name tag identifying him as the general manager stepped out.

"Could I have your attention, please?" The general manager spoke loudly, as if to override the chaos. His bald head was smooth and as shiny as a new penny. "We don't have much information at this point, but I can tell y'all one of our housekeepers discovered a body in the restroom. She's been positively identified as Miss Trinity Solomon."

No one stirred, out of respect for the deceased or perhaps just plain old curiosity.

"We're willing to give anyone their deposit back if they want to leave, but the police need to talk to you before you go. That is, *if* you go."

The moment he hushed, whispers rose on the air like dandelions blown about by a headwind as people traded information back and forth. The overwhelming majority standing with me on the lawn seemed to be in town specifically for the wedding.

A lady to my left announced she'd write up a little something for the Baton Rouge Women's Club newsletter. A soft-spoken older gentleman wondered whether the flowers could be donated to a local hospital. And a young businesswoman questioned the fate of Mr. Solomon's oil company now his only child was gone. It was all very civilized, but also chilly, for such a sudden turn of events.

I glanced at my shoes. Ivy's beautiful hat lay in the grass. *Such a pity.* She never had a chance to wear it for the competition, and now it was ruined, or nearly so. If I brought it back to my room, there was a chance I could reshape its crown using my travel steam iron.

Since I didn't have any other way to help her, I scooped up the hat. We awkwardly stood there for a moment longer until Ambrose touched my arm and began to lead me away from the crowd.

"C'mon, Missy, let's get out of here."

I studied the faces as we walked. Like it or not, a dead girl had been found in the hotel's bathroom, even though she appeared to be as right as rain during our tour yesterday. True, she was in a family way, but she'd been downright feisty with her daddy when he challenged her about the wedding.

Someone had wanted Trinity gone and, for all we knew, that someone could still be among us. A few weeks back I ran into our local police chief at the Food Faire. He told me about a thief he'd arrested who videotaped his victims when they returned home. Apparently the guy wanted to record their expressions when they noticed the smashed windows, broken locks, and scuff marks on the front door. Especially if they began to yell, shriek or argue with each other because they didn't know what else to do.

To sit back and enjoy human suffering was horrible, but that didn't mean those types of people didn't exist. While most sane folks would catch the first Jefferson Transit out of town, most wouldn't murder a young bride right before her wedding. I eyed all the spectators equally as we made our way to the front of the house and up the stairs. I collapsed into one of the rocking chairs on the porch, still clutching the crushed hat to my chest.

Ambrose followed suit and sat beside me. "Well, I didn't see that coming."

"Ambrose! Don't be so flippant."

"Of course, I feel awful for the girl's family."

"That's better." I started to fluff up the pheasant quills on Ivy's hat, but my heart wasn't in it. She and I had walked right by the restroom where the maid found Trinity. Heavy panel door, brass doorknob, leaded glass window. Nothing unusual about any of it. "Who do you think would do such a thing?"

"Now that's hard to say. No telling who had motive. Could've been anyone. Even someone they didn't know."

I rolled my eyes. "It had to be someone they knew. Why would you even say that? It's not like a stranger would wander onto this plantation out of the clear blue."

"You're only saying that because it makes you feel safer."

No doubt he was right. The thought of a stranger killing someone two floors below my bedroom was enough to send me packing. But, if it was someone who was upset at the bride, or her family, that would be a whole 'nother story.

The waiter I'd seen earlier ambled up the stairs and joined us on the porch. "Maybe the ghost did it." He was handsome, even with the prematurely gray hair, bless his heart.

"Now that'd be the day," I said.

"People were talking about it this morning." He leaned against the rail that separated us from the river beyond. "One guy told me he almost called the cops last night because he heard so much noise. People moving furniture around, banging walls, having a regular party."

"Do tell," Ambrose said. "I'd be mad too if someone kept me awake all night."

The waiter crossed his arms. "Or some*thing*. By the way, I'm Charles. I'll probably be your server while you're here."

"Nice to meet you, Charles. I'm Missy and this is my friend Ambrose."

He looked doubtful when I said *friend*, but that was neither here nor there at this point.

"By any chance, did you hear anything last night?" I asked.

He shook his head. "There's too much stuff going on in the kitchen. The chef has to practically scream whenever my orders are up."

"You mean Cat? I met her this morning by the Jacuzzi. So you didn't hear anything?"

Ambrose shot me a look because he knew full well my questions usually led someplace else.

"Not a thing," Charles said. "If anything weird happened last night, I wouldn't know. Guess it's time to drive back to school."

"Let me guess. LSU? I went to Vanderbilt and Ambrose here went to Auburn—"

Charles's eyes flitted away from my face and landed somewhere behind me. At that point, I could have been speaking Swahili, for all he knew, because he only had eyes for the front door, which had squeaked open.

I turned. Beatrice stepped onto the porch with her cell phone once again at her ear. There was definitely some history between those two.

"Charles?" I asked.

His head snapped 'round again. "Uh-huh. Auburn."

"Never mind. It's not important."

Ambrose chuckled at our exchange. "Girlfriend?"

"What, her? Oh, no. No."

"Do tell." Ambrose was toying with him now.

I was about to intervene when Beatrice finally lowered the cell. "Mr. Jackson, can you come with me?"

"Me? Is something wrong?"

With everything that had happened, it was anyone's guess what new crisis lurked around the corner. Maybe the police wanted to question Ambrose about what he'd seen while he was at the front desk. Or maybe they wanted to know if he'd heard anything the night before.

"You had a call," Beatrice said. "She said you weren't answering your cell. Something about a problem at the store."

"Criminy. My guess it's the Fitzgerald dress." Ambrose grimaced. "I didn't do a very good job of training my assistant to handle things when I'm gone, now, did I?"

"Don't blame yourself, Ambrose. She should be able to figure it out, don't you think?" I said.

"I should tell *her* that." Reluctantly, he rose from the rocker and motioned to Charles. "Want to hold my seat for me? Best view in the house."

"No, that's okay. I have to get back to school pretty soon. Finals are coming up."

Beatrice didn't even glance Charles's way, which seemed a trifle sad. "They have the number in the registration cottage," she said to Ambrose, instead.

"Gotcha." He lingered by the rocker, and neither he nor Charles seemed anxious to leave.

"Speaking of which," I asked Beatrice, "did they ever tell you what happened to Trinity Solomon?"

"No. All I know is a maid went into the handicapped stall this morning to refill the toilet paper and there she was. Must have been an awful sight."

"So there was lots of blood?" What a horrible fright to walk in on a crime scene—first thing in the morning, no less.

"No, there wasn't any blood." Beatrice pursed her lips. "They didn't ask for a mop or anything. Just said we couldn't use the bathroom until a crime-scene investigator came by."

"Well, they wouldn't use a mop, not until they'd had a chance to analyze the splatter pattern, if there was one." Thank heavens I took a criminal-defense course at Vanderbilt when I thought about going to law school. Never imagined I'd use the information, though.

"But they wheeled the stretcher right by me and they didn't cover up the body very well. It looked like she was only sleeping."

"Did her skin look gray or purple?" I asked.

"Now that you mention it, her skin *did* look purple. What does that mean?"

I shrugged. "Nothing." No need to provide a police procedural out here on the front porch. Although it meant Trinity had been lying in the restroom for some time, at least a few hours.

"We should go see about that call," she said to Ambrose.

"Are you going to be okay out here by yourself, Missy? This shouldn't take more than a minute or two."

I waved away his concerns. "Fine and dandy." With Ambrose gone, I could question Charles to my heart's content. "I need to catch my breath anyway."

Before they left, Beatrice blessed Charles with a throwaway smile. The boy looked ready to melt into a puddle of happiness.

"Breathe," I said, once they were gone. No need to have two bodies lying around the plantation.

"Excuse me?"

"You stopped breathing when she spoke. Sit." I pointed to the chair Ambrose had recently vacated. Sometimes it was best to take the bull by the horns and lead him around the corral. "You were telling me about ghosts and such."

Charles reluctantly sank into the rocker. "You hear things when you're waiting tables."

"I imagine. If you were to gamble, who would do something like that to the Solomon family?"

He didn't hesitate. "There was a big accident at her father's oil refinery last year."

"Really? I kinda remember reading about it in the newspaper. Baton Rouge, wasn't it?"

"Yep. A fuel stack exploded in the middle of the night."

"Did a lot of people get injured?"

He narrowed his eyes. "Yeah, but it was more than that. There was the money too. Half of Baton Rouge had invested in the refinery and when it shut down, they got aced."

"What do you mean, 'aced'? Did Mr. Solomon lose everything?"

Now he looked disgusted, with his face all pinched up. "*He* didn't lose anything. But everyone else did. Even my dad had money in it."

"Sometimes they'll sell off the assets if there's been an accident and give the money to the survivors. Why didn't they do that?"

"There wasn't anything left to sell. How much would someone pay for a burned-out fuel stack? 'Course, Mr. Solomon got off scot-free. Turns out he'd invested his money somewhere else. Didn't have a dime in his own property."

Gracious light. That would give a lot of people motive to get back at Mr. Solomon. But why go after his poor daughter? Why not the man himself?

Charles rose from the rocker and stretched. "I'd better head back. Time to hit the books."

"Okay, then. I'll probably see you tonight."

By the time he left, my thoughts were a million miles away. Not only did Mr. Solomon cause a lot of physical harm to people in this area, but it seemed he'd caused a lot of financial damage too. Hard to say which of the two would be a better reason for revenge.

No sooner had Charles started back down the stairs when the top of Ambrose's head appeared over the landing. He seemed a little winded from all the coming and going, so I motioned to the rocking chair, which had been getting more than its fair share of use that morning.

He shook his head. "Missy, I hate to do this, but I have to get back to the shop."

"Really? If it's not one thing, it's another. Or as my granddaddy used to say, It's always somethin', never nothin."

"The wedding next weekend is going to be a disaster if I don't take care of this. I need to come up with a whole new design or the mother will want my head on a platter."

I sighed heavily. "Oh, Bo." Ironically, one of the things I liked about Ambrose when I first met him was his passion for his work. But why did that passion have to interrupt the only weekend we'd had together in a month of Sundays?

"We're talking major disaster here. Now she wants her mermaid dress to be a ball gown. Trust me, there's not enough fabric for that."

"I understand."

Once he made up his mind, it was like trying to tame the wind to change it.

"I'll only be gone a few hours. Then I'll come right back. You probably won't even notice I'm gone."

I worked up a respectable pout. "You know that's not true. Maybe I'll leave too and go back with you."

"Now don't be silly. Didn't you want to go swimming? I'll tell you what: You go get some sun, and I'll be back as quick as anything. This place costs a lot of money, so you might as well enjoy it. Even with everything that happened this morning."

Maybe that wouldn't be *too* bad. There were a few things I'd wanted to do around the plantation that Ambrose might not enjoy. Reading in the library was one, along with getting my toes done at the day spa. "Well, if you insist."

He smiled, which brought out the blue in his deep-set eyes. "Try to stay out of trouble for once, okay?"

So much for the day's plans. I settled back in the rocker, but then changed my mind and snatched up Ivy's hat. Even though Ambrose was determined to fix things at his store, I could always help him by finding him something to eat on the way. I walked across the porch, but before I got very far, a shrill noise sounded below me. It landed a half-note shy of being on pitch as someone whistled away. Sounded to me like an off-tune rendition of "When the Saints Go Marching In."

Curious now, I peeked over the rail as the front door closed behind Ambrose. Someone stood over a clump of impatiens next to the house, tugging at a weed. Thinning hair, blue coveralls, and a low-slung tool belt around the waist. It was the gardener from before. The one who'd ordered everyone to stay away from the house once the maid discovered Trinity Solomon.

Despite the horrible morning, he seemed calm as he casually pulled at a stalk.

"Good morning," I said, as I began to descend the staircase. "Crazy times we've had this morning, right?"

He didn't bother to rise to meet me; though he did glance my way.

"You can say dat again. Crazy 'nuf to scare da guests away."

Judging by the man's pale face and watery blue eyes, he looked to be about eighty or so. His accent reminded me of the Cajun store owner in my building.

"You were very brave this morning," I said.

"Tank ya. Didn't know what else ta do, ta be honest."

"I'm Melissa DuBois." I stopped and held out my hand. "You do a great job with the gardens here. They're absolutely beautiful."

"Gotta cover da soil in acid. Git it from da coffee. Pour dat stuff on da plants and never tink twice 'bout dem again." He slowly straightened and held out his left hand. He'd pinned the empty sleeve on his right side to the blue coveralls.

"Nice to meet you." I gently shook his hand. "I'll have to remember that about the coffee, Mr. . . ."

"It's jus' Darryl. Darryl Tibodeaux. Nice ta meet ya."

"Sounds like you know a lot about plants. Been here long?"

He ducked his head. "Not dat long. Use ta work at da oil refinery. Dat's water under da bridge. Water under da bridge."

"I heard about the big accident there."

"Da refinery weren' so good ta me." He glanced at the empty sleeve of his coverall. "Happy ta have dis job. Happy ta have any job."

"I think they're lucky to have *you*. I mean, look at those flowers!" A low rumble careened through my empty stomach. "Say, Darryl. What with all the craziness this morning, I completely forgot to eat breakfast. Do you know if the kitchen's still open?"

"Should be. Dat Cat works round da clock. If'n it's not, she'll open it right up for ya."

I smiled gratefully. "Good to know. Thanks." It was probably time for him to get back to his work and for me to snag a bite to eat. "See you around the plantation."

My mind swirled as I reversed course and began to ascend the stairs. First, the maid's horrible discovery of Trinity in a bathroom stall. Then, I'd already met two people who'd been affected by the fire at Mr. Solomon's oil refinery, and I'd only been talking to folks for a little while.

Finally, there was the assistant back at Ambrose's store, who couldn't breathe without his help.

I'd almost reached the top landing when something else sounded. Unlike Darryl's whistling, this noise sounded downright pitiful. Someone was gagging. Or were they retching?

I took stock. While I couldn't see the person, I definitely heard them. And even though Ambrose always said my feet moved faster than my brain, I didn't see any other option but to help if I could.

I turned and went back down the stairs, following the noise. Sure enough, a figure on the other side of the staircase had bent over an azalea bush and was retching. It was none other than Cat, the chef I'd met by the pool. She still wore a beach towel around her waist, only now her hands clutched at it for dear life.

"Cat!" She'd probably be mortified to know someone had witnessed her baptizing the bushes like that. But, in my book, protocol took a backseat to practicality, and she'd stained the front of her towel something awful with the vomit.

She looked ready to crumble, so I quickly jogged over, after first tossing the smashed hat onto the lawn. No need to deface *that* any more than necessary. "Are you okay?"

"Yeah, I think so." She looked up from the mess in the bushes, clearly disgusted.

"Do you want water or something?" Poor thing looked as pale as a bedsheet, which was saying a lot since her skin looked like fresh milk to begin with.

"No, I'm fine. Really."

The strain of the morning must have been too much for her. "Was it someone finding that poor girl's body? Is that what set you off?"

Cat didn't answer right away, but she didn't have to. She stared at the ground as if it took too much effort to lift her chin. "I guess so. I'm not really good around blood and stuff. It makes me queasy."

There hadn't been any blood, according to Beatrice, but that was neither here nor there at this point.

"Come on," I said. "Let's go sit on the porch and rest until you feel better." She let me lead her away like a newborn calf, her knees knocking all the way to the stairs, after I'd first stopped to retrieve Ivy's hat.

We climbed the steps together and ambled to the same old rocker I'd just left. At this rate, the thing was going to mold itself to my backside, but I slid into it anyway.

She wiped her mouth again, although her skin looked clean now. The same couldn't be said of the towel, though. "Look at me. Yuck."

"It's okay. It's a natural reaction to stress." I wished for a handkerchief at that moment, or at least a paper towel, to clean her up. "We should get you a washcloth or something."

Cat shook her head. "No, really. I'm fine. Don't go to any trouble. Look, I shouldn't even be here. You're one of our guests—"

"No biggie. You rest a spell and then we'll get you cleaned up."

She must have realized I was right because she sagged into the rocker beside me. "Something must have upset my stomach."

"Bless your heart."

We rested on the porch like that for a few minutes, rocking and chatting about this, that, and the other thing, until the color slowly returned to her face.

After a bit, she straightened. She must have seen something near the river because she pointed. "Look. A police car."

A white squad car cruised along the road in front of the plantation.

"Wonder why they don't use the parking lot?"

"Beats me. Maybe they're checking the area for evidence." But contrary to my opinion, the squad car stopped right in front of us. A tall African-American man ambled out, hopped over the low garden fence, and began to walk toward the main house. He wore a navy blue uniform with gold piping and shiny doodads on his chest. This definitely wasn't the same trooper I'd seen earlier, and he was headed in our direction.

Cat and I waited while he climbed the stairs. His dark uniform against pure white paint stood out beautifully. Didn't I almost say the same thing to Ivy when she'd complained about the dress designer? The one who suggested the bridesmaids wear black? Ambrose was right. It would've looked stunning against the snowy paint.

Once he reached the top of the stairs, the policeman tipped his hat to expose a thinning head of hair and two bushy black eyebrows. A crescent-shaped scar followed his left brow.

"Well, shut my mouth and call me Shirley," I said. Whatever was Lance LaPorte doing standing in front of me in a policeman's uniform? Last time I saw him, he'd pestered me in our church's social hall as we both graduated from Sunday school. Had a twin brother, if I recalled correctly. But twenty years had passed, not to mention a slew of meals, judging by his waistline.

"Missy DuBois?" He looked surprised to see me too, and he tilted his head like a kitten with a twirly piece of twine. "That you?"

"Sure is, Lance." Nice to find there were still some surprises left in this old world. "Now, you start at the beginning and tell me whatever it is you're doing here in that uniform."

He laughed. "Didn't you hear I graduated from the police academy? My brother took up law and I took up order. I'd have thought everyone back home knew that by now."

"We sorta lost track of you after your family moved. Someone said you'd all gone south, but no one knew for sure."

"That right? My brother and I came down here with my mom after she divorced."

"How is your mom?" Near as I could recall, Mrs. LaPorte left her no-account husband after he lost one too many factory jobs.

"She's good. She'll be tickled to hear we met up. She got married again, but to a nice guy this time."

"Well, that's good. But what brings you here? Is it about the body they found this morning?"

When he finally noticed Cat, he fell silent. Maybe it was the mess on her towel, but more likely he didn't know whether he could trust the stranger sitting next to me.

"This is Cat. She's the chef here. And she knows all about the body in the restroom."

"That's why I'm here," he said. "I'm a detective with investigative-support services for the Louisiana State Police. Got a promotion last month."

"Your mama must be so proud." What a stroke of luck! I'd never been this close to a real police investigation before. At least one that didn't involve smudged newsprint at a grocery-store checkout counter. It awoke my natural curiosity, like that kitten with the twirly twine.

"It's so good to see you again, Lance. Can't wait to spend some time with y'all."

Chapter 4

Once Cat was feeling up to it, Lance and I helped her through the front door and into the foyer. Thank goodness she wanted to return to the kitchen to prepare the night's supper, since I had every intention of following Lance around as he did his police business, whether or not my stomach complained. I didn't think Lance would mind, given we'd known each other since he was a little boy in short pants and I wore pink flip-flops to that Sunday-school graduation.

"Are you here alone?" He led the way as we walked past the golden ballroom, obviously headed for the bathroom by the restaurant.

"No, I'm with my best friend, but he had to leave for a bit. The woman who was murdered was to get married this weekend. He designed the wedding gown."

"Terrible shame." Yellow caution tape dressed the closed bathroom door like a satin sash on a prom queen's gown.

Carefully, Lance peeled back the tape and pushed open the door. I snuck in behind him as quiet as a church mouse, since I knew police normally didn't want the public in the primary area of a crime scene.

An investigator had already come and gone, though, because a fine silver powder dusted every flat service. Magna powder. Looked to me like they scrounged whatever evidence had been left behind.

Everything seemed in place. Everything except for the last stall, the handicapped stall. Here someone had ripped the receptacle for sanitary products clean from the wall, leaving behind bits of tile grout, crumbled caulk, and milky-white dust.

Lance pulled a camera out of his pocket and began to take pictures.

"Interesting," I said.

"Missy!" He whirled around. "What are you doing in here?"

"Helping?" It was worth a shot, albeit a long one.

"Please wait outside. I'll be done in a few minutes, after I've taken some pictures."

"Sure thing. By the way, you know the bride was pregnant, right? Wouldn't have any need for that maxi-pad bin."

Lance squinted. "Now, just how would *you* know that?"

"I saw Trinity Solomon arguing with her daddy yesterday, and she was clearly showing." I backed out of the handicapped stall and left him to do his work, if that was how he wanted it.

I managed to peek into each stall as I strolled along, but they all looked perfectly normal. This police business was tedious work. Not nearly as exciting as what I read in the *National Enquirer.*

Next, I stepped over to a trio of pedestal sinks. Magna powder dotted the surfaces, along with tape marks where an investigator tried to lift prints. Since Lance was busy with his pictures, I sidled over to a trash can built into the tiled wall. Someone had whisked the plastic bag away and hadn't bothered to replace it yet. Everything looked perfectly normal there too. I was about to leave when something sparkled from behind the first sink. Glimmered, really. It was a tiny starburst I'd have missed if I'd blinked.

As it was, the wall and crown molding merged together since both had been painted beige. The bit of sparkle I'd seen had lodged itself in the crease.

I glanced back. Lance was so busy he didn't pay me any mind. So, I leaned over the sink, grabbed a paper towel, and then bent to re-trieve something shaped like the spore of a honeycomb: Golden, soft to the touch, and pliable. Like it had been spun from amber plastic. If I squinted just so and imagined the piece missing, I could see it was the outer casing of a pill.

Lance coughed, which startled me to no end. Like it or not, the piece of trash I held in my hand was part of a crime scene. I shouldn't even have held it, so I returned the pill to its spot in the crease and tossed aside the paper towel. "Looks like the investigator missed something."

Lance left the commode and strode over, glancing at the spot I pointed at. As I thought, the plastic wasn't visible unless the light hit it just so, and the light didn't seem to want to cooperate at that mo-ment.

"Here." I grabbed another paper towel from the wall holder, reached down and plucked out the casing. Tampering with evidence was one thing, but leaving perfectly good evidence behind was quite another. Sheepishly, I handed it over to Lance. "Now, don't you scowl at me like that. You know you'd have missed it if I hadn't pointed it out."

Lance held the capsule in the palm of his gloved hand. I'd been right about the casing part. It was clearly meant for a medicine of some sort.

He pulled a small paper baggie from his pocket and dropped the honeycomb spore into it. "Glad you found that, Missy."

Well, that's better. I hadn't meant to intrude, but two sets of eyes were always better than one. "Looks like medicine to me."

"I'll get it to the lab so they can analyze it."

"Any idea when you might get the results back?"

"Hard to say, but it shouldn't take more than a day or two."

"That's good. Say, is it cold in here to you?" Truth be told, the place was starting to give me the heebie-jeebies. It had been exciting, at first, to be smack-dab in the middle of a real police investigation, but now, the silence was getting to be a bit much. Not to mention that someone had died right near where I stood on the cold tile floor.

"Say, Lance, how do you know if the killer struck here or brought the body to the bathroom when she was already dead?"

"There'd be scuff marks on the floor. Lots of little details determine the place of death." He glanced at his watch and then at me. "You should probably go now. I've got to finish in here and then get back to the station. I'd appreciate it if you didn't tell anyone else you were here."

"Of course." Not that there was anyone left to tell, what with Ambrose back in Bleu Bayou. In fact, not one person in this huge, hollow mansion would care a blessed thing about what I did, and that seemed downright pitiful. "I have a wonderful idea, Lance. Why don't you call your mama and tell her we'll all have supper here tonight?"

He stared at me blankly.

"My treat. It'll be nice . . . like we're all back home sitting around your kitchen table." Well, not exactly like that, but I could sure use some company. Even though Ambrose insisted he'd be back in a few hours, I knew better. Brides were a breed apart, and she probably wouldn't release him until after nightfall.

"All right." He finally smiled. "Let me call Mom and get it squared away. It's a little fancy, though. Sure you don't mind paying?"

"Wouldn't hear of anything else." After all, I had twelve hundred dollars due me for the wedding here. "What about your brother? He can come too, if he's in town."

"Naw. Larry decided to set up shop in Baton Rouge. Guess he got a little bigheaded once he got that law degree."

"No matter. I'll see you and your mama here tonight at seven. Does that sound good?"

"Sure. Let me guess. You'll be the one wearing a Sunday hat to supper?"

"But of course." Sweet of him to remember. I always wore a sunbonnet bigger than me to church, even when I was a little thing. "See you at seven. Good luck with the investigation. Such a tragic thing." I turned away from him, the powdered surfaces and the crime-scene tape that limped against the paneled door.

Although my stomach might complain, I still had a mess of things to see around the plantation. Supper would be here soon enough.

I decided to explore the front of the mansion next. The hall leading to the foyer was empty this time. The hotel must have refunded everyone else's money; but I had no intention of asking for mine back. How could I ever look my new neighbor, that sweet Maribelle Girard, in the eye again unless I tried to help find the killer?

The beveled glass door swept open, and I stepped onto the porch. A paved road lay just beyond the white picket fence, but not a single car was on it. The only sound was a trickle of water that lapped against stone somewhere in the distance.

I reveled in the peace and quiet, especially after all the hubbub of the morning. Now might be the perfect time to look around the plantation. I walked down the stairs and took the brick path traveling east, to the far side of the property. I had all the time in the world and no one for company but me, myself, and I, so the three of us walked until we arrived at the source of the gurgling noise. A stone fountain stood smack-dab in the middle of a round garden with four benches and a plaster statue of a Roman lady watching over it all. Why, I'd discovered a secret garden in the middle of Morningside Plantation.

Jutting out from the garden were two more paths. One path must have led to the registration cottage, which sat at the front of the property, while the other path probably headed to the back, toward the pool and spa. It all looked perfectly symmetrical.

I headed for one of the wood benches and sat, surrounded by the sweet smell of star jasmine. The flower beds shimmered like the crown of a hat made from shot silk when two pieces combined to look iridescent in the sun. In fact, these colors looked like they'd been stroked on with a paintbrush, which made my plants back home seem pitiful by comparison. "Wonder if Darryl siphons off any of that special water from the Mississippi?"

The plaster statue behind me chuckled at that. At least it sounded like the statue, until I whirled around and saw Darryl poke his head out from behind.

"*Mo chagren* . . . I'm sorry."

My, but that man did get around. "You scared me half to death! Thought I was hearing things."

He ambled over to where I sat. "Sorry 'bout dat."

Everywhere I turned this morning, I ran into Darryl. Wonder how he did that?

"No matter. Since we're both here, you might as well join me and rest for a few minutes." No use in him working himself to a frazzle since the wedding had been cancelled.

He carefully eased onto the bench. "Been meanin' to take da rest, but da work never gits done."

"I can imagine. This garden is beautiful too, like those other flower beds. My snapdragons wither once we get this close to summer."

He glanced at me. "Remember, it's da coffee. Git it from da kitchen. Keeps dem blooms from fallin' off."

"That's right. You mentioned that. I'll have to try it sometime."

"Don' go crazy. Jus' a lil bit. 'Nuf to give it da acid."

"See? This place is lucky to have you."

He shook his head sadly. "Can't do much else now. Jus' tendin' da plants and keepin' bugs off 'em."

"At least you get to be outside all day. So, Darryl, can you believe all the hubbub around here? What a horrible shock for the Solomon family."

Darryl didn't blink. "Truth be told, dat family axed for it. Hurt lotsa folks 'round here wit' dat refinery."

"Really? You think they got what they deserved?" Hard to imagine the mild-mannered gardener sitting beside me might actually condone violence like that. "I don't agree. I don't think it gives anyone the right to go after his daughter. Do you have any idea who could've done something like that?"

"Naw. Mostly I keeps ta myself. It's da bes' way."

"I suppose. But just the same, you must have a theory. Maybe someone came around who didn't belong here or you saw a strange car in the parking lot?"

"I told ya. I keeps ta myself." His brow furrowed. "Why you be askin' me all dese questions?"

"I met Mrs. Solomon this morning and it turns out we have a lot in common. A lot. I want to help her if I can, but no one seems to have seen or heard much of anything."

"I dink ya bes' be leavin' dis to de police. People don' take kindly to snoopin' 'round here. Makes folks wonder 'bout cha."

"Me? I only want to help out Mrs. Solomon. I can't do that if no one's willing to say anything. Surely you must have seen something unusual. Maybe you thought it was nothing at the time—"

"Like I said, bes' be leavin' dis to da police. Ya don' know wot you be gettin' into. I gots to go. Weddin' or no, there's still lotsa work ta be done."

With that, Darryl abruptly rose from the bench and left. Strange how he refused to speak to me about the morning's turn of events, and stranger still that he felt no pity for the Solomon family.

His voice stayed with me as I left the garden by way of a cobblestone path. I was so busy replaying the scene in my mind I didn't pay attention to where I was going until I found myself on a route that led to the back of the house. The general manager had announced the maid's discovery here. And this was where everyone else was so preoccupied with the details that no one seemed to mourn the poor girl. I couldn't help but shudder when I saw the glossy back door.

Something was different, though. I hadn't noticed anything earlier but the sheen of the paint and the bald man who'd emerged from the mansion. Now I could tell the wall's bricks were discolored. The ones on the left were weathered and worn; the ones on the right looked clean and much newer. Maybe the bricks to the east had been added later, which would explain the difference.

I crossed the lawn and approached the wall. Sure enough, this part of the house looked like it had been added to the original. I pulled aside a scrim of vines and discovered a door few people probably even knew existed.

Someone had nailed a small bronze plaque to it with the words *Andrews Family Museum*. The only thing I loved as much as hats was history, and seeing that plaque made me smile like a child who'd stumbled upon an OPEN sign in a toy-store window.

The doorjamb was warped, so I put my shoulder against the panel and pushed for all I was worth, which sent me stumbling into a darkened room. A row of smudged windows allowed weak sunlight to pool on the hardwood floors. Half a dozen glass display cases loomed around the room.

I stepped in and approached the nearest exhibit. It featured something called *gasoliers*, which apparently were the lights Horace Andrews had installed in most of the plantation's rooms. Black-and-white photos and artists' renderings gave examples of the newfangled lights, from simple to ornate, from brass-coated wall sconces to a ballroom chandelier that dripped crystals.

The next display case held a hodgepodge of things from the Civil War. One picture showed a young Confederate soldier with a rifle clasped across his chest, as if the gun's barrel could stop grapeshot from entering his heart. Military insignia of various shapes and sizes hovered protectively around the photograph. Eagles and arrows, monograms, circles and stars.

I moved on to the next photo. This one showed a delicate young mother with a child on her lap. The two wore matching linen dresses with thick blue sashes, and the child's feet swung over her mother's knees. While the toddler stared off in the distance, the mother eyed her lovingly. Tears came to my eyes the longer I studied the photo.

I barely remembered my mother, and when I did, the scenes resembled a dream. A lady leaned over me once as I lay in my bunk bed and held a washcloth against my burning forehead. She smelled like peppermint.

The same pretty woman picked daises with me as soon as I recovered, which she strung into a chain. The next memory always left me winded: The chain broke when someone in a uniform whisked me away from my bunk. I never saw that bed again, and I refused to get my driver's license until I was at Vanderbilt. Losing two parents in one car accident was more than any child should have to face.

I blinked away a tear. Funny how the memories ambushed me. I willed myself to walk to another display case and peer through the glass. Military uniforms filled this one. A soldier's hat, called a *kepi* and made of wool, perched above a plain military vest with a standing collar. But something was missing. While artifacts filled every inch of the other cases, this one had an empty spot near its top. Only a shadow of something long and boxy remained, along with some pushpins. No other spots had a hole like this.

Could the plantation have loaned out whatever was there? Maybe, but normally a museum director would include a note card that explained the item was on loan. That way, any guests who wandered into the museum wouldn't wonder about this particular display.

Instead, the original text remained, beside the empty space. There were two paragraphs of type so miniscule they were impossible to read in the dim light. *Interesting.* Everything else in the museum was pristine. They'd restored and dusted the photos, matted the artist's renderings three times over, and cleaned the military insignia until it sparkled. I'd have to ask Charles about the mistake when I finally got around to visiting the restaurant later.

Speaking of which, the day had dragged on and on, and I was no closer to finding something to eat. Maybe it was time to finally trade my curiosity for a beignet and a nice, tall glass of sweet tea. The museum could wait, while I wasn't sure my stomach would hold out much longer.

Chapter 5

I closed the museum door and pondered my options. I was hungry enough to eat the backside of a skunk. But I was tired too. The day's excitement had worn me to a frazzle, and I longed for a soft bed and an even softer pillow.

What good would it do to visit the restaurant if I couldn't even stay awake during my meal? Perhaps I'd have to ignore my stomach a little longer and head for the hotel room instead.

Feet dragging, I walked up the main staircase, which seemed longer and much narrower than before. The plush carpet sucked at my shoes, like wet clay, all the way to the third floor, where something winked at me from my hotel-room door. It looked like a note, even from twenty feet away. I walked closer. It *was* a note. Who'd leave me a message in a place like this, where I didn't know a soul?

I plucked the paper off the door. It said something about Ambrose needing more time in Bleu Bayou and I should go ahead and have supper without him. Curses! I thought the bride might kidnap him for hours and hours, but part of me had hoped she wouldn't. Could it be I missed him already, and he'd only been gone for one afternoon?

Grumpy, I slogged through the doorway and into the bedroom, where nothing had changed. My oversized sun hat still lay on the window seat, across from the frothy pink bed with the wooden posts. I'd looped a sparkly fascinator onto one of the posts in hopes I could wear it this weekend, which didn't seem likely to happen now.

Maybe a good, long nap would make me feel better. The frilly bed looked especially inviting, even though a triangle of sunshine slanted through a nearby window and neatly bisected the pillow. Some delicate lace curtains were bunched behind brass tiebacks, so I set a panel free and let the lace fall against the glass. Although it didn't do much to staunch the brightness, the fabric created a pretty snowflake pattern of light through holes the size of needles' eyes.

Before I set the second panel free, I spied a smudge in the lower left corner of the window. Three crudely drawn splotches, each the size of a quarter, marred the wavy glass.

I leaned closer to the pane. The marks weren't perfectly smooth. Like hieroglyphics, the corners didn't quite meet up and flat lines drove across the spots that should have been curved.

After a minute, I realized what they were: letters from the alphabet. Initials spelling out *EBA*. What was it Beatrice had said about the Andrews family on the tour yesterday? Something about how their youngest daughter, Eugenia Andrews, had become engaged while living here. Apparently in this very room, since the hotel had christened it the Eugenia Andrews bedroom.

During the Civil War, girls carved their initials into their bedroom windows with their brand-new engagement rings. Supposedly, it symbolized the girl's love for her fiancé, although more practical sorts thought it was a sneaky way to test whether a diamond was real. No scratches on a windowpane meant the ring was nothing more than cheap crystal, white glue, and tin.

I imagined Eugenia Andrews stooped at this very window to scratch her initials into the glass. How many nights had she practiced that in the hopes of becoming engaged?

Being the youngest daughter in a large family, she probably did a bunch of things like that. She'd no doubt squirreled away a piece of wedding cake after each of her sisters got married, then stuck them under her pillow so she could dream about her future husband. While it seemed sweet and innocent more than a hundred years later, I couldn't imagine the family's housekeeper would like *that* practice very much.

I bet Eugenia turned down her suitor at least twice before she agreed to marry him. No one took those first refusals seriously, since everyone knew a girl had to play hard to get back then. If a girl said yes the first time around, she was too desperate.

Unfortunately, the love story here had a tragic ending, Beatrice had said. The night before Eugenia was to say her vows in front of God and man on the front lawn of Morningside Plantation, a messenger galloped across it on horseback to deliver a bloody missive from the Battle of Mobile Bay. Dozens of young soldiers had died, including Eugenia's fiancé. The grief-stricken girl had insisted on wearing her wedding veil for weeks afterward, even to her beloved soldier's funeral.

Despite my fatigue, I knelt again to study the monogram. Something moved beneath my window in the garden two stories below: A pair of figures, one tall and one short. Both were easy to recognize, even from a couple stories up. The general manager, with his bald head and navy suit coat, and Cat, who had changed out of the soiled towel and now wore a green sweat suit.

My, but the room felt surprisingly stuffy all of a sudden. I grasped at the window and gave it a firm tug until the ancient wood casing gave way and the pane slid up. In order to catch more of a breeze, of course. Various sounds wafted up to me, including the whoosh of a car on the road beyond, the trill of a songbird from somewhere in the garden, and a man's troubled words.

"You can't leave now," he said.

Cat turned sideways, as if more interested in the deep emerald hedge than in her boss. "I have to." Her words sounded muffled and weak. "Maybe I shouldn't have told you."

"That's not it."

Since my room still felt stuffy, I carefully pushed the window open a bit more.

"Here. Don't cry." He reached into his jacket pocket and pulled out a square of white. Instead of giving it to Cat, though, he tenderly dabbed the handkerchief against her cheek. *My word.* What an interesting display of affection between a boss and his employee. "Does anyone else know?" He continued to press the handkerchief against her cheek.

"Not really. Don't suppose we can keep it a secret much longer, though."

"Maybe we don't have to."

"What do you mean?" she asked.

At that moment, a semitruck, the only one I'd ever seen use the surface road out front, barreled past the plantation, canceling all other sound with its enormous tires and confounded diesel engine. Not that I'd wanted to overhear a private conversation, mind you, but my curiosity had been piqued. Like the cat with a twirly piece of string again.

When the general manager finished wiping Cat's face with his handkerchief, he held it out to her, like a gift. She tucked it into the pocket of her sweat-suit jacket, and then they both turned and walked away until I lost sight of them.

The crunch of those darn rubber tires against asphalt faded too, as the semitruck barreled farther down the road. Of all the times for someone to come roaring past the plantation, why did it have to be now? I'd have given anything to know what had caused that sweet gesture. And why didn't he want Cat to leave?

Chapter 6

Try as I might, it was impossible to nap after that curious scene. After rolling around for a good half hour, I finally gave up. My mind replayed the conversation between Cat and her boss over and over again and, by the time I rolled off the bed, I was more restless than ever.

Maybe it was time to finally put my curiosity on hold while I satisfied my stomach. I left the room a few minutes later and headed for the restaurant, which Cat had opened up again. After ordering a sandwich to go, I took my feast to the garden outside and ate half of it as I strolled among the star jasmine. Once finished, I rewrapped the other half, since there was no need to spoil my dinner with the La-Portes later that evening.

I stayed outside for more than an hour, reading the headstones in the graveyard and counting the live oaks scattered across the property. Before long, the sun hung low in the sky and it was time for me to return to my room.

The minute I entered the bedroom, I headed for the closet, where one of my favorite hats peeked out from its box on the top shelf, next to Ivy's damaged pheasant quills and tangled lace.

Now, normally I'd save a fancy sinamay for outdoor weddings and such, but I hadn't seen Mrs. LaPorte in forever and that struck me as reason enough to reach for that particular hat. I pulled it from its box and fluffed up the black and red bow. Paired with a Pucci sheath and platform heels, it'd be perfect for our little get-together tonight.

Some fifteen minutes later, my hair backcombed and lips colored, I left the room and proceeded down the stairs. I managed to navigate them in high heels, even though I would have preferred to have Ambrose by my side to steady my climb, and arrived at the restaurant with five minutes to spare.

The minute I spied Mrs. LaPorte with her son, twenty years disappeared into the walls. "Hello."

She smiled and there was the sweet-faced mother who'd doled out Gatorade in plastic cups to Lance and me. "Why, Missy, you look prettier than a pat of butter on a stack of wheat cakes!" She enveloped me in a hug of clean cotton and sparkly pearls. She wore a simple cream dress and a loose chignon of snow-white hair at her neck. "Couldn't believe it when Lance told me you'd run into each other. Thanked my lucky stars you were sitting on the front porch when he showed up."

Poor Charles tried to intervene at this point and whisk us into the restaurant, but we chatted for a good minute before either of us felt inclined to move. For his part, Lance had no choice but to follow behind when we finally allowed Charles to guide us to a sparkling table by one of the picture windows.

We read our menus over glasses of sweet tea, while I discreetly devoured a roll. In between bites I provided a respectable report on my comings and goings at the store, until I decided to launch right into it. "Did Lance here tell you what happened this morning, Mrs. LaPorte?"

"First off, do call me Odilia." She gently patted my hand. "And I heard a girl died right here in the bathroom."

"Her name was Trinity Solomon."

"That's what I heard." She shook her head. "One of the Solomons out of Baton Rouge, but can't say as I'm too surprised."

I nearly choked on my roll. "Really? It's not like a girl gets murdered around here every day."

"No, dear, but she's part of the Solomon clan. I'm sure you've heard about her daddy."

Lance squirmed, probably uncomfortable with our gossiping. Since we had yet to say anything mean-spirited, I didn't see the harm. "I did hear about him, more than once. Heard his refinery in the Gulf exploded about a year back."

"Yes, which was bad enough. But then to find out Mr. Solomon had been pinching pennies since the day it opened. That was the last straw."

I couldn't imagine I'd heard correctly. "Come again?"

"No one knows for sure, Mom," Lance said. "Could have happened at any refinery."

She wagged her finger at him. "Tell that to the night crew. It takes skill to keep those stacks from catching fire. When Herbert Solomon took the staff down to next to nothing, it was only a matter of time before something bad would happen."

"I heard all about that from some of the people here. The man was cheap?" It was hard to imagine anyone who'd pay a full orchestra to serenade wedding guests with "Here Comes the Bride" could also pinch pennies.

"Only when he wanted to be. That's what got everyone so angry," she said. "He cut his staff by half and then bought himself a fancy new car. One of those be-and-w's."

Lance laughed a little. "It's *BMW*, Mom. Can't a man buy himself a new car around here without everyone getting riled up about it? They're jealous, is all. People didn't like him because he made money."

I took a sip of tea. Plenty of people had probably made money in these parts. The very building we sat in had been the work of a wealthy sugar plantation owner. Too bad he'd chosen to make his fortune on the backs of others.

"Whenever there's a loss of life, that changes everything." I set the glass aside. "It makes people want to strike out and hurt back."

"True enough," Odilia said. "He didn't have any friends. I knew Ivy Solomon personally and told her more than once it was a miracle how she stood by that man after everything came to light. Believe me, I know a bad husband when I see one, and he was tighter than the skin on a grape. Like the way he made her sew curtains for her sitting room and then went out and bought real estate. Or the way he made his future son-in-law sign a prenuptial agreement before the boy's big day."

"Do tell." I leaned forward.

Odilia glanced over her right shoulder, then her left. We were the only ones in our corner of the restaurant, but one could never be too careful. "You know how my boy Larry is an attorney up in Baton Rouge?"

"Lance here told me about that." I glanced at Lance, who was picking at a roll from the bread basket. Smart of him to realize we weren't going to slow down the conversation so he could catch up.

"He graduated first in his class at Louisiana State. Always did have a mind for memorizing."

"I know that's true." We'd gotten sidetracked. "I remember how Larry memorized the Book of Psalms when we were only little things. I bet his clients love him. Was Mr. Solomon a client?"

"Sure enough. Called on him a few months back and said he needed legal help. Didn't like the boy his daughter was set to marry and wanted to protect the family fortune. That's according to my Larry, anyway."

As she spoke, Charles made the unfortunate mistake of trying to approach our table to take our order. I raised my eyebrows, which was all the signal he needed to turn tail and leave. There was time enough to hear the daily specials once Odilia and I swapped stories.

"Anyway, Herbert Solomon came to my boy's office angry about how his only baby was being taken advantage of. Between you, me, and the tabletop, his baby wasn't much to look at and her fiancé could have had any girl from here to Texas."

"I know that's true. I saw the girl on my very first day here. God rest her soul."

"Well, Herbert Solomon was convinced her fiancé was only after Trinity's money. Didn't imagine anyone could love his daughter as much as he did."

"So he had your Larry write up a prenup? That's a little extreme."

"Told my son he was going to make a big deal out of presenting it before the wedding to see what the boy would do. Sort of like playing King Solomon in the Bible when those two women wanted the same baby. Figured if the boy really loved his Trinity, then he'd sign the piece of paper and give away his rights to her money."

"That must have come as some surprise. I can only imagine how *that* conversation went."

"It happened not more than a week ago." Odilia held out her menu. "Apparently, Herbert told my Larry that the boy asked if he could bring home the prenup to study it."

"See—" apparently Lance had been paying attention, after all— "he *did* care about her."

Men can be so delusional. If, in fact, the fiancé had been after Trinity's money, the last thing he would've done was tussle with her daddy without looking for another way around the prenup.

"Don't be too sure, Lance. Could be he hoped to change his bride's mind. Or her father's. Thought if he bought himself a little time, he could turn things around."

Lance looked thoughtful as he finished the last of his roll. Crumbs littered his plate like birdseed on a white feeder.

"Guess it's time to order." I felt a bit more charitable by now. Strapping guys like Lance needed their supper, and he'd already put in a full day's work, so he must have been starving. Not to mention I hadn't eaten a proper meal since who knew when. "Order whatever you want. Tonight's a special occasion."

Even more so now I'd learned such interesting information about the Solomon family. Amazing how many tidbits could be revealed over a basket of supper rolls and a glass of sweet tea.

The rest of our meal passed uneventfully. Once again I marveled at how Odilia knew exactly what to order and how it should be prepared. She always did know her way around a kitchen.

It was good to see her and Lance, just like when we were back home chatting over something fresh baked from her oven. I always could count on her to make Lance and me laugh at her stories, and she could turn a phrase better than most anyone else I knew. Too soon, it was time to say good-bye and watch them leave.

I began to walk back to my room. My feet had bloated up, along with the rest of me, and I slogged through the carpet like a skater on a rough patch of ice.

Two hallways loomed ahead of me. One was the main hall I always used to get to the stairs, which normally was wide and welcoming. Since I was full on bread and sugar, it seemed much longer and narrower than before.

The second hall was definitely the shorter of the two. I opted for the shortcut and entered a dark corridor. A few steps along, something tingled against the back of my neck, beginning at my shoulder blades and shimmying higher to my skull.

I was being watched. From somewhere above, as if the observer was perched near the ceiling.

I raised my gaze. On the wall next to me was an enormous oil painting of a glowering Confederate general. Colorful epaulets decorated each shoulder of his boiled wool coat, and shiny brass buttons closed the lapels. It looked like Stonewall Jackson, but it was hard to tell Civil War generals apart, what with the overgrown beards and all.

I peered down the length of hall. A row of oil paintings unfurled before me. *Butter my biscuit.* Most were seascapes and military battles, with a few portraits, like Jackson's, thrown in for good measure.

I studied each one as I walked. P.G.T. Beauregard, the Battle of New Orleans, the state capitol in Baton Rouge. All were unique to Louisiana and looked priceless. The last painting was an oversized portrait of a dusty battle on an open field.

Something seemed off, though. The painting tilted lazily toward the floor. When I tried to straighten it, I realized it hung against an uneven section of wall. Deep cuts around the frame made the wall dip on one side.

The picture was nailed to a hidden door. A small door, but a door nonetheless. With no keyhole nor knob. Why would someone build a door into a wall and then not attach a knob?

Since it'd be a shame to dirty the canvas with my fingerprints, I pushed against the elaborate gilt frame instead. Slowly but surely, the door gave way and exposed a gaping black hole.

Cautiously, I stepped inside. There were no shadows or edges or corners in this space. Nothing but emptiness, dark and as cool as an abandoned coal shaft.

I felt along a wall beside me for a light switch. One click and the room instantly brightened. A brick fireplace rose floor to ceiling in front of me, the hearth taken up by a pair of velvet wingbacks. Nearby stood an elaborate writing desk covered with mother-of-pearl inlays.

Lorda mercy. There were enough curiosities in this room to fill any Ripley's Believe it or Not! Museum. Like the bejeweled hookah on the writing desk and the emerald turban in a glass case. Didn't Beatrice say something or other about a Turkish craze that once swept through the South? People couldn't get enough of anything and everything having to do with the Middle East, which would explain the hookah, the turban, and an embroidered prayer rug on the wall.

Even the air smelled different. Like burnt leaves, earthy and dry. Cigars, maybe, or perhaps a pipe. I stepped up to one of the wingbacks and sniffed. Sure enough, burnt tobacco.

This had to be a smoking room. A place where men disappeared after dinner to talk politics, play cards, and gamble to their hearts' content. Of course, no self-respecting Southern belle would *want* to stay in a room full of smoke and foul language, but the gentlemen insisted these rooms be built into their mansions.

I moved closer to the writing desk and the trove of oddities. Beside the turban lay a sterling-silver cylinder, about the length of a rolling pin, engraved with flowers, stars, and whatnot. I delicately pulled the ends apart and discovered something shiny and round, like the pin and notch of a key, nestled on a bed of burgundy silk: An old-fashioned brass key as long as my finger.

"Hello?" someone called out.

I almost dropped the cylinder as I turned. The hotel's general manager peered from the doorway.

"My goodness, you frightened me."

"What are you doing in here?" He didn't look particularly pleased to see me.

"Thought I'd take a little stroll after dinner." I tried to sound nonchalant, although my breath stalled. "And I went through that wonderful gallery of yours. You really should—"

"Guests aren't allowed in here." He whisked the antique tube away from me.

"I'm sorry. I didn't mean to intrude." I took a deep breath for courage. "Couldn't help myself when I saw this beautiful room."

"That may be, but I'm going to have to ask you to leave."

"Sure. No problem. But can I ask you something?" Might as well go for broke. "What's that? I've never seen one of those before." I pointed to the strange cylinder.

"It's a scroll holder."

"Wow. It's beautiful. Especially all of the silk on the inside." Was it my imagination, or did he flinch?

Instead of responding, he carefully replaced the antique on the desk.

"Too bad the scroll's missing," I said. "All I saw was a key inside."

"Impossible. It's empty. Can I walk you to your room?"

Interesting. "I'm pretty sure of what I saw. Where did you find all this stuff?" My eyes swept over the crowded space.

"Most of it belonged to Mr. Andrews. He was a collector. There's a lot more in the attic. You really should go."

"It's a shame to hide it. Especially with all the knickknacks."

"I suppose. Look, it's getting late. I'd be happy to escort you upstairs."

"That's okay. It's been a heckuva day, but I can manage on my own."

The manager waited for me to move. When I didn't, he gently took hold of my elbow and guided me away from the desk.

"You're lucky. Most people never get to see this room. It's time for me to lock up."

I tugged my arm away. "But there's no keyhole in the door. I checked."

"Did I say *lock*? I meant to say that I need to set the alarm in here. Off you go."

Of all the nerve! He treated me like a bothersome child who refused to go to bed.

"I can find my way back. Thanks a lot."

"Have a pleasant evening, Miss DuBois. Sleep well."

Before I retreated through the opening, I glanced over my shoulder. The manager opened the top drawer of the writing desk and stashed the cylinder inside.

I took my time navigating the stairs. Strange he'd hustled me out of the smoking room so quickly. It wasn't as if I'd sprawled across the velvet chairs or tried the turban on for size. My presence there made him nervous, although there was no telling why.

I climbed the stairs until I arrived at the third floor. When I approached my door, there was a blotch above the peephole. Someone had taped a note there. *Not again.*

This note said something about Ambrose being stuck with another crisis, so he wouldn't be back until morning. *Dadburnit!* I shoved the note into my purse and turned the key in the lock.

The room was as quiet as always and silence overwhelmed me as I went about organizing my nightclothes. Once I'd changed and used the facilities, I combed my hair a hundred times and brushed my teeth. I rushed through the rest of my routine before switching off the light and flopping into bed.

I couldn't stay mad forever, though. And the bed *did* feel nice, what with a canopy of pink silk and a tuft of matching comforter. Downright comfortable, in fact. All that was missing was a twirling ballerina like they stuck in a music box and a tiny violin to play *Swan Lake* in the background.

Soon all sound disappeared. I couldn't have been sleeping long, though, when I awoke with a start. Something had fallen out in the hall. Was I dreaming? I sat up under the canopy of pink and held my breath, listening.

Crash. There it was again. Unmistakable. A cold fear passed through me, stitching me to the spot. I wanted to call out for Ambrose, until I remembered he was nowhere near the plantation. Maybe if I closed my eyes and put my hands over my ears, the noise would disappear.

No such luck. Another crash, this time a bit farther down the hall. Whatever could someone be doing banging around like that in the middle of the night?

By the time I flung back the comforter and jumped from the bed, my fear had hardened to anger. Some people had no respect for others. Probably a drunken guest trying to find his room with the floorboards swaying as he stumbled from door to door. I debated whether to call the front desk or give the noisemaker a piece of my mind.

As usual, my feet moved before my brain could engage, and I moved to the door and threw it open. The hall was empty. Whatever had awoken me from my sweet sleep was gone. Or was it?

A shadow slid along the opposite wall, like a puff of cigarette smoke against paper. A bit of gray felt cloth was visible. More curious than frightened now, I followed the blot down the hall and onto the stair's landing. For a moment, the shadow froze, silhouetted by moonlight. A dark hat was above and heavy brogans below. If I wasn't a practical sort, I would've sworn the figure on the stairs wore a uniform. A Confederate uniform, like the one I'd seen in those pictures in the history museum downstairs. Like the one of a soldier holding a musket across his chest.

"Hey, you! What're you doing?" I knew the person would answer, since he'd been caught red-handed, snooping around in the middle of the night.

The figure turned and tumbled down the stairs in a flurry of gray felt and black boots. *Oh my!* I moved to help, but the figure disappeared as quickly as that puff of smoke.

When I finally allowed my brain to catch up, the chill returned. It was foolish of me to confront a stranger like that. Ambrose would have lectured me twelve ways to Sunday about the importance of minding my own business.

Slowly, I backed away from the stairs. Bravery was one thing, but foolhardiness was quite another.

I returned to my room, with my tail tucked between my legs. Whatever had awoken me from my sweet sleep was gone, as ethereal as the moonlight that splayed across the carpet. Why couldn't Ambrose have returned sooner? At least I'd have someone to tell about the figure that tumbled end-over-end down the long stairway. Someone to comfort me and stroke my hair until I fell asleep.

I dropped onto the music-box bed, which didn't look nearly as inviting now. Odds were good I wouldn't sleep another wink.

Chapter 7

Sunlight glimmered against the hardwood floor in my room the next morning, patiently nudging me awake. I'd caught only a few winks of sleep after the commotion in the hall, and my head was as heavy as wet sand.

After a long stretch, I headed for the bathroom. Maybe a steamy shower and some mint toothpaste would revive me.

Somewhat awakened, I dressed and grabbed my favorite cloche from its hatbox on a shelf in the closet. Although Ambrose didn't much care for this one and once compared it to an oversized French beret, now would be the perfect time to wear it, with him being gone and all.

I schlepped to the staircase, where sunlight poured through a beveled window and hopscotched over the stairs. I continued to walk down the stairs and through the hallway by the restaurant. Nothing much registered until I passed the bathroom where Lance had reaffixed the crime-scene tape, and then I shuddered.

No use starting the morning off on a sour note, though, so I veered to the bar, where fat leather armchairs clumped around tables made from old wagon wheels. The smell of cut limes, spilled gin, and Ivory dish soap rose above it all.

Everything was ready for the day. Glasses hung from a rack above the bar like shiny raindrops poised to fall on a pile of folded towels. To one side of the bar, they'd installed a fancy double dishwasher, like the kind they advertised in *Southern Living*. Couldn't help but read those ads when I sat under the hairdryer at A Cut Above. Turned out the really fancy dishwashers had a drawer above and another below, so single people like me could wash a small load and not feel so guilty about it.

Since I was all alone, I walked up to the bar for a better look. Before I got very far, my purse snagged on the counter and plummeted to the ground, spilling the contents every which way. I bent behind the bar to retrieve a Tampax that was careening across the floor.

"You shouldn't be here," a woman said.

Another voice immediately joined the first. I sucked in my breath and silently slid to the ground.

"I had to talk to you." It was a man, breathy and rushed. "What am I gonna do, Beatrice? They're gonna think I killed her."

"Gee, you're worried about yourself," Beatrice said. "What a surprise. Don't you even care that she's dead?"

"Of course I care. I'm not an animal, you know."

"You could've fooled me. Look, Sterling, what do you want *me* to do?"

Since I had no choice but to overhear this conversation, I might as well get comfortable. I twisted sideways and stretched my legs in front of me. Thank goodness I'd opted for the snug cloche and not one of my oversized hats, which would surely show above the bar.

Beatrice continued: "You're probably being followed. I wouldn't doubt if they get an arrest warrant for you today."

"That's why we have to leave. Come with me, Bea." A swish of fabric, as if someone had grasped at clothing.

"Trinity's dead." Her retort was harsh. "Like you said, they'll think you had something to do with it. You're not going to drag me down with you."

"But that's where they're wrong," he said. "Why would I kill her before we got married? I'd be stupid. I was gonna be a millionaire. You have to believe me."

My lips automatically pursed. According to Odilia LaPorte, Herbert Solomon forced the groom to sign a prenup that would leave him high and dry after the ceremony. Might he be talking big for Beatrice's benefit?

"It doesn't matter what I believe," Beatrice said. "Go home and let me figure out what to do. Don't make a move until I call you. Got that?"

Her voice was like broken glass; so different from the chipper greeting I'd heard before.

"If you say so, but I'd rather stay here with you."

"I told you . . . go home. Stay there until I call. Don't even think about coming back or trying to contact me."

"But I can't go back there." His voice softened to a whimper; like a puppy dog begging for a treat. "The rent's due and I haven't got it."

"Not again." Although I couldn't see a thing from my hiding spot, I imagined Beatrice shaking her head. "What happened to the money I gave you last month? Don't tell me you blew it already."

"It's those acting lessons, Bea. They charge so damn much. How can they expect us to pay for it? They know we're starving artists, but they don't care."

"Why do you always come to me for it? I don't have any more money than you. Guess you should have asked your fiancée."

"You know how her father was, tightfisted bastard. I'm only two weeks behind. That's all I need. I promise I'll pay you back. Every dime of it."

More rustling, and then a hand slapped something on a bar stool not too far away. Hallelujah I was up to date on my prayers, or else I'd want to confess something right then and there and beg God to hide me. As it was, I simply held my breath and hoped for the best.

"There. That's all I have," Beatrice said. "Take it. But don't ask me for anything more until the end of the month." Her voice quieted. She must have stepped away from the bar. "And be careful. The police are probably checking out your apartment now."

"I will. And I'll pay you back. Promise."

"Yeah, right. Any day now."

Finally, the bar fell silent. I snatched up the Tampax, along with some Altoids and my cell phone, and tucked them all in my purse. Not that I wanted to overhear a private conversation, mind you, but I couldn't very well have stood and excused myself to go use the ladies' room. No, proper etiquette dictated I let them finish their little chat, even with me listening from not more than four feet away.

Surprising how different Beatrice sounded. She couldn't have been nicer to Ambrose and me, while she sounded ready to bite that guy's head off and spit it out the nearest window. More like a parent giving a scolding.

Not that either of them sounded a bit sorry Trinity was dead. They seemed put out, inconvenienced. Like they wanted to save their hides instead of find out who murdered the young bride.

Which meant I'd have to chew on their words, along with some biscuits and gravy, at breakfast. As if on cue, my stomach growled, so I smoothed down the cloche before straightening and moseyed over to the maître d' stand.

Sure enough, Charles stood sentinel behind the wooden podium as fresh-looking as one of the linen tablecloths draped over the tables.

"Morning, Melissa. Is your friend still upstairs?"

I focused on closing my purse so the tension had time to dribble from my face. No need to let Charles think something was wrong. "No. He's not coming this morning. He had to put out some fires at his shop yesterday, and he never made it back. And please call me Missy."

"Will do. And that's too bad about your friend." Charles led me through the restaurant to a table near the window, where he expertly scooped up the unneeded place setting.

"His assistant can't seem to get along without him," I said. "Someday he's going to have to cut that apron string."

Charles handed me a menu as I slipped into the seat. "Sounds like they need him."

"Must be." Since Charles and I were the only two people in the restaurant, perhaps now would be the perfect time to chat. "Has everyone recovered from yesterday?" While Trinity's body had surfaced only the day before, these people still had a business to run.

"Guess so. It would've been a lot worse if we'd known her better. I mean, I never met the girl until last week."

"Really?"

He offered a basket of rolls as round as pond stones and lightly glazed.

"Still, it must have come as a terrible shock when they found her body so close by," I said.

"That's true. Kind of creepy, when you put it like that."

"I should think so." Daintily, I placed a roll on my plate. "Where do you think they took the body?" While this wasn't the best meal-time conversation, Charles would have the inside scoop.

"There's only one funeral parlor in town. It's right next to the Baptist church." He set down the rolls and hovered over me, as if waiting for me to look at my menu. He should have known by now he'd have to wait a bit longer.

"That must make it very convenient. Back in Bleu Bayou, the funeral parlor is way across town."

"Riversbend is much smaller, so our church pastor works at both places."

"Do you go to church there?" I asked.

"Yeah, when I'm not working."

I glanced around the empty restaurant. I was probably the only person within a ten-mile radius sitting down to breakfast instead of sitting in a pew at the Baptist church. Shame on me for forgetting today was the Sabbath.

"Where did you say the church is?" There was no telling how much longer Ambrose would be away, and I *was* wearing my favorite hat. It could be interesting to see how the people around here worshipped, especially if it meant being closer to the place where they'd taken Trinity. Might be downright fascinating.

"Half a mile down the road, on your left. You can probably make the morning service if you leave right now."

I glanced out the window. Bright sunshine and a few wispy clouds. Perfect weather for a stroll. And I could always use some fresh air to get over my encounter in the hall the night before. "Say, Charles, I think I saw something outside my room last night. Or some*one*. Wearing a uniform, of all things."

"That right? Must have spooked you with all that talk of ghosts yesterday. You know there's no real evidence."

"Of course." When he put it like that, it *did* sound silly. "I'll tell you what. You get me some coffee to go and I'll head over to the church and put that nonsense about ghosts and such out of my head."

"You got it." Charles left, which gave me a moment to slip a breakfast roll into my purse. I could always repay the hotel later with a big supper order. After a minute or two, he returned with a Styrofoam cup filled to the brim with something black and steaming.

"It might be fun to visit a new church," I said. "Want me to say hello to anyone for you while I'm there?"

His face softened a bit. "If you see Beatrice, tell her hey."

"I'll do that. If I see her." Now that I had a plan, I slid out of the seat, renewed by our little chat. If I was ever going to help sweet Ivy Solomon, there was no time like the present. And there was no telling how long until Lance got an official police report. By then, whoever killed Trinity could be miles and miles away, and it didn't seem right to be so close to the person doing the investigating—my old neighbor, Lance LaPorte, all grown up—without helping if I could.

Coffee in hand, I left the plantation. The only other souls out on this bright May morning were two broodmares who watched as I walked along their fence line. They looked recently brushed, with manes that lay flat against their crests.

"Morning, ladies."

The smell of dry willows, spent wildflower stalks, and dusty pea gravel followed me as I hiked down the road. I longed for a sketchpad so I could capture the way the willows bent in the morning breeze. Even though I normally used feathers for the trims of my hats, I could always replicate the pussy willows with some rolled organdy or silk. I tried to memorize their exact bend so I could sketch the stalks when I returned to my hotel room later.

Once I'd passed the horse pasture, I came upon columns of spiky plants grown chest-high, spaced a foot apart. Sugarcane. Not a kitchen garden, by any means, but a commercial operation that stretched back as far as a football field.

A bit farther along, the church/funeral home/coroner's office Charles had described came into view. First up was the church, made with white clapboards, rounded windows, and flower boxes full of purple irises. The picture of a quaint country church. The building stretched back a ways, and it had sired an identical building next door. The two were joined by a fabric awning that arched over a cobblestone path.

It all looked perfect. Too perfect, as a matter of fact. When I drew closer, the wood clapboards were actually plastic and the flowers made of silk. Even the roof's shingles were so evenly spaced they must have come off a roll. A marquee in front of the first building announced the Rising Tide Baptist Church, while a smaller sign pointed to the Riversbend Funeral Home next door, like an afterthought.

Church had yet to begin. An old man in a gray suit guarded the doors like a stone lion. I automatically walked toward him until I remembered the real reason for my visit. Niceties would have to wait if I wanted to explore the funeral parlor next door.

I ducked my head and pretended to be searching for a trash can for my coffee cup, which I found by the cobblestone path. I made a big show out of tossing the cup, then dashed toward the funeral parlor, which had the same plastic siding, indoor/outdoor grass mats and artfully arranged window boxes as the church. I was beginning to feel like a tourist at Disneyland, where artists used paint and plywood to create the illusion of actual charm.

Fortunately, the door was unlocked; probably left that way by the church's cleaning crew. The moment I stepped through the doors, I paused. The room was dark compared to the parking lot, and a stained-glass window at the front provided the only light. In it Jesus wore an enormous halo, which looked more like an oversized sombrero, truth be told, and raised his hands heavenward. A half-dozen folding chairs separated me from the figure's embrace.

The only thing missing was a casket. A stand was there, with four wheels and thick hospital-grade steel bars, but the space between the front and back of the cart was empty.

I quietly slid into one of the creaky folding chairs and pondered my options.

"Lookin' for sometin'?"

"Darryl! You gave me a fright." The voice nearly brought me to my knees, and I placed my hand on my chest. "You've got to stop sneaking up on me like that. It's not polite."

Darryl, the gardener at Morningside, kept popping up when I least expected it. He tucked his head, hopefully because he realized he'd done something wrong.

"Yer too early for da memorial service, an almos' too late for da church next door." He jerked his thumb toward the Baptist church. "Deys asked me to take care of te chapel here. Keep her clean. Whatcha doin' here?"

"Me? I'm out for a stroll. Thought I'd check out this place before my friend gets back. The door was open. It's a quaint little chapel."

His eyes narrowed. "Dis be te funeral parlor, Miz DuBois. Notin' quaint about dat. Ya best be gettin' to church, and I'll lock up te place."

His tone made the hairs at the nape of my neck bristle. "I didn't mean any harm. Honestly, you act like I broke in here for fun."

"Didn' mean no offense, Miz DuBois. Guess all dat talk about te family burnin' up dat girl's body done make me crazy. Poor ting, so young an all."

"Really?" Casually, I leaned back. After spending so much time in psychology classes at Vanderbilt, I knew plenty of tricks to get people to tell me more. One of my favorites was a little something called "reflection," where you simply parroted back what a person had just said. It made people want to prattle on. "They want to burn the girl's body?"

"Dat's what te fater said. Goin' on about cremation. An him bein' Cat'lic an' all." By this time, Darryl had moved his good hand forward, so I quickly moved my hand too. That was another trick called "mirroring," but that was neither here nor there at this point.

"If they're Catholic, then they'll probably have the funeral back in their own parish, don't you think?" I asked.

"Lots of dem churches don letcha bring te ashes in. Could be te priest be makin' em stay here for dat. Hard ta say."

"I'm surprised she's being cremated. Doesn't sound like the kind of thing most parents would agree to."

"Dey be gettin' bad information." Darryl shook his head. "Someone be tellin' em what ta do."

I hadn't thought of that. But what could they possibly gain by cremating the girl's remains instead of having a proper Catholic burial in their own parish? I'd have to ask Ambrose when he returned.

"I guess I should get to the church service, then." I rose and wandered past him. "Are you coming?"

"Oh, no." His face grew even more somber, if that was possible. "I don' belong in tere. Dey don wan' me any more ten I wan' tem." He stood with his legs pressed tightly together, which was definitely a defensive position, according to the textbooks.

"All right, then. See you back at the plantation." I waved and ducked past him into the bright sunshine, relieved to be free of Darryl's stare.

Compared with the gloom and doom of the funeral parlor, the church positively glowed. I hurried under the awning to the church's double-wide doors, which were closed. They never do seem to latch right, though, so I gently depressed the handle and pushed them open without a sound.

The place was small. Two columns of pews ran front to back and held about four-dozen people in all. I could tell from the back of the heads it was a family crowd, with parents bookending their offspring at the ends of the aisles.

A baldheaded man sat a few rows up on the left. When he turned, I glimpsed the profile of the general manager of Morningside.

I sauntered over to his aisle and tucked into the row as inconspic-
uously as possible. Once again, I thanked my lucky stars I hadn't
worn a more showy hat, because I'd surely put folks to whispering
about my appearance. As it was, only a few people seemed to notice
my arrival, including the general manager, who nodded.

"Morning," I whispered.

He opened his Bible and turned it my way to give me the chapter
and verse. I lifted a book from a holder in front of me and located the
day's passage in Psalms. Pretty innocent stuff, compared to Revela-
tions, and since I'd memorized most of it anyway, I let my mind wander to the people who sat around me.

The smallish group was well-behaved, with most of the families
keeping their toddlers in check. In my book, there was a fine line between family togetherness and tempting fate, but butter my biscuit if
these children didn't behave as well as a convention full of librarians.

Once the pastor finished dissecting the passage, he turned our attention to a man who sat in the first row. The stranger popped up
from his pew and joined the clergyman, all the while waving a bulletin in the air.

"Thank you, Reverend," he said. "Good preaching today. Mighty
fine. If y'all will open your bulletins, there's a little something in
there about the ladies' fashion show tomorrow night."

Fashion show? My ears immediately perked up. A spaghetti supper I could understand. Same thing with a bake sale or bingo night.
But fashion show? Be still my heart.

"Now, we planned to put on the show tomorrow night in the social
hall. Heaven knows we need the money for our new choir robes. I'm
sorry to say the organizer's backed out, so we're going to have to cancel the event."

The congregation groaned in unison, like a choir exhaling at the
end of a long whole note. Whatever did he mean? Seemed a shame to
cancel on account of one person backing out.

"Yes, it's true. I know how disappointed y'all are, but there doesn't
seem to be any other choice. We've already sold a bunch of tickets, and
we'll return everyone's money as quick as we can."

I couldn't, could I? The way I figured it, I needed more time at
Morningside if I was ever going to help Ivy unravel the horrible tangle of events. It might give me the perfect reason to stay in town, plus
a little privacy to look around the plantation, since everyone else

would be at the church tomorrow night. I could always offer up Ambrose as master of ceremonies and then sneak away from the show when the opportunity arose.

My mind made up, I rose from the pew. "Y'all don't know me, but my name is Missy DuBois."

Heads turned my way in response.

"You may have heard of my shop, though. It's called Crowning Glory, and we make couture veils and whatnot for bridal parties."

That caused some nodding and general agreement among the crowd.

"Anyway, the way I figure it, you need someone to organize a fashion show tomorrow night. My best friend happens to be Ambrose Jackson. He's been on television and everything."

The whispers came back now as loud as a kettle brought to boil. Just like I thought. The mere mention of Ambrose got them riled up. Ever since he did a reality show for the Learning Channel, where he turned ordinary girls into princesses, there weren't many places we could go without being recognized. Sometimes I wondered if the women we met were more interested in his dress designs, or in Ambrose.

"Between the two of us, we can come up with enough fashion to make your head spin."

"That's a wonderful idea, Miss DuBois!" The speaker with the bulletin looked positively ecstatic.

"It'd be a shame for you to have to cancel your event." Guilt should have overcome me by then, offering up Ambrose on a silver platter, but in my experience, it was better to act first and seek forgiveness later. It wouldn't hurt him to help out the locals here. "He'll be thrilled, I'm sure."

Since I'd spoken my piece, I sat again. It felt good to help other people, even if the other people hadn't exactly asked for my help.

"We would be most grateful," the speaker said. "Guess the good Lord works in mysterious ways. Sounds like we're going to have an amazing fund-raiser tomorrow night. Make us forget all about the violence here this weekend. Praise the Lord, and let's pass the plate."

Chapter 8

Now that I'd done my part to help the Rising Tide Baptist Church, I simmered in a warm gumbo of helpfulness until the preacher blessed us with the benediction. Even though fashion shows involved endless details, like pulling dresses, matching accessories, and hiring models, it was like falling off a greasy log backward if you'd staged them enough times, which I had. In fact, the Ladies' Auxiliary League asked us to produce a similar fashion show just last month, and I still had all of the notes and contact info at my fingertips.

As I made my way to the narthex now, someone touched my elbow. It was the speaker with the bulletin, and his eyes shone like new pennies.

"Can't thank you enough, Miss DuBois, for helping us out. I don't know what we would have done otherwise." His cheeks shone too, and were as pink as the blush on a rose.

"It wasn't anything. Figured you could use a hand. Like you said, the good Lord works in mysterious ways."

"When people hear a TV star is helping with our fund-raiser, they'll burn up the telephone wires wanting to come. We'll start the program at dusk with a choir number or two and then turn it over to you and your friend. If that's okay with you."

"Don't you worry. Give us a runway and a microphone, and we'll be good to go."

He nodded briskly. "We'll be in touch. I'm guessing you're staying at the plantation?"

"Sure enough." He still seemed a tad nervous, so I decided to put him at ease. "Please don't fret. It's nothing Ambrose and I can't handle." Really, he was going to age something awful if he worried about every little detail in life.

That did the trick, and he smiled. "Thanks again. It's a miracle you came here today."

"I don't know about that." Truth be told, my idea had been to visit the funeral parlor next door and hunt up anything I could find about Trinity. I never expected to offer Ambrose and me to a roomful of strangers like a slab of sponge cake on a dessert plate. The way I figured it, this would play out nicely, as long as Ambrose didn't mind me steamrolling him like that.

By now the congregation, including the lion-like deacon, had left. I had a lot of time to think as I wandered back to the plantation. Time to ponder how I'd line up my ducks when I talked to Ambrose. Maybe that was why I barely noticed the sugarcane stalks or the two old broodmares or the rattle of a truck that approached me on the road.

In fact, I didn't notice it until the tires ground to a halt not more than five yards ahead, spitting pea gravel and chalk dust. The driver's window was open and a hand with tattooed knuckles and blue fingernail polish gripped the steering wheel, which pretty much gave away the owner's identity.

Sure enough, after killing the ignition, Cat Antoine threw open the door of the Ford dually and proceeded to throw up in the crabgrass by the side of the road.

"Oh, my." I picked up my pace and soon reached the truck.

After she once again baptized the ground—like she'd done with the azalea bushes earlier—she slithered out of the truck and bent over. She seemed even tinier without her chef's coat.

"Are you all right?"

Obviously, she wasn't and she didn't answer me right away. Finally, she nodded. "Guess so." She wouldn't look at me, which was probably for the best since a trickle of ooze dangled from her chin.

I fumbled around in my purse for a stray Kleenex. "Here, Cat. Use this."

"*Uuuggghhh.*" She wiped her mouth, which was a good sign she wasn't too far gone.

"You need to get right back to your room and go to bed." Honestly, sometimes people had no sense. Here she was, running around like a rooster with its head cut off, when she should have been lying under a quilt with a cool washcloth and a hot-water bottle.

"You don't understand." She still wouldn't look at me, but kept her eyes trained on the dirtied ground.

"What I understand is you're sick and you shouldn't be going anywhere but right back to your room." I took hold of her shoulder and squeezed it gently to show her I meant business. Somewhere along the line I'd switched to the voice I used with children who ransacked my store.

She shrugged out from under my grasp, which meant she truly was feeling better. Whatever stomach bug had possessed her to stop by the side of the road now lay in a puddle at our feet. "I'm not sick, Missy. I'm pregnant."

Oh, my. Now the conversation between her and her boss in the garden the day before made sense. This changed everything.

"Okay, then." I tucked back into my purse and found one of the Altoids I'd rescued from the bar's floor. I blew on it softly and gave it to her. "Have this. First things first. How far along?"

She accepted my offering and shrugged. "About three months."

"Does the daddy know?"

"Not exactly."

"Imagine you're going to have to take maternity leave." There was no way she could manage those big pots and pans with a baby growing in her belly, and maybe that was what had upset her boss so.

"I suppose. I think I'll go back to my room now. Want a lift?"

The question stumped me. On the one hand, it was a lovely day. On the other, here was my chance to find out more about one of the employees who worked at Morningside Plantation. My curious nature won out, of course. "I'd love a lift."

We both climbed into the Ford dually. A jumble of notebooks, magazines, and Louisiana road maps cluttered the dashboard and floor, and torn plastic seats stretched from side to side like a dirtied church pew. The only feminine touch was a strawberry air freshener dangling from the rearview mirror.

"This was my dad's." Once Cat fired up the engine, we pulled onto the road. "He passed away last year. Mom gave it to me since she couldn't drive it."

That made sense. It looked tricky enough to drive at any age, although Cat was doing a fine job as we bumped and banged and jostled our way toward the plantation. Her cheeks were even pink again. With her green jacket and reddish cheeks, she reminded me of the strawberry air freshener on the rearview mirror.

"I can't bring myself to clean it out," she said. "Everything reminds me of him. Is that weird?"

"No. I think it's sweet you want to keep your daddy's memory around." That explained the tin of Skoal wedged against the front window and the hardhat I'd spied in the truck bed. "What did your daddy do?"

"He was a journeyman at the refinery."

"Really? Would that be the same place everyone's told me about?" I asked.

She didn't answer. By this time we'd arrived at the plantation, and she swung the truck around to park by a massive pin oak.

"Doesn't much matter now." She opened the door of the cab and heaved herself up and out. She seemed winded by the effort, even though she was only three months along.

I followed her lead and did my best to make a ladylike exit. "Sure you're going to be okay?"

"Always am. My stomach's feeling queasy, though. Might get something from the kitchen to settle it down."

I'd spent a lot of times in kitchens through the years, baking cookies for the store, making umpteen casseroles for Ambrose, who doesn't cook, and helping my friends with their Derby parties. Seeing someone else's kitchen was like exploring an overgrown bayou. You never knew what lurked behind the sauce pots, inside the cupboard, or next to the teakettle. "Mind if I tag along?"

She shrugged and shoved the truck's keys into her sweat-suit pocket. "Help yourself. It's closed to the public, since our Sunday brunch is already over."

We fell silent as we walked through the clipped garden and under an overhang shading the entrance to the kitchen. Inside, an enormous Vulcan range monopolized the back wall. It was as slick as a mirror, with more knobs than a rocket ship. Everything was coated in aluminum or polished brass, which made me worry for the poor staff that had to clean it.

Over our heads hung a rack of bright copper pots. You could always tell a real chef by the condition of her pots, and Cat's looked well-loved, judging by the dented sides, scraped bottoms, and wobbly handles. The kitchen walls had the same used brick as the floor, and a single window welcomed daylight into the space.

Cat moved to a door by the entrance and turned the knob, which made a gaping black hole appear. Pasta boxes, produce crates, and spice tins lined the pantry, and, like the rest of the kitchen, seemed frozen in time, even with the fancy range. I half expected to see a Revolutionary woman in a calico dress and floppy bonnet come waddling along to fix her family lunch.

Cat reappeared from the pantry. "Keep forgetting to take these." She held a bottle that looked like prenatal vitamins.

"Do you want something to eat with that?" I asked. "You might feel worse taking them on an empty stomach." Heaven only knew she'd need her strength since she was eating for two. "I've whipped up a few meals in my day."

"You'd cook for me?" She looked surprised. "Okay. As long as it's not too spicy. Don't want to lose my lunch too."

"Put up your feet and I'll make you an omelet." I pointed to a spot by the kitchen island, which was as wide as the counter at my store and nearly twice as long. I heaved open a double-sided refrigerator next to the stove and found enough eggs to feed a starting lineup. I brought out the eggs, a jug of milk, and some cheese, all of which would be nice and bland, but good for her too.

"You seem pretty handy around the kitchen." She watched me warily.

I dislodged a skillet from the pot rack and began to crack eggs on its side. "Should be. I've been living on my own long enough to figure out the difference between braising and poaching."

"Do you like to do it?" she asked.

"Guess you could say that." I poured some milk in the skillet and swished it around with a whisk that hung from a corkboard above the burners. "As long as I have company in the kitchen."

Cat seemed to think on that. "I don't like to work that way. People tripping over each other. That's how it was at my cooking school in France, and I couldn't wait to get out on my own."

"Well, there's good and bad to it." I flipped the eggs with a turner. "No sense in making four-dozen cookies all by yourself. Don't you have any help around here?"

"A sous-chef comes in to get supper started, and my pastry chef works Saturdays." Cat began to rock back and forth. The more she rocked, the younger she seemed, and I almost forgot she was in a family way. "By the end of the night, it's only me, though, unless we're talking about a weekend."

"Can't imagine that's much fun. Sounds kind of spooky."

"It can be, since I've been hearing all those ghost stories. Guess I should know better than to listen to 'em."

"Hmm."

"You're going to think I'm crazy, Missy, but I swear I saw a ghost here one time. Gray felt coat and everything." She pointed to the ancient window next to the stove. "There at the window. It happened one night when I was by myself. Nearly scared me to death."

Doesn't that just beat all? "Why, Cat, that sounds like the figure I saw last night. But don't you think it might have been a guest?"

"What kind of guest comes up and taps on a window?" She held out her arm. "Look, I still have a scar from when I jumped back from the stove." Sure enough, a thin brown line cut across her wrist.

Since she and I were getting to know each other, I decided to share my story. "Something like that woke me up last night. Something loud."

"A ghost?"

"Hard to say. It moved so fast I only saw a blur." I sprinkled some cheese on the omelet, then grabbed a plate from a rack next to the stove and flipped the eggs onto the platter. "It was wearing a gray felt coat, though, and heavy boots, like a uniform. But I doubt it was a ghost."

The minute I set the steaming plate in front of Cat, she lifted some omelet with her fingers, dripping cheese and all, and shoved it into her mouth. "Whah makes you say daht?"

"Careful! You'll burn yourself." Honestly, how could this girl be trusted with a baby if she didn't have enough sense to let her food cool?

"No biggie," she said, once she'd swallowed. "Can't feel a thing in my fingers anymore." She held up her hand to prove her point and darn if she didn't have the smoothest fingertips I'd ever seen. "By the second year of cooking school, you've burned your fingers too many times to count." She tucked back into the omelet, oblivious to any pain.

"Anyway, I heard a crash. When I came around the corner, it tumbled down the stairs, all gray coat and black boots. Then it ran away."

"Was there a hat?"

"Now that you mention it, there was."

"Sounds like the same guy," she said.

"Hmm. Maybe you're right. *Why* would someone do that?"

"Beats me."

We chatted for a few more minutes. After a bit, Cat took one last bite from the omelet.

"Looks like you're good to go now. Don't forget to take your vitamins. Wouldn't want your little one to be puny."

Once we'd said good-bye, I left the dark kitchen and stepped into the bright hall. So much brickwork was a tad oppressive. How could Cat stand to cook there night after night, all by herself?

A blurry figure darted past me as I stepped over the threshold to enter the main hall. My purse smacked into it something awful and a bunch of paperwork flew in the air. "Oh!"

Beatrice, of all people, should've known better than to go tearing around the mansion like that again. She bent to retrieve the papers scattered around our feet.

"I'm so sorry, Miss DuBois. It's my fault. Most of our guests went home once they got done with the police. I forgot some people are still here."

"You really should stop running around the halls. You might hurt yourself." I bent to help her. "And please, call me Missy. Looks like we've messed up your things."

"That's okay. They weren't in any order."

As I helped her sort through the pages, I lifted a formal-looking note card. A wedding announcement, of all things, printed on cream linen with beveled edges and embossed gold ink. "This one's got a little tear on it. Hope that's okay."

Beatrice plucked the announcement from me and slid it into a manila envelope. "I'm sending these things back to Mrs. Solomon. She'd planned to display them at her stepdaughter's wedding."

"So sad." I reached across and picked up another paper, this one a color picture. It was a photo of Trinity on her daddy's arm, God rest her soul. She wore a burgundy dress and matching hat. Why, it was a beautiful broad-brimmed hat with an enormous satin trim.

I glanced at the photo again and noticed a familiar face behind her. Wholesome good looks, big smile, prematurely gray hair. It was Charles, wearing a white tuxedo jacket, no less. A far cry from the black vest and wraparound waiter's apron I usually saw him in. "Well, I'll be. That's Charles, from the dining room." I handed the picture back to Beatrice.

"It can't be." She shoved it into the envelope, along with the other things. "Mrs. Solomon told me all the pictures came from the Baton Rouge Country Club. Well, I'd better pack these up. She'll be expecting them in the morning."

She closed the envelope and walked away, a trifle slower this time. Part of me wanted to yell at her to stop and to yank that picture back for a good, long look. It *was* Charles. I just knew it. But didn't he say he hadn't met Trinity until last week? That didn't make sense, since he'd obviously been to a shindig with her and her daddy.

Could he have been a waiter there? Maybe. But something about that photo was downright strange. Put most men in a tuxedo jacket and they stiffened up like shoe leather. But Charles seemed completely comfortable, like he wore that kind of jacket every day. No, something was off, and I'd have to ask him about it the very next time I saw him.

Chapter 9

With my thoughts still on Beatrice and the odd photograph, I wandered toward the main hall. Sooner or later I'd have to see about getting lunch, which would be the perfect time to ask Charles about the strange picture of him and Trinity. In the meantime, I'd only seen about half of the mansion and still had the other half to go.

Maybe it was finally time to visit the front section, which was the part closest to the Mississippi River. I began to walk that way and soon reached the golden ballroom, where the ceiling glowed and the painted floors glistened. Hard to imagine Ambrose and I had toured this room less than forty-eight hours before.

I stepped into the room, which immediately reminded me of a bottle of amber cognac, or the inside of a priceless Fabergé egg.

The portrait of Mrs. Andrews watched as I walked along and then paused under the crystal chandelier.

Unlike most chandeliers, this one had a large glass bowl at the end of each arm, instead of a teardrop bulb. I guessed it was a gasolier, like the ones I'd read about in the plantation's museum. Mr. Andrews's neighbors probably thought he was crazy to plumb such an elegant ballroom for gas. But there was no telling how many couples had waltzed under this very light until dawn broke over the Mississippi River.

"Hey there, Missy." Lance stood in the doorway, holding that special black notebook of his. It was part of his uniform now, as ever-present as the thick utility belt or the State of Louisiana patches sewn on his sleeves.

I didn't expect to see him so soon. "Hi there. Don't tell me you're still working. You know it's Sunday afternoon, right?"

He chuckled. "It's all the same to me. I work four on, four off. I'm right in the middle of my week. What're you doing?" He joined me under the gasolier.

"Having a little look-see around. Do you think that's real gold on the walls or just paint?"

"Hard to say. Can't imagine anyone having enough money to cover a whole room in fourteen-karat gold. You never know, though. The mirror looks real."

Across the room, an enormous mirror in an elaborate gilt frame dangled inches above the floor. Its top leaned away from the wall.

"You know why they pointed their mirrors down like that, right?" I asked. "So girls could see their skirts and make sure they covered their ankles. Didn't want to give the men any ideas."

"Can you imagine?" Lance shook his head. "Nowadays it's the last thing anyone worries about. Kind of miss that modesty."

Something skirted across the mirror's reflection before I could reply. Something quick and dark and out of focus. It dashed from one end of the mirror's frame to the other. I whirled around. The mirror was reflecting the open doorway. Someone must have been listening to us from the hall.

"Did you see that?" I asked.

"See what?"

"Someone just ran by the door. I saw them in the mirror."

Lance cocked his head. "You're probably getting spooked by what happened here. Are you sure you're okay?"

The doorway was empty now. "I'm fine." Slowly I turned back again. "But someone ran past this room. Don't look at me like that. I'm not imagining things."

"Okay, then. Whatever you say."

"I'm telling you, someone ran by. Do you think they were eaves-dropping on us?"

"I guess there's no telling. What were we talking about?"

"I asked why you were still here. Are you doing more inter-views?"

"No, I'm working on the supplemental report. I'll give it to the forensics lab when I'm done."

"But they found the body in the bathroom. Not here in the ball-room."

"It doesn't matter. The victim was all over the mansion before she died. This report will give them some info about what happened in the vicinity of the murder."

"Do you have any suspects yet?"

Lance raised his eyebrows. He wasn't going to dignify my question with a response.

"Okay, okay. I get it," I said. "Everything goes into that precious report. How about this: Is there anyone you've ruled out at this point?"

"That's better." He finally flipped open the notebook to a spot near the middle. "We can discount any employee who wasn't on duty this weekend. That's about a third of 'em. Then there's the guest list. A lot of people only had a passing acquaintance with the Solomons. Mostly bankers and other business owners. Oh, and a few politicians."

"Plus the family. Guess you can automatically rule out the parents."

He shot me a curious look. "Now, why would you say that?"

"C'mon, Lance. I know there are some strange people in the world, but no one would murder their own daughter."

"You'd be surprised." He puffed out his cheeks, as if he'd seen it all before and would probably see it again by dinnertime. "But you go right on believing that, baby girl."

"Don't patronize me. I'm not Pollyanna. I just can't imagine anyone would do that to their kid. Especially right before her wedding, and especially since she was pregnant."

A picture flashed through my mind of Mr. Solomon and Trinity, his face contorted with rage. A good old-fashioned hissy fit, from what I recalled.

"Uh-oh," I said. "I may have forgotten to tell you something."

Lance's eyes immediately widened. "What's that?"

"I heard them fighting on my first day here. It was Mr. Solomon and his daughter. He said something about how she shouldn't have a say in the wedding. But the worst part was what she said to him."

"Go on." Lance pulled a pen from the spine of his notebook and held it over the paper.

"Now, it may be nothing. Just family talk. You know how you get so mad at your family sometimes you want to scream? Well, Trinity told her dad she wished he were dead."

Lance didn't flinch, but he began to write on the notepad. Impressive that he could watch me and scribble at the same time. "What time did that happen?"

"It had to be a little after four-thirty on Friday. We'd begun our tour when we heard them."

"They came into the room with you?"

"No. They went in through the front door. Mr. Solomon first and then his daughter. He looked ready to spit nails. I thought he was going to lose it right there in the foyer."

"What did he say when she told him that?"

"Nothing. She turned around and left, and he just stood there. Can you imagine?"

Lance stopped writing for a moment. "Hmm. Anyone else see this?"

"Yeah. Ambrose was with me. And Beatrice. And the others on the tour. We were all kind of embarrassed. But they didn't seem to notice we were there."

"Interesting."

"But it doesn't mean anything, right? People get angry all the time and say stuff they don't mean. She was mad at him and she spouted off the first thing that came to her."

Lance fell silent.

"C'mon. You can't really believe Mr. Solomon killed his daughter." My mind swirled with possibilities. Even though I didn't know the family, there were a few facts everyone could agree on. It was well known that Mr. Solomon and his daughter didn't get along. "Everyone knew Mr. Solomon pinched pennies," I said. "Why would he waste all that money on a wedding if he knew it wasn't going to happen? He wouldn't do that."

"Funny you should say that." Lance replaced the pen in the notebook's spine and began to rifle through the pages until he reached a clear plastic sleeve jammed against the back cover. It held some random papers, starting with a pale pink sheet. "Got a look at the catering bill this morning." He didn't open the sleeve, but merely nodded at it. "This is the catering invoice. Look how much he paid for a deposit."

I moved closer for a better look and quickly scanned the page, crammed full of letters and numbers. After a while, I found a line next to the word *deposit*, which was blank.

"You mean he didn't put down a deposit?" I asked. "That can't be right."

"It *is* right. Normally the plantation asks for ten percent. Anywhere from twenty-five-hundred to five-thousand dollars or more. But not this time."

I double-checked the sheet. Dollar amounts filled every other line. Come to think of it, the wedding planner had asked me to waive *my* deposit until after the wedding. Normally I'd have said no, but this was a special case. Any client who could afford such a massive wedding at Morningside Plantation wouldn't stiff me on the bill.

"I spoke with the catering manager this morning. She thought she'd insult Mr. Solomon if she asked him for a deposit. Called it a 'professional courtesy'."

"You don't say." I wondered if Ambrose had waived his deposit too. He hadn't mentioned it, but then I hadn't mentioned my waiving it, either. "So, Mr. Solomon didn't put any money down for his daughter's wedding?"

"Looks like it. Otherwise he would have paid about seventy-five-hundred dollars. Maybe more. But he put down zero. Zip."

"Seriously?" It was hard to wrap my head around. "But that doesn't mean he murdered his daughter. It only means everyone's afraid of him. No one wants to get on his bad side because he has so much money."

"Exactly. But you wanted to automatically exclude the family. Sometimes that's not a good idea."

"I suppose. But I still can't believe any father would murder his daughter. Even someone like Mr. Solomon."

"I would have agreed with you a few years ago. Now I don't know. I stopped trusting people. Makes my job a whole lot easier."

"That's the most pitiful thing I've ever heard." And I hoped more than anything, Lance was dead wrong about Herbert Solomon. By the time I said good-bye and left the ballroom, I'd lost my enthusiasm for touring the mansion. Somehow the shine had dimmed during our talk about parents and children and murder.

I retreated to the back of the house instead, where I felt more at home. After a moment, I reached the restaurant entrance, where someone with salt-and-pepper hair stood at one of the first tables.

Watching Charles from behind was like watching a magician. Like an illusionist before an audience, he whisked something shiny from a washtub next to him and then flipped it into a napkin in his other hand. His final trick was to wrap the silverware up all nice and tight with a quick flick of the wrist. All that was missing was an "abracadabra!" and a round of applause at the end of his show.

Never let it be said I didn't know a golden opportunity when I saw one. I sidled into the restaurant, as if by accident, and then casually walked up behind him. My heels must have given me away, though, and he turned.

"Why, hello, Missy. I'm sorry, but we're closed." He glanced around the quiet restaurant as if to prove his point.

"I know." I pulled a chair away from the table, all nonchalance. Moist knives and forks winked up at me from the tub like shiny coins tossed into a fountain. "And how are you doing today?"

"Okay, I guess. It's my turn to prep the silverware."

"I can see that." Watching him roll the flatware had reminded me of making pigs in a blanket for Derby parties. It's another chore I'd done dozens of times for dozens of parties. Since my hands were clean, I might as well make myself useful. I reached into the washtub and immediately felt warm, moist metal.

After a bit, Charles and I set up a comfortable rhythm in our silence. I retrieved some silverware, shook it off, and then passed the pair to Charles, who rolled up everything all nice and neat. The give-and-take, back-and-forth, provided me with the perfect distraction.

"I saw the strangest thing earlier," I finally said. "A picture. I could have sworn it was of you."

"Me? What was I doing?"

"That's the thing." I reached into the washtub and casually withdrew a wet fork. We were in no hurry, since dozens of the pieces lay waiting and supper wasn't for several hours yet. "Hard to tell. Looked like you were at a party. A fancy party too."

"Probably wasn't me, then."

"But it *was* you." I married the fork with a knife and passed the pair to Charles.

The way he accepted it, so gingerly, reminded me of a museum curator with a precious artifact.

"In a tuxedo, no less. Do you belong to the Baton Rouge Country Club?"

"You're kidding, right?" He began to chuckle, but stopped when he looked at me. "I'm sorry. I don't mean to be rude. But I doubt they'd let someone like me join, even if I could afford it."

"That so? You must have a twin, then. A spitting image too. So you've never been to the Baton Rouge Country Club?"

"Well, I didn't say that."

"I'm sure they have lots of parties there. Did you happen to go to one, maybe with Trinity Solomon?"

"No . . . maybe . . . I don't know." Clearly discombobulated, Charles reached across me and plucked a fork from the washtub, essentially taking away my job. Strange how he refused to look at my face.

Well, this will never do. I decided to steer the conversation back to something neutral. "So, Charles, I'm guessing you grew up around here. It's such a pretty area. Everything looks so green."

Luckily, he paused and waited for me to hand him a knife, instead of taking one out of the bin. "I grew up down the road, and you should see my parents' backyard. The cypress trees are so big I could hide behind them and no one would ever find me."

"That *is* big. And to think you stayed right here after high school. So many people don't do that. I didn't."

"I didn't have much choice. After the refinery blew up, my dad lost all his money. Didn't have a cent to pay for room and board at college. The only thing he had for collateral was a shrimping boat, and they took that away too."

"I'm so sorry."

"Nearly killed him. The day the sheriff got the boat was the worst day ever."

"You were there? How horrible."

"I'll never forget it." Charles's eyes glazed over. "Dad thought I was sleeping, but the dog went crazy, running around in circles and stuff. I woke up and went outside to see what was wrong."

Instinctively, I laid my hands in my lap, since Charles's story was ten times more important than wrapping silverware.

"It was frosty out. I didn't have time to grab shoes and my feet got wet in the grass. Dad didn't know I was there because I ducked behind a cypress before he could see me."

"Hmm." I pictured Charles, hiding behind a tree trunk, in his bare feet.

"Dad always told me he was gonna get rich off that refinery. Said putting his money there was safer than in a bank."

"That should have been a good plan," I said. "Until the refinery exploded." Not to belabor the point, but the accident had devastated so many people in the area.

"My dad lost everything, and then the sheriff came for the boat. It was the last straw. He fetched his Smith and Wesson, because he thought someone was trying to steal his baby. Who could blame him, right? But he saw it was the sheriff before he fired. He told me I must have dreamt the next part."

"Next part?" Was it my imagination, or did Charles's eyes mist over, like the flatware, which was slick with condensation?

"I saw my dad bring the handgun to his own head when he realized what the sheriff wanted."

"That's horrible! Do you think maybe you made a mistake?"

"I know what I saw, Missy. He was scared to death. I'll never forget the look on his face when he did that. He dropped his hand after a second, but it was too late."

We both fell silent. The memory seemed painfully fresh for him. So fresh it looked like he wanted to reach his hand through the window and touch the cypress, the weathered fishing boat, and the father with a handgun at his head.

"I blame Mr. Solomon. That bastard."

I flinched.

"I mean, he was such a jerk. Sorry to cuss, but that's how it is. That oil refinery hurt a lot of people around here. A lot of people." There was no mistaking the edge in his voice.

"I've heard all about him," I said.

"It was over a year ago, but it's why I still live at home and drive to LSU three days a week. To save money."

"That makes sense to me. And I'm so glad your father didn't pull the trigger."

Ever so slowly, I passed Charles a fork to see what would happen next. But he fell silent and we stayed that way for several minutes, until I remembered something.

"I have friends who are counselors back in Bleu Bayou. In case you want to talk to someone about what happened."

"Thanks. But I don't like to talk about it. I don't even like to think about it. So, let's talk about something else. Anything new with you?"

"Goodness, what isn't new? I still can't believe everything that happened yesterday. Turns out I know the police officer in charge of the investigation. We grew up together."

"That so?"

"Yeah. We lived next door to each other about a million years ago. The police still don't have any leads. Or any leads I know of."

Charles looked at me quizzically. "It's only been one day."

"True. But I've heard the first twenty-four hours are critical. We're way past that now."

"I've heard that too."

It felt like the right time to ask him what I really wanted to know. "What do you think happened? I mean, with Trinity and all. I know you said some people complained about noise on Friday night, but you never told me what *you* think."

Nothing stirred then, save for the blur of silverware as we passed it back and forth. Even the birds outside had fallen silent, as if they wanted to hear what Charles would say.

"To tell you the truth, I've never trusted that Sterling guy."

"You mean Trinity's fiancé?"

"Yeah. He didn't act like a guy who was going to get married. I mean, it sounded like he was trying to hook up with someone yesterday when I heard him talking on the phone."

"Hooking up? What makes you think that?" Of course, the memory of Sterling and Beatrice talking in the bar flew to the front of my mind. Maybe it was common knowledge around here that those two were a couple and I was the last person on earth to figure it out.

"He was mumbling into the phone like he didn't want anyone to hear. And he must have been talking to a girl, because he kept calling her 'baby'." He looked disgusted, his eyebrows pulled tight. Obviously Charles didn't care a lick for Sterling Brice.

"That's a pretty good clue, all right. Who do you think he was talking to?"

"I don't know for sure, but I have a bad feeling about this. I mean, if that guy was seeing someone on the side, he'd have a good reason to kill his fiancée."

"Maybe."

Charles lowered his eyes to the tabletop. "What gets me is he didn't even deserve her. She could've done a lot better."

"You don't say." Carefully, I pulled a fresh fork from the bin. "Sounds like you were a fan of Trinity."

"It was hard not to be. She always made you laugh. Great sense of humor—" He stopped short. The words lingered in the air, fat and bloated, for several seconds.

"But I thought you didn't know her, Charles."

His eyes shot from the table to my face. "Well . . . um. That's what I've heard."

"You know you can tell me anything. I've heard everything there is to hear, so don't think—"

"I've gotta go." Charles didn't bother to accept the fork I tried to hand him. Instead, he looked desperate to leave the restaurant. "Cat probably needs me in the kitchen. I'll do this later. Thanks."

In a poof, he was gone. Like the magician I'd imagined him to be when I first arrived. *Abracadabra.* A puff of smoke and a hasty exit . . . and there went Charles.

Maybe I'd underestimated him, after all. Maybe there was more going on behind that friendly smile and those dancing eyes than I cared to admit. But what?

I rose from the table. The best thing I could do was hike around the plantation and sort out everything in my mind. The stiff breeze might blow away some of the doubts about Charles that had begun to cloud it.

Time was running short. First there was the crash in the hall the night before, then I'd learned the head chef was pregnant, not to mention seeing the photograph of Charles and Trinity. At this point I had a thousand more questions than answers.

Maybe that was why the sight of Darryl, as I walked down the hall and toward the front door, perked me up. Next to Charles, Darryl was one of the best sources for information about the plantation.

"Hello, Darryl." Yes, it was definitely time to enlist his help. "How're you doing?"

He was watering a potted fern and glanced up. "Good. Got time ta do tings, wot wit all da guests done gone."

"Guess so. Sorry if I held you up from your work at the funeral home. And the church service was pretty good. You should go sometime."

He grunted at the fern instead of speaking.

"I mean it. As a matter of fact, I'm putting on a fashion show there tomorrow night and I could sure use some help. We'll need lots and lots of flowers. Are you interested in some freelance work?"

"Maybe. What ya got in mind?"

"Several tall vases for the stage and something special for the wings. Definitely a boutonniere for Ambrose." Which reminded me. If he didn't reappear at the mansion soon, I'd have to call him at his shop and explain about the show tomorrow night.

"I can do dat. Mixed flowers, or ya want sometin' special?"

"Your snapdragons are gorgeous. I don't want you to take any from the plantation, but do you have a garden back home?"

"Ya, a big one. Let me tink on it."

I mentally calculated the number of arrangements we'd need for the show. "It'll probably take two four-foot vases for the front and maybe a couple of five-footers for the wings. And Ambrose likes delphiniums."

"What kinda budget ya got?"

I clucked my tongue. "Now don't go crazy. This is for a church, after all. The last time we did this, we spent two-hundred and fifty dollars on the large arrangements."

"Sounds good. Wot ya up ta now?"

"I've been looking around the plantation. Trying to see as much as I can before Ambrose gets back. I can't stop thinking about what happened here yesterday."

"Ain't dat da truth."

"I feel so bad for Mrs. Solomon. She and I know the same people back in Bleu Bayou. I can only imagine what's she's going through."

"Her child be sainted now, is wot we say."

I blinked. "What an interesting way to put it. No matter how you say it, she must be devastated. I wish I could do something for her."

Something had occurred to me while I was in the restaurant, but I'd have to phrase it carefully for Darryl to say yes. "There is *one* other thing I could use help with. Is there any way I could see the room where Trinity stayed? I keep thinking the investigators came and went so quickly. What if they missed something? What if they overlooked something important?"

Darryl shook his head. "Dey's give me a key ta da rooms. But dat's not for me ta decide."

"Nobody's talking about what happened here this weekend. The only way we're going to find answers is to pull together." I didn't back away, though Darryl stared at me as if I'd asked him for his bank-account password instead of a room key. "We could wait for Officer LaPorte, but we're running out of time. Or we can look around on our own. Maybe they missed something in her room. They might have."

"Dat's breakin' da law, Miz DuBois. Deys don't want us in dere."

"Of course they don't want us in there. But nothing else has worked so far. The killer could be halfway to Baton Rouge with all the evidence by the time the Riversbend Police Department gets its act together. Honestly."

Darryl paused. His decision could go either way.

"All right," he finally said. "I can get ya in dere. But dat's it. Dat's as far as dat goes."

"Fair enough. You show me her room and give me the key, and I'll never tell another soul how I got in. I'll even stand in the doorway so I don't make footprints. But sometimes things get overlooked and there might be evidence begging to be discovered. *Begging*, I tell you."

He didn't look convinced, but he straightened anyway and walked to the stairs. He moved like someone half his age, and I rushed behind to keep up, especially when he took the stairs two at a time.

As soon as he reached the landing, Darryl turned and pulled something from his pocket. "Here ya go." He furtively offered it to me. "Room two-one-five. Do wot ya's got ta do and den get out."

I clutched the key. "Of course. Thank you." The second floor was as deserted as the first had been, but I quickly ducked around him and tiptoed down the hall.

The door to room 215 stopped me cold, but I managed to turn the key in the lock and watch a shadow sweep across the carpet as it opened.

The outline of heavy furniture appeared. A divan, the same type as the one in my room, sat next to the window, and a bookshelf ran across the far wall. An enormous four-poster bed piled high with throw pillows held center stage.

My heavenly days. Trinity couldn't have slept in her room Friday night because the pillows formed a perfect triangle on the bed. I knew from my studies at Vanderbilt first responders wouldn't touch anything at a crime scene unless it was critical to the investigation, and they certainly wouldn't make up a bed.

Trinity must have spent Friday night somewhere else. But where? Not in her fiancé's room. According to Beatrice, Sterling didn't know Trinity's whereabouts when she disappeared before the hat competition.

I kept my promise to Darryl and stayed in the doorway. It was dark and still, and I gradually noticed something else: a strange smell. Like the Cutex fingernail-polish remover I kept on my vanity back home. Which meant an investigator must have used a fuming wand to scan objects, like an alarm clock on the nightstand.

Lance told me about those things when we combed the restroom downstairs. He said the same smelly superglue people used to repair kitchen chairs and smashed pottery and whatnot would also build up ridges on a fingerprint so it could be photographed. While I couldn't pretend to understand the science behind it, the whole idea amazed me.

Lance seemed wistful when he talked about the wands. The Riversbend Police Department couldn't afford them at five thousand apiece, so they drove their evidence to a bigger county. He hoped to get one during the next budget cycle, if I recalled correctly.

So why did the Riversbend Police Department suddenly have a fuming wand? The smell made my eyes begin to water. Either the officers ranked this investigation as a number-one priority and coughed up the money somehow, or someone else was bankrolling it.

I wiped away a tear sliding down my cheek. Except for the strange smell, the bedroom was ordinary enough. Messy, but ordinary. Shirts trailed half on and half off their hangers in the closet, a pair of shorts puddled on the ground, and a paperback fanned open on the divan.

Someone had confiscated the wedding dress. In fact, the room didn't seem to belong to a bride. No jewelry or box for fancy shoes or lace garter. But maybe they gave those things to Trinity's stepmother once they'd been fumed for evidence.

I wiped another tear and pulled the door closed. Heaven only knew it'd take a proper search warrant to do more, and I'd seen and smelled enough. I pocketed the room key and made a mental note to return it to Darryl as soon as I could.

By the time I swept down the hall, my stomach was growling like a vacuum cleaner set to *high*. Enough was enough. It was time to dry my eyes and find something to eat.

I headed for the stairs. There was only one problem: I desperately needed a Kleenex, but the bathroom downstairs still gave me the heebie-jeebies. Since my room was only one flight up, it'd make more sense to go there first.

I climbed the steps to the third floor. My eyes still watered from the chemicals, and I almost tripped on the landing and landed face-first on the carpet.

This hall was empty too. Only a few people had chosen to remain at the plantation, and most of them had nothing to do with the wedding. Heaven only knew whether the hotel even told them about the weekend's grisly events.

I steadied my hand against the wall for balance. The hall was wide and not nearly as intimidating as the night before, when the ghostly figure trailed past like a puff of smoke. In fact, I felt a little foolish now as I walked along the carpet.

Halfway down, I paused. Someone had left a package by my door. I rubbed my eyes and glanced at it again. Was it a package, or something else? It seemed more green than brown, and it stood about a foot tall.

Of course. That sweet, sweet Ambrose. He'd ordered a flower arrangement to cheer me up since he had to leave and return to Bleu Bayou.

I should have expected as much. He always put my happiness above his own, often when I least expected it. Like the time I held a grand opening for Crowning Glory on a summer day with unusually stormy weather.

How I struggled to make it the best grand opening ever. I spent six months beforehand ironing out the details. I ordered five hundred business cards and five hundred glossy postcards to mail to banquet halls, wedding planners, and photographers all up and down the Great River Road.

When the printer returned the postcards—awash in beatific brides and frothy veils—I addressed each one by hand, since mailing labels seemed too impersonal. Then I bought rolls and rolls of stamps and dropped the cards into the mailbox two weeks before the big event.

That same day, I began to bake. Trays and trays of pralines, macaroons, and anything else that wouldn't stain lace. Even though I planned to exhibit my wares up high on shelves, I knew one or two would make the rounds through the shop as guests passed them back and forth.

With a week to go, I broke out the Borax. I mopped the floor two times, wiped every surface, whether it needed it or not, and cleaned both the inside and outside of the front window.

Ambrose arrived for the grand opening an hour early. He even vacuumed the rug, my protests notwithstanding, and Windexed the glass again for good measure. By then, sheets of rain had fallen and his collar was soaked through, but he didn't care.

I threw open the front door at the stroke of ten. When no one arrived that first hour, I started to make excuses. It was too wet, it was too early, they'd come at lunch.

Ambrose tried to distract me with games of gin rummy and crazy eights. He even let me win when he could have played the eight in his hand.

Time dragged on and on, and still the store resembled a church on New Year's Eve. Ambrose finally laid down his cards and mumbled something about getting us lunch. Soon after he left, the front door swung open and I assumed he'd forgotten his keys. But in trotted a wedding planner, who bemoaned the weather and her busy schedule and blah, blah, blah. She even whipped out her cell and called a client on my behalf.

On her heels came a photographer. And then a group of caterers. Before long, so many people stood shoulder to shoulder in the store no one could see the shelves. But it didn't matter. All anyone wanted was a business card, along with a praline or two.

When the trickle swelled to a throng, the truth dawned on me. Ambrose must have called in every favor that anyone in town owed him.

He finally got back to the store an hour later. I glimpsed him through the window, as he stood on the sidewalk. When a guest left the store they passed him my business card and he handed over some cash. It looked like a drug deal in broad daylight, with the pusher selling cardstock instead of cocaine. Every transaction was the same: card, then cash; card, then cash.

It went on all afternoon. Ambrose finally elbowed his way into the store twenty minutes before closing time.

"Where have you been, Bo?"

I remembered the look on his face. He casually leaned against the counter, as if he'd never left. "Nowhere special. Tried to get us some Chinese, but then a client called. Oh, well. Looks like your opening was a smash."

Two could play at his game. "I know. It's been crazy. I talked to people and passed out business cards all afternoon. Guess that postcard I mailed out worked, huh?"

"It *was* a nice postcard," he said.

I tried to be angry, but couldn't. "You didn't have to pay all those people off. But I'm glad you did."

Over the next few weeks, I tried to figure out how he came up with the money to bribe my guests. He ate ramen noodles for a month afterward and never once complained. And now this. Fresh flowers delivered right to my doorstep.

I stepped closer to my hotel-room door. The flower arrangement was more wide than tall, and it spread in front of the kick plate. My eyes had stopped watering, and I paused some twelve feet from the door. The colors were a jumble of greens, golds, and tans. But no cut flower I knew, even a fresh one, shimmered quite like that.

Plus, the arrangement seemed jagged, much too jagged for a professional bouquet. I crept a foot or two closer. Was that a feather sticking out from the top? It *was* a feather, although that didn't make much sense.

I froze. My eyesight had cleared. It wasn't an arrangement of blooms and bulbs, leaves and stems. It was fabric, poking out from a greasy paper grocery sack. It had been left on the ground where I'd be sure to find it.

I forced myself to walk the last few feet to the door. I bent to pluck the feather from the sack. It was a quill, of all things. A pheasant quill, with barbs ripped out at random spots. A quill like the one used in Ivy's Victorian hat.

My fingers released the feather, and it twirled to the floor. Whoever destroyed Ivy's hat must have been angry, because the cuts were jagged, unplanned. They must have found the hat on the front porch, where I'd forgotten it once Lance arrived.

Why would someone destroy her beautiful hat like that? Even smashed, the hat was exquisite and obviously expensive. Now it sat in a ripped grocery sack, a jumble of tulle, ribbon, and felt, topped with a bedraggled pheasant quill.

It was a message, obviously. Someone wanted to frighten me. I'd been holding my breath for the past few moments, which I slowly exhaled. If that was the person's goal, they'd accomplished their mission.

I backed away from the hideous pile, then turned and ran down the hall to the stairs. I almost smashed into the front door before I remembered to open it, and then I stumbled out onto the porch.

What to do now? Ambrose was down the road in Bleu Bayou, and

I'd apparently spooked Charles with my questions. Even Cat said she wanted to close up her kitchen for the day once she ate my omelet.

My eyes swept the grounds. The parking lot was empty, except for a lone car next to the registration cottage. It was a Louisiana State Police car, covered with mud. Dirt was smeared across the windshield, grime spread across the side panels, and the whitewall tires were black. Which could mean only one thing: Lance LaPorte was back. He never could take care of his toys, even when we were little. He always was as reckless as a tornado.

Yes, Lance LaPorte must be close by. I could tell him about the chilling discovery by my hotel-room door.

I gazed over the front lawn as I descended the stairs. A dark form stood amid the green grass and wispy willows. Lance stood in the small graveyard beside the mansion, which Beatrice had mentioned during our tour. The cemetery held the remains of Mr. and Mrs. Andrews and most of their children.

There was no telling why Lance was in the graveyard, with no one for company but a bunch of headstones. Every once in a while he shifted, and the blue of his uniform blurred for an instant.

Thank goodness he was still at the mansion. I skirted the perimeter, the sound of willow wisps rubbing in the breeze following me. Lance didn't know I was there, and I was about to call out to him, when something else moved. Hidden behind Lance was another man, only this one wore coveralls and carried a pair of mud-caked garden clippers.

Darryl stood by Lance beneath a canopy of willow branches. In the Andrews family graveyard, no less.

The meeting piqued my curiosity. Any thoughts of interrupting Lance to tell him about my discovery gradually faded away.

The conversation seemed cordial enough. Lance spoke loudly, probably due to Darryl's age, while Darryl responded by methodically rubbing the garden clippers against the sleeve of his coveralls.

Nothing stood between me and them but an expanse of wide-open lawn. Since it wouldn't be polite to interrupt the conversation at this point, I hightailed it back up the steps and walked out on the balcony of the restaurant. I stood above them now, looking down on two dark forms in the deserted cemetery.

I shouldn't eavesdrop. Since Ambrose wasn't there to whisper *no* in my ear, I soon caved and ducked behind a fat column.

Luckily, Lance continued to raise his voice and it boomed in the quiet. I grabbed a nearby chair and scooted it behind the column, since I had no way of knowing how long they'd been speaking or how long it'd last. Then I settled in, which might not have been the morally right thing to do, but I felt God would forgive me, even if the two gentlemen below might not. There would be time enough to tell Lance about my chilling "gift" once the men finished their conversation.

"You're saying you never met him," Lance said. "Not once?"

I peeked around the pilaster. Lance withdrew his notebook.

"Hard ta say. Lots of dem folks come 'round dis weekend. Strangers, dey were." Luckily, Darryl had raised his voice to match Lance's.

"Surely you'd remember him, though."

"Lots of folks come 'round. Can't remember dem all, can I?"

Lance scribbled something on the page before looking up again. "Think hard, Mr. Tibodeaux. Maybe you ran into him *before* the wedding. You must have spoken to him at one time or another."

Were they talking about Sterling Brice, the dead girl's fiancé? Why would Lance care whether Darryl had spoken to him? That seemed like a stretch, even though I couldn't read Lance's mind.

"Ya be askin' de wrong person," Darryl said. "Ya gots lots of people 'round here who don' like de Solomons. Ask some of dem. *Pardonnez-moi.*"

"Just a minute."

I peeked around the column again. Lance had closed the notebook and now grasped Darryl's shoulder. Everything stilled at that point, from the shuffling willows to a few cicadas in the bushes and even the dull roar of traffic on the highway.

"You're officially telling me you've never met Herbert Solomon or his daughter, Trinity?" Lance's posture was rigid. "Think carefully, Mr. Tibodeaux, before you answer."

"Dat's what I'm sayin'." Darryl roughly shrugged out from under the officer's grasp.

I must have been hearing things. Or maybe it was Darryl who didn't understand the question. Of course he knew Herbert Solomon. He'd worked for the man, for goodness' sake. And Mr. Solomon had confided to him that the family would be cremating Trinity's body.

I was about to call out to Darryl when I remembered my predicament. He didn't know I was listening from the balcony.

"Thank you for your time, sir," Lance said. "I might need to question you again, so don't leave the property."

"Where am I gonna go? I'm crippled, ya know. Not much strength in dis ol' body."

"Yes, I can see that." Lance's tone was wary.

He must have figured out what Darryl meant. How could Darryl, with only one hand, have murdered a healthy young woman? That was probably what he wanted the officer to think about.

"No, sir," Darryl said. "Dis ol' body good for nuttin'."

"I see. Thank you for your time."

Lance pivoted and retreated through the garden gate. The interview ended so quickly. Did Lance believe Darryl, or did he feel guilty about badgering him?

Either way, the conversation did *not* sit well with me. Why would Darryl lie to Lance and say he'd never met Hebert Solomon?

There was only one way to find out. I rose and made my way downstairs. Darryl had finished cleaning the clippers by the time I crossed the lawn, and he shoved them angrily into his tool belt, like a gunslinger in the wild, wild West, as I approached.

"Afternoon," I said.

He glanced up, startled. *"Bonjour."*

For once I'd surprised Darryl. I strode through the garden gate and into the cemetery. "Nice day out. A little humid, but when isn't it?"

"Say dat again."

"Wasn't that Officer LaPorte just now?"

"Ya. Know 'im?" Darryl's eyes narrowed.

"We go way back. I used to go to Sunday school with him and his brother."

"He be nosin' around dis place, askin' all kinds 'a questions."

I pretended to read a nearby headstone. "You don't say. So what did he ask you?"

The headstone was almost hidden by the sparse crabgrass. Darryl leaned over it and plucked at some blades. "Sometin' about Mr. Solomon. Don' know why he be askin' me. I stay outta trouble. Dat's da key."

"You know he probably asks everyone the same questions." I pointed to the fallen marker. "Did that belong to Mrs. Andrews?"

"Yep. Poor ting only lived ta thirty."

"What happened to her marker?"

"It's da soil. Like quicksand. Wants ta bring tings down."

All of this talk about gravestones and soil was well and good, but I had other things on my mind. "You know, Darryl, I couldn't help but overhear a snippet of your conversation with the police officer. Why did you tell him you'd never met Herbert Solomon? I know you have. You told me about it when we were in the chapel."

"Did I, now?" He didn't seem surprised by my question, or that I'd eavesdropped on his conversation with Lance.

"Yes. Yes, you did."

"Better fix dis here stone before da ghost of Miz Andrews come back." He hoisted up the stone, using his left hand. He handled it as easily as a wisp from a neighboring willow.

My jaw dropped. The marker weighed at least a hundred pounds, if not more. That was about as much as an old rain barrel behind my store after a good, long thunderstorm, which I never could seem to budge without Ambrose's help.

So much for any talk about Darryl's handicap. The man was incredibly strong; there was no denying it. And apparently, he didn't plan to answer my questions about Hebert Solomon. There was no denying that, either. An uneasy feeling washed over me.

Chapter 10

Darryl walked away once he righted the gravestone. Why did he tell Lance he'd never met Herbert Solomon, when I knew otherwise?

It reminded me of my conversation with Charles. He'd denied knowing Trinity, only to later admit he knew her well. It seemed as though everyone at the plantation harbored a secret or two. My job, if I wanted to help poor Ivy, was to separate the truth from the lies, like peeling away one of the wisps from a willow.

With Darryl gone, I decided to track down Lance before he left the plantation for good. My heels sank as I walked across the grass, the soft blades tickling the sides of my feet.

The lawn was unusually lush—probably May's rainstorms—and the blades continued to squish beneath my feet. Soon my thoughts retreated to the last time I traveled across a lawn so vast and green.

The skies had been clear, like today. The smell of turned earth had encircled me, and my feet sank in the moist grass. My conversation with Darryl had sparked the memory, and the rolling expanse of lawn must have inflamed it.

A call had come from First Baptist Church in Texas. They wanted me to speak at a women's conference about trends in fashion during a garden party with a Mardi Gras theme, of all things, which they'd stage on several acres behind the sanctuary.

Although east Texas is known for summer showers, on the day of my speech, brilliant blue stretched out as far as the eye could see.

Women were buzzing around the property when I arrived. Stirring this and passing that, bustling between a giant punch bowl and a hors d'oeuvres table. They'd strewn colorful beads everywhere.

The women were so happy to see me they swarmed around me when I arrived at the party, like bees with a queen. They fired off so many questions I didn't know who to answer first.

Potato salad. The smell of onions in potato salad had wafted over to me, trapped in a Pyrex dish held by one of my questioners. The way she balanced the dish on her hip was downright impressive. We walked past tables decorated with harlequin masks, king cakes, and fleurs-de-lis.

"Where's your husband? Is he parking the car? Surely he came to hear you speak."

It was a genuine question. The lady didn't seem particularly mean-spirited, so I mustered an answer. One I'd practiced in front of my bathroom mirror many times before; it wasn't the first time I'd been asked it, and it surely wouldn't be the last. "I don't have one. Work keeps me so busy, you know."

"But I assumed—"

"Guess I haven't been lucky."

The most amazing silence enveloped us. No one spoke for several seconds, until the lady with the Pyrex broke the tension. "Really? A pretty girl like you? I can't believe that. By the time I was your age, I had three children in elementary school."

"I'm afraid it's true," I said. "But I like to think I have plenty of time for that. Wouldn't you agree?"

Their frowns told me otherwise.

"Anyway, thank you for inviting me here today. Everything looks so lovely."

"Of course. We wanted to make you feel welcome." The first speaker gazed over my shoulder, as if she couldn't believe me and expected to see a wayward husband magically appear on the lawn behind us. "We have a lot of work to do. I hope you don't mind if we go set these things down." The minute she spoke, the group dispersed like a puff of dust in the wind.

Just like that, they disappeared. Here they'd made a big show out of welcoming me, until they realized we weren't so alike, after all.

When they discovered my shortcoming—my inability to muster even one measly man at the advanced age of thirty—it was as if I'd told the group I had scarlet fever and was highly contagious.

They'd assumed something about me, only to discover it wasn't true. I'd always remember the lesson they taught me: Never rely on a first impression.

No matter how much we want to believe something about another person, that doesn't mean reality will cooperate.

My head still bowed, I continued to walk toward the registration cottage, where I'd spied Lance's car. Late-afternoon sun cast long shadows from the pin oaks and crepe myrtles onto the emerald grass.

Supper would soon be here. I hadn't eaten anything all day, unless you counted the breakfast roll I stashed in my purse before church or the handful of Altoids I'd nibbled on during it. Funny how whole meals could come and go now, and I was none the wiser without Ambrose to remind me.

After a few more steps, I discovered Lance was gone. By this time I was not only starving but parched, and I seemed to recall they had an enormous ewer of sweet tea on a side table in the registration cottage.

I made my way to the building and swung open the door. Instead of sweet tea, though, the hotel's general manager sat perched in front of a giant Dell computer. That man worked way too hard, considering it was a Sunday afternoon.

I ducked around a table piled with brochures—no ewer in sight—and approached the desk. The cottage looked much newer than the other parts of the plantation, with smooth drywall, recessed lights, and whatnot. "Hello, there. Don't the owners ever let you rest?"

The manager held out his hand. "Good afternoon. I don't think we've officially met. I'm Wyatt Burkett. And no, the owners don't really care."

"That's a shame. Let me call them up and I'll set 'em straight." I grinned to let him know I was teasing. "By the way, I enjoyed sitting next to you in church this morning. You seem to have a nice little congregation there."

"Yes, we do. And it was mighty nice of *you* to offer your services for the fund-raiser tomorrow night."

"It wasn't anything." Which was true, considering Ambrose still had no idea I'd volunteered him. "Say, Wyatt. Do you always work Sundays? Surely the Andrews family must give you the Lord's day off and not just a few measly hours for church."

"I work every afternoon. We're owned by something called a real-estate investment trust. Do you know what that is?"

"I'm afraid not." I leaned against the counter. Paying bills was one thing, but I'd rather suffer through a month of root canals than learn about investment trusts, tax-sheltered annuities, and those sorts of things.

"It means a group of people owns this place. In our case, a group of hotel owners out of Dallas."

"Can't imagine the Andrews family would up and sell their home to perfect strangers. My grandma would call that goin' back on your raisin'. I'd never do that."

He smiled. "Everyone believes that. Until they get that first electric bill from Louisiana Power and Light. The heirs didn't have enough money to keep the place going. Oh, they tried. Let's see... it was a boarding house, a French restaurant, and then a day spa. You should've seen it a couple of years ago; it was a total wreck."

"That's pitiful. There should be a law against it."

"You'd think the locals would've been thrilled to see new owners come in and spruce it up." His smile disappeared. "Just the opposite. Someone started a trash fire at our grand opening and nearly burned the place down. Trying to send us a message, I guess." He stared at the computer screen. "In fact, April was one of our worst months ever."

"Do tell! I'd have thought you'd have brides lined up from here to Alabama, trying to get married in that beautiful golden ballroom of yours."

"You'd think so, wouldn't you?"

The things one found out through idle chatter. Here I'd come into the cottage for a glass of sweet tea, and I'd picked up a big cup of information instead.

"Say, where are you hiding that sweet tea I saw here before?" I asked.

"It's almost gone, so I put it in the tour guides' office behind me. Help yourself."

"Thank you, kindly." I glanced at the computer screen. "I'm sorry about the business dropping off. Maybe it'll pick up come summer."

That didn't seem likely, though, since the check-in counter was as bare as a bald cypress in winter. I skirted the desk and ducked into the tour guides' office, sad to see the mansion in such poor straits.

In contrast to the rest of the plantation, the tour guides' office was nothing special. It housed a cheap laminate desk, two plastic chairs, and a giant poster board held up by thumbtacks. The owners obviously didn't spend money on places hotel guests wouldn't see.

The poster board was a calendar, with entries for guides named Charity, Mary Kate and, of course, Beatrice. I sashayed over for a better look. Oddly enough, Charity was supposed to be on duty today, not Beatrice. Strange I'd run into Beatrice a little while ago in the hall.

She must be filling in. Below the calendar sat a side table with the sweet tea, but by now only a cupful of brown liquid skulked around on the bottom. I dropped my purse to the floor and it hit the side of a trash can, which wobbled before tipping over. A stream of papers flowed out, starting with a picture of Trinity and her father, followed by the wedding announcement I'd seen earlier.

I bent and retrieved even more papers out of the trash, including a wedding invitation and a program for Trinity's ceremony. Wasn't Beatrice supposed to mail those to Ivy? If so, why did scuff marks crosshatch the special picture of father and daughter and an ugly tear bisect the wedding announcement? How could Beatrice have been so careless?

"Missy?" Beatrice hovered above me, her face rigid.

I hadn't heard her come in. Although I wasn't a bird-watcher, I must have looked like a screech owl caught in the light of a birder's lantern, my eyes three sizes too big.

"What are you doing here?" she asked.

"Getting some tea?" I swept my hand over the debris on the carpet. "I found these in the trash. They must have fallen into the wastebasket by mistake."

Now Beatrice looked stunned. "I—I was going to mail those. You're right. They must have slipped off my desk by accident."

I glanced again at the wedding announcement. The nasty tear was no accident. "Maybe we can fix these things up a bit."

"You never told me why you're here," she said.

"I came in to find the sweet tea. By the way, according to the schedule you don't work on Sundays."

"I've got finals coming up and I left my notes in here, so I had to come back. That's all."

"Interesting." I straightened and forced myself to smile. "What are you studying at the university?" Anything to distract her while I arranged the papers in my hand into a neat pile. Damaged or not, these belonged to Ivy and not in a trash can.

"Science. I'm on an academic scholarship at LSU." She took the papers from me before I could react.

"How interesting. I wouldn't have pegged you for the science type. More like business or advertising. Something like that."

"No, I'm a chem major. Shooting for my pharmacy degree. I'm almost done too."

"Good for you. And please tell me you're going to mail those things to Mrs. Solomon in the morning. Wouldn't want her to wonder what happened to them."

"No, of course not." Beatrice bent over and swept what was left of the pile into her hand. "Can't imagine how they ended up in the trash like that." She straightened and glanced over her shoulder.

I followed her eyes to the door. Wyatt stood under the threshold with a key in his hand.

"I'm afraid I need to lock this office up, ladies. You two all through?"

"Why, yes." The tea was a tad dark for my tastes, anyhow. "I think we are."

I nodded to both Wyatt and Beatrice on my way out of the office. She'd grown awfully chilly after I found those things in the trash. Not to mention she'd whisked them away from me so quickly.

Finally, where were the chemistry notes she needed? Unless she was going to return to the office, which was highly doubtful since Wyatt planned to lock it, she hadn't retrieved any notes at all.

The questions tumbled through my mind as I slowly trekked back to the main house. The stairs seemed higher than ever, and I gripped the rail for support. Enough was enough already. If I didn't get something to eat or drink soon, I surely would pass out.

It was time to eat a proper meal. I made my way through the foyer and down the hall, until the door of the restaurant finally appeared.

Hooray! Charles had taken command of the maître d's stand, like I'd hoped.

"You're a sight for sore eyes," I said. "Table for one, please."

"Sure thing." He seemed subdued as he led me into the restaurant.

My favorite table by the picture window was already occupied. I cursed my luck until I drew closer and realized it was none other than Ambrose, back from Bleu Bayou and looking none the worse for wear.

"Hello, Missy!"

I dropped my purse next to the table and planted a big ol' kiss on his forehead. Only a day apart and already I missed him so.

"I was going to call you," I said. "How did you know I'd come here?" He'd even had the decency to wait for me before nibbling on something from the bread basket.

"I went to your room first, but you weren't there. I know you don't always remember to eat lunch, so I figured you'd come here for dinner."

"You know me too well."

As I settled in, Charles returned to our table, still looking miserable. "Why, Charles, whatever is the matter?" I asked. "You look like someone stole all your marbles."

"A police officer was here." He quietly handed us menus. "Asked me a bunch of questions about Trinity. I didn't know what to tell him."

I took a fat roll from the bread basket and bit into it. *Heaven on earth.* When I finished chewing, I delicately placed it on my bread plate. "You can always start with the truth. We have a saying in Bleu Bayou: *Tell the truth and shame the devil.*"

"That's the thing, Missy. I got the feeling the officer didn't believe me."

"Exactly what did you say?" I knew better than to glance at Ambrose, because he'd no doubt give me one of his patented mind-your-own-business-Missy looks he was so good at conjuring.

"I didn't see anything strange yesterday," Charles said. "But he wanted to know all about my past. Why does he think I had anything to do with the murder?"

"For all you know, he asks everyone the same questions," I said.

"Can I speak plainly with you?" By now Charles had noticed Ambrose was more interested in the bread basket than in our conversation, and he turned to me. "I wasn't exactly honest with you this afternoon. I did know Trinity. I knew her well."

It was about time he admitted it. "Why didn't you just say so?"

"It's complicated. I'm not supposed to know her, or her family. They're part of that rich crowd at the Baton Rouge Country Club."

"And?" He wasn't making this easy, and if he didn't get to the point soon, I'd have to wrestle Ambrose for leftover bread crumbs.

"I sort of worked there last summer. I was supposed to be busing tables."

"There's nothing wrong with that. Sounds like a good summer job."

"It was. I'm not ashamed of it. Working at the club and a scholarship got me through my first year at LSU."

"So you met Trinity there. Seems simple enough. Doesn't mean you were best friends or anything."

The way he sighed said more than any words could.

"Right?" I asked.

"Like I said, it's complicated. Instead of working at the restaurant, her daddy wanted me to escort her to parties and stuff. Said she couldn't very well show up at her own parties without a date. No one ever asked her out before that Sterling guy came along."

Finally Ambrose glanced from the bread basket to Charles. "Did you do that for her daddy?"

"It was either that or have no job," Charles said. "Mr. Solomon is one of the owners at the country club, like he owns everything else. He would've had me thrown out of there. He even threatened to yank my scholarship at LSU."

"He shouldn't have done that," Ambrose said. "He should be ashamed of himself, not you."

"Truth is, I got to know Trinity pretty well," he said. "She was so funny, and we had such a good time together. I felt bad about taking the money, but I needed it."

"I hope you told the police the truth," I said. "That's all you can do."

"But my scholarship . . ."

"You're afraid they'll pull your scholarship over this?"

"My dad lost his business, Missy. I can't graduate without it." He looked as miserable as a house cat in a rainstorm.

"Then here's what you should do." How could I resist offering advice at a time like this? "You tell the officer everything you know, but tell him it's between you, him, and the fence post. No need for the whole town to learn about your past."

"I can't do that. If anyone talks, Mr. Solomon will know I ratted him out. I can't take that chance."

I didn't want to be the one to bring it up, but lying about his relationship with Trinity would no doubt put Charles at the top of Lance's suspect list. "You need to tell the truth, Charles. Tell him how you met Trinity."

His shoulders slumped. "The last time I saw her was Valentine's Day, right around the time that Sterling guy showed up. I didn't know they were getting married until this weekend."

"But that was only three months ago." I'd assumed we were talking about something that had happened years before. I didn't want to be indelicate, but there is *some* math I do understand. "How well did you get to know Trinity?"

Before he could answer, Cat appeared at our table, wearing a chef's toque. She looked fit to be tied as she approached Charles and whispered in his ear. When she finished, the two of them disappeared in a flurry of black and white.

"Well, *that* was interesting," I said.

"Which part? The part about a dad paying someone to date his daughter, or the fact Charles would actually do it?"

"Both. Something doesn't sit right with all of this." Which was true enough. "There are more secrets around this place than fleas on a stray cat."

"Don't get started. This isn't any of our business." Once again, it seemed like he wanted to save me from myself.

"It's not my fault people keep confessing their sins to me. Maybe I should've become a priest."

He chuckled before biting into the shreds of his biscuit, probably feeling more charitable now that he had a little food in him.

As for me, if Charles didn't return to our table soon, I'd have to make do with Ambrose's leftover bread crumbs. Not to mention a slew of unanswered questions.

An hour later, after I bent Ambrose's ear about the shadow in the hall, my accidental eavesdropping on Beatrice and Sterling and the mansion's money woes, our meal drew to a close. We were full-up on roast duck—my choice—and medium-rare steak—his—when I pushed my chair away from the table. There was one last thing we needed to discuss before we could call it a night.

"We had some excitement at the church I visited this morning." It was better to break it to him in dibs and dabs, instead of running off at the mouth and giving him indigestion. "Do you know they're planning a big fund-raiser for tomorrow night? A fashion show. They're trying to raise money for new choir robes."

"That so."

"You know we work so well together. Organizing new collections, finding just the right accessories, and then me adding the perfect hat. When you think about it, we're kinda like those magicians—Penn and Teller—only we do our magic with silk and satin." I was rambling, but I needed time to work up to a point.

"You're right." Ambrose even grinned, until he must have realized what I was up to. "All right, Missy—spill it. What've you done?"

He knows me so well. "Nothing you wouldn't have done yourself." Which was the truth. "I kind of volunteered you to host their fashion show tomorrow night. Okay, more than that. I kinda said you and me would run it. You're so good at it, Bo, and you know that's true."

He groaned. "We're supposed to go home in the morning. Remember?"

"C'mon. You love to do this kind of thing. Show off your ball gowns, throw in a few mother-of-the-bride dresses. It doesn't have to be extravagant. We just need the Ambrose touch."

Luckily, he didn't seem too angry. Irritated, maybe, but not downright hostile. "If you don't stop flattering me, I'm gonna say no."

Maybe I pushed too hard. "Everything else is under control. *Everything.* They'll hold it right there in their social hall, and it's only a hop and skip away from here." I had saved my best ammunition for last, like when Cat glazed her plain old biscuits with a dollop of shiny egg whites to make them sparkle. "After all, think about the new clients you could get. I'll bet women come all the way from Baton Rouge for the show."

He squinted. "Maybe you're right. And if you've gone and done it, there's not a whole lot I can say."

Hallelujah! I wouldn't have to eat my words with the church and take it all back. "You won't be sorry." I grasped his hand, happy as anything. "Since you've been so nice to me, we can explore anywhere you want tonight. There's not much open, but maybe we can stroll around the grounds some more. I even found a museum out back with pictures and everything."

"I can do what I want, huh?" He smiled. "Now *that* would be a miracle. The museum sounds good."

We both finished our coffee and then strolled out of the restaurant arm in arm. My feet weighed about a thousand pounds apiece. Cat definitely knew her way around a duck, even if she did have more tattoos than a Navy midshipman.

Once we'd walked for a few minutes, the museum appeared. Surprisingly, the door stood ajar. We entered, and I searched for a light switch on the wall and flipped it on.

"Here, I want to show you something." I purposefully avoided the picture of the mother and her child and pulled him over to the photo of Morningside Plantation in its prime. Here, every gas lamp was lit, an elegant carriage hovered in the drive, and a uniformed liveryman stood at the ready. "Isn't it beautiful?"

Even though the trust did a bang-up job of renovating the place, my heart fluttered at how things used to look. A parade of women in enormous bonnets posed on the limestone stairway, while men in top hats and tails lined the drive. One gentleman even carried a silver-tipped walking cane.

"Just like in Bleu Bayou, this whole area used to belong to Cajuns." I enjoyed putting my newfound knowledge to use. "But then business-men came down from the East. Once they figured out how to make money off the river, shipping their lumber and whatnot, it was only a matter of time before they built plantations like Morningside to keep their wives happy. Course, the women probably still grumbled about trading New York City for a swamp."

"Sounds reasonable." Ambrose studied the picture for a moment. "Where's everyone else?"

"That's the shame. The slaves lived in cabins out back." Another gritty black-and-white picture showed a group of people sitting be-hind the mansion, only this time the women wore handkerchiefs in-stead of bonnets, the drive stood empty, and none of the men held a walking stick. "The family hated the practice of slavery, even though they needed people to run this place. So, they paid their staff wages, which almost no one else did. One of the Andrews sons joined the Confederates, but his brother chose the Union." I led Ambrose to the next display case, like a docent at a museum. "That's the boy who went to war for the Confederates, Jeremiah. He looks a little young to me."

Ambrose leaned forward and began to read a note card next to the photo, his voice rumbling in the quiet. "*Jeremiah Andrews fought for the Confederacy against General Farragut in Baton Rouge. He died on the eve of his seventeenth birthday.*" He shook his head. "Such a shame. So many soldiers lost, from both the North and the South."

"And so sad for Mrs. Andrews."

After a moment, he straightened. "Look at all the other displays in the room. Notice anything different?"

I glanced around. Plenty of muskets, gunpowder, and military bric-a-brac. Not to mention an empty spot near the top of the cabinet in front of us. "Just that bare place up there. I noticed it yesterday too. What do you suppose used to be there?"

"Hard to say. But it was pretty big; bigger than a lot of things here. Looks like they forgot to take down the notes on it."

"I know. I saw that too. Only I forgot to turn on the light yesterday and I couldn't read it."

Ambrose leaned again and began to read. *"The centerpiece of a Confederate soldier's uniform was a gray shell made of wool. This one was unearthed on the battlefield of Charleston, South Carolina."* He paused. "Looks like they had an actual Army coat here once."

It couldn't be. Could it? "That's what the person in the hall wore last night."

"Are you sure?" He frowned. "I don't want you going out into that hall again without me. As a matter of fact, I'm staying in your room tonight."

"Do you really think that's necessary?" I did my best to look nonchalant. *Please think it's necessary.*

"Absolutely. I won't take *no* for an answer."

"All right, then." I waved away his concern. "Only because you insist."

Chapter 11

Since we'd seen most everything, I doused the light in the museum and sashayed past Ambrose, who shut the door behind him.

Shame on the hotel for not locking the place up. Anyone could come in and waltz away with a piece of history, which was apparently what someone had done.

"Tomorrow night will be here before you know it," Ambrose said. "Why don't we go upstairs and start pulling some notes together for the fashion show."

"Sounds good."

My body ached from the lack of sleep, but I knew he was right.

Hallelujah—the museum wasn't far, and we soon passed the restaurant. My heels shuffled along the carpet as I followed Ambrose.

"Well, what do you know?"

He stopped so abruptly I almost ran into him. "Ambrose Jackson!"

We were at the bar; the one where I'd overhead Beatrice and Sterling earlier in the day. This time, though, a handful of people milled around the room.

"Isn't that the officer you were telling me about?" Ambrose asked. "The one you grew up with?"

A tall African-American leaned against the bar. It was Lance, all right, still in his police uniform and still carrying that notebook.

"Wonder what he's doing here," I said. Even police officers had to go home at some point.

"Maybe he never left."

"You're right." Truth be told, the sight of that notebook drew me like a magnet to steel. But I also had Ambrose and the fashion show to think about.

"I need to find the washroom," Ambrose said. "Why don't you say hi to your friend for a minute."

"Good idea." Dilemma solved. I sidled up to Lance at the bar. "Hi again. Whatever are you doing here so late? Don't they give you guys any time off?"

"Hey there. I've been doing interviews all day, but I'm almost finished up." He motioned to the bartender. "Two coffees, please."

Maybe one more cup won't hurt. While the bartender poured our drinks, I pointed to some club chairs across the room. "Mind if we sit for a second? My dogs are barking and I'm waiting on Ambrose."

"Sure. I've got a few minutes now my interviews are done."

We took our coffees and walked over to the chairs. I deliberately picked a spot out in the open so Ambrose would see me.

"How'd it go today?" I steadied the coffee and carefully sat.

Lance did the same. "Good. Think I've spoken to everyone but the statues outside, and they're not talking."

"Give 'em time. You've spoken with everyone?" I took a gulp and nearly choked. The coffee was strong enough to float a pistol. "*Gahlee.* Now, you don't have to tell me everything. I just want to hear the good parts."

"You know I can't do that." He shot me a look copied straight from Ambrose's playbook. The mind-your-own-business kind of look I'd come to loathe.

"Can't or won't?" I asked.

"This is an open investigation, and I'm not at liberty to talk about it."

"Did you memorize that line from your police manual? It's me, Missy DuBois. We grew up together. If the girl next door can't keep a secret, then I don't know who can. Honestly." I steeled myself against the bitterness and sipped from the coffee again.

"Guess it couldn't hurt to tell you who I talked to."

There, that's more like it. "Tell me you started with the housekeepers. I'm sure they know more about what goes on here than everyone else."

"Of course." He opened the notebook halfway. The letters looked all catawampus on the page. "Along with a waiter, a tour guide, and a gardener."

"That would be Charles, Beatrice, and Darryl." Amazing how quickly I'd come to know the hotel's staff. "They're all nice enough, near as I can tell, but it's hard to know who to trust."

"None of them had much to say. That Charles had a motive—his father lost a lot of money with the refinery—and he was at the right place at the right time."

"Well, I don't know about that."

Someone emerged from the men's room who looked like Ambrose, but he was immediately intercepted by another man at the bar. The interceptor wore a navy blazer with a name tag on the lapel.

"What else do you have?" I asked.

"Spoke with a housekeeper by the name of Laney Babin." Lance double-checked his notes. "Guess it wouldn't hurt to let you know she found the body in a stall at oh-eight-hundred hours. Didn't think to check for a pulse, but she knew the victim was dead."

"How could she tell?" Finding someone on a bathroom floor could have meant a lot of things: A fainting spell, a pratfall, maybe even a drunken stupor. Didn't necessarily mean the person on the ground would stay there. I mulled things over with another gulp of coffee.

"She noticed the victim's eyes were wide open. It reminded her of a fish on a platter. She said, and I quote, 'The victim eyed me like a black drum on a bed of rice.' She was too afraid to get close, so she turned tail and ran out the door."

"It probably scared her to death," I said. "Imagine she wouldn't see many dead bodies, being from a small town and all."

"I didn't tell you that." He looked surprised. "How do you know the housekeeper is from a small town? Riversbend, to be exact. Population nine-hundred and fifty, at last count."

"Everyone knows you find black drum in the bayous. And she had to be local with a French name like Babin."

"You're right. She also didn't like the color of the victim's face. Thought it looked like grape Kool-Aid."

"You never should have talked to her so early in the morning." The caffeine was clearing the fog from my mind, so I took another sip. "You interviewed her before breakfast, right? No wonder she had food on her mind. She probably said the victim was as plump as cooked boudin. Next time, wait until later in the day."

"We'll know more once we get the autopsy report back. Coroner got the body yesterday, so we're probably looking at Wednesday for the report." He yawned. "I need to call it quits, though. These shifts are gonna kill me yet. Take care of yourself, Missy."

"Don't worry about me. I have Ambrose for protection." I glanced over. The stranger was talking Ambrose's ear off.

"Glad to hear it. By the way, you seem to have your own ideas about what happened here this weekend."

"I do. You can be sure of that." And most of them involved a certain tour guide and the victim's unfaithful fiancé. Everyone knows people usually murder for love or revenge. Why should this case be any different?

Once Lance said good-bye, I finished my coffee and rose. Funny how I felt like a brand-new person. Like I could square-dance all the way to Bleu Bayou and back again.

I skipped over to the bar and grabbed Ambrose by the arm. "Time to get that meeting underway. We need to get busy, busy, busy."

The stranger speaking with him stopped mid-sentence and then turned and walked away.

"I'm so sorry, Bo. I should have let you finish your conversation."

"Are you kidding? That guy wouldn't stop talking." He grinned. "And you're right. We need to get our act together. But where'd you get all this energy?"

"I kinda had some coffee."

"Oh no." Ambrose knew all about me and coffee. He once said it was like giving uppers to a jackrabbit: totally unnecessary.

"Maybe I should walk it off. Wanna come with me?" Sundays for us usually meant an early night since we both had to be at work come Monday morning. But all bets were off this weekend.

"Maybe a little one. But we've got lots to do."

"Let's get at it, then. Time to go, go, go. Maybe we'll even run into Wyatt. He's the general manager. That guy works all the time."

I left the bar with Ambrose two steps behind me. When we got to the registration cottage, though, someone new sat where Wyatt should've been. The lady seemed bored as she twisted paper clips into a chain.

"Darn. Wyatt must be off duty," I said. "Well, there's always tomorrow morning."

"Speaking of which . . ." Ambrose glanced at a clock over the woman's head. "I know we need to go over our plan for the show tomorrow, but I'm dead on my feet. How about we go back to the room and then get up early? Otherwise, I don't know if I'll be able to think straight."

"Okay. I guess. Why not? I'll race you."

"Whoa." Ambrose draped his arm around my shoulders. "How 'bout we walk back to the room like normal people?"

He kept me in check the whole way there. It took me three tries to get the room key in the lock with my trembling fingers once we arrived. Instead of waiting for me to walk through the doorway like he usually did, Ambrose strode ahead of me.

"It's okay," he said. "Everything looks clear."

I debated whether to leave the light off. Part of me wanted to see his handsome face, so I moved to the nightstand and fumbled with the Tiffany table lamp. By the time I figured out how to work the antique lamp, my fingers still twitching like crazy, a noise sounded behind me.

Someone was snoring. It was Ambrose, sprawled across the divan.

"Really?" I stomped my foot. I had half a mind to march over there and shake him awake, but he looked so cute scrunched up on the dainty divan. And here I thought we might actually move our relationship in a new direction. Apparently not tonight.

I sighed and grabbed a cotton blanket from the foot of my bed and then draped it over him.

Might as well get ready for bed. Once I changed into my pajamas, I combed my hair and washed my face. Then I doused the bathroom light and returned to the bedroom.

Sleep wasn't an option, so I grabbed a book from the shelf and curled up next to the divan to be close to Ambrose. The smell of Armani cologne made it almost impossible to focus, but I somehow managed to read the book's title: *Famous Plantations of the South*. The cover featured a beautiful picture of a crepe myrtle ablaze in reds and pinks. Such a nice coincidence we happened to visit Morningside in spring, when the myrtles caught fire and catalpa trees dusted the ground with snowy petals.

Speaking of which . . . hadn't we paid extra for rooms with a garden view? I'd only looked out the window once or twice the entire time I'd been at Morningside, so I rose from the floor and peered through the window over the divan. Only a sliver of the moon's light graced the sky, when I needed the whole thing to see anything but shadows and splotches.

I leaned in toward the window. At that moment something—or someone—scuttled by the garden hedge. It stood out, even in the pale moonlight: square shoulders, long coat and hat. After a second, the apparition disappeared.

Well, I'll be. What hotel guest would wander the garden at night, with no moonlight to speak of? That didn't make sense, but what could I do since Ambrose was asleep and I had on nothing but pajamas?

Besides, it was probably my imagination. After I settled on that, I dropped to the floor again near Ambrose and flipped open the picture book. First up was a picture of a mansion painted like an Easter egg in yellows and blues. A fat headline said it was the San Francisco Plantation, even though we were nowhere near the Golden Gate Bridge. Such a funny name for a Southern plantation.

I turned the page. *Crashhh!* Something sounded outside in the hall. I dropped the book and jumped to my feet.

Amazingly, Ambrose didn't stir. So I moved across the carpet to the door. But this time around I decided to arm myself. My umbrella hung from the doorknob, ready to protect my hats against spring showers. The sharp end might come in handy, or I could always swing the wooden handle like a baseball bat. I grabbed it, turned the knob with my free hand, and then stepped into the hall.

I probably wouldn't find anything. But then a figure came right at me like a bullet down the barrel of a .22. I immediately took aim with my umbrella and swung high and wide. Surprisingly, the crack of wood against bone rang out, and the form crumbled to the ground.

I stared at the person twitching on the floor. It was one thing to be an intruder, but quite another to see him or her at my feet. Tentatively, I poked my toe somewhere near the person's midsection. No response. I tried again, only this time I kicked higher. That did the trick, and the form below me moaned.

I leaned over the body. The cheese-wedge moon provided just enough light to illuminate a gray felt coat, cloth haversack, and navy hat. A buckle twinkled from the hat's epicenter, like a starburst in the night sky. I'd downed a soldier. A Confederate soldier. No doubt the visitor from the night before; the one who floated down the stairs and left behind only shadows and splotches.

I looked again. Yes, it was definitely a uniform, the wrists circled with ribbon, the neck stiff with starch, with a felt hat. My curiosity piqued, I reached for the hat and plucked it off. Wyatt's head appeared, as shiny and smooth as the twinkly buckle. The man hired to drum up business for the plantation, not to scare it away. The general manager who found me in the smoking room and scolded me for being there. No doubt the key I saw there belonged to the plantation's museum.

"Ambrose!" Hang any more niceness on my part. I couldn't very well leave Wyatt lying on the carpet like a deer downed by a hunter. What if I'd killed the man, since I hadn't heard another peep? "I need you!"

When he didn't respond, I turned my face toward the room and tried again. "Help me, Ambrose!"

That did the trick, and Ambrose appeared in the doorway, rumpled and confused, like a little boy missing his teddy bear. Bless his heart.

"I think I killed him!" I stood and moved to Ambrose's side, where I'd be safe. Now that I'd swung my umbrella like a Louisville Slugger, what next?

"What is this man doing lying on the ground?" Ambrose ran his fingers through his hair, which didn't do a lick of good. "And why is he wearing that uniform?"

"It's the general manager, and I have no idea why he's wearing it. I was sitting on the floor looking at a picture book, when I heard a terrible noise in the hall."

"Why didn't you wake me?"

"You were so tired, Bo. I didn't have the heart. I came out here with my umbrella and he ran at me."

"This doesn't make sense. Why did you hit him if you knew it was the general manager?"

I shot him an exasperated look. "Obviously, I didn't know who it was. I swung first and asked questions later." Although that seemed to sum up my entire life, I hoped Ambrose would spare me the sarcasm.

"We can't leave him here. Help me get him into your room."

We dragged the unconscious man into my bedroom. Fortunately, I hadn't broken skin, but a knot the size of a billiard ball slowly erupted on his forehead. Why did I have to be such a good aim?

"What should we do?" I asked.

"Call the front desk. They'll know how to reach the night manager."

I ran to the phone and lifted the handle. After two rings, a voice picked up on the other end.

"Night manager. May I help you?"

"I hope so. This is Missy DuBois. You have to send someone to the Eugenia Andrews room right away."

"Is something the matter?" She sounded awfully relaxed for such an important emergency.

"I'll say. I've got Wyatt Burkett up here, and he's knocked out cold." No need to provide details. There'd be time enough to sort out the whole mess later.

"I see. That's on the third floor, right? I'll send the guard."

A short time later, someone clamored up the stairs. It was a security guard who didn't look too happy about walking up two flights of steps at this time of the night.

"You called, Ms. DuBois?"

He sounded dubious, as if I'd made a ruckus for the fun of it. I stepped aside to expose Wyatt, who was slowly recovering from the blow.

"Oh, my." That woke the guard, and he hustled over to Wyatt.

"Who did this to him?"

"It's a long story." I shrugged. "There was a noise in the hall. Turns out it was Wyatt here, running around in one of those uniforms y'all keep downstairs in the museum." My Southern twang tended to come out particularly strong when I had to deliver bad news, which I think makes it easier to digest. "Guess I hit him just right."

"You hit him in the head?"

"She thought it was an intruder." Ambrose jumped in to defend me, like I knew he would. "Good news is he's breathing regular. He's got a lump, but it's on the outside of his head, so the blood's not pooling on the inside, which is always a good sign."

Both of which were true, and that seemed to appease the security guard some. He took Wyatt by the shoulders and began to hoist him up. "Mind giving me a hand?" he asked Ambrose.

"Not at all. Will you be all right by yourself, Missy?"

"I think so. I'm a little jittery, but it's probably just the coffee."

Ambrose got under Wyatt's other shoulder, which elicited a loud moan, and they angled his body to move him down the stairwell.

Once they left, the hall fell silent. I couldn't imagine the night would turn out so. No use trying to go to sleep, so I returned to my spot by the divan.

Why did Wyatt dash through the building like a bat after a mosquito, dressed in a stolen Confederate uniform? What did he hope to gain? Or, more likely, what did he hope the plantation would lose? If another guest had heard the noise instead of me, she might have been scared half to death. Was that his plan all along?

The picture book lay open on the floor. A fake ghost in a stolen uniform wouldn't exactly help Morningside become one of the "Famous Plantations of the South." Between Wyatt's shenanigans and an unsolved murder, odds were good no one would pay to stay here again.

Ambrose finally returned to the hall an hour or so later. This time he went to his own room, darn the luck, and I lay wide awake for several hours.

When sleep finally came, I dreamed of shadows and baseball bats and crime-scene tape, until the sound of someone rapping on my door woke me.

"Missy. You up?"

"Oh, Bo." It seemed like midnight and I'd only been sleeping for fifteen minutes or so.

"C'mon, wake up. It's time for breakfast," he said.

I rolled out of bed, inched open the door, and stuck my head in the hall. Why would Ambrose rustle me out of bed at the crack of dawn?

"Really?"

"I got a call from Beatrice," he said. "She wants us to meet her for breakfast."

"That's nice." I yawned loudly. "She probably wants to apologize for last night."

"I don't know." Doubt clouded his eyes. "She didn't seem too happy."

"Don't be such a worrywart. My guess is she wants to apologize for what Wyatt did. Make sure we don't bad-mouth the plantation to other people."

"Could be." Ambrose didn't look convinced, though. "Get dressed and we'll see what she wants."

Which was easier said than done. I retreated to the room and slogged past the warm bed. More than anything, I longed to hide my head under the covers like a turtle in its shell. But then I'd disappoint Beatrice, who was only trying to make things right with us.

Thank goodness for makeup, especially under-eye concealer. After doing what I could in the bathroom, I studied the hats lined up in my closet. Maybe it was time to bring out the big gun, the green velvet trilby with the burnt coque and hackle feathers. The velvet would play up my eyes, which was exactly what I needed this morning.

Between that and a slash of Chanel Rouge lipstick, I prayed I looked respectable as I stood outside Ambrose's door fifteen minutes later.

"I'm ready."

He, of course, looked amazing in a crisp black polo. Remnants of the Armani cologne lingered.

"Wouldn't want to keep Beatrice waiting."

Ambrose led the way as we traveled downstairs to the restaurant. Unfortunately, Charles was nowhere to be found, but then I remembered it *was* Monday morning, and he was probably sitting in a lecture hall somewhere on the LSU campus.

"Hello." Beatrice had arrived before us, and she met us at the maître d' stand. "I picked a nice table in back." She proceeded to lead us through the empty restaurant to a table by the window. Even though it wasn't my favorite table overlooking the old oak, it was pretty, nonetheless.

"Thank you." I draped the strap of my purse over the back of the chair before sitting down. "So nice of you to invite us to breakfast like this. By the way, shouldn't you be in class right now?"

"No, it's finals week. I don't have my first one until tomorrow. Besides, the hotel asked me to stay today so we could sort out some things."

"Now please don't think we're upset about last night." I scooted my chair up to the table. "It's not the plantation's fault Wyatt went crazy like that." I fanned open my napkin, like the ones Charles and I had wrapped up quite nicely, and placed it in my lap. "We're willing to let bygones be bygones."

Beatrice kept staring at the tablecloth. Funny she wouldn't look at me.

"That's why you invited us here, right? To make amends?" I pushed the coffee cup away from my plate, since I had no intention of ever drinking caffeine again. "Like I said, we're not angry, so don't think the hotel has to make it up to us."

She finally eyed me. "That's not it. We're going to have to ask you to leave."

I must have misunderstood. Probably just the lack of sleep playing tricks on me. "Come again?"

"The night manager called the paramedics last night. You gave Mr. Burkett a concussion. Now, I know he was probably asking for it, but he's already talking about a lawsuit."

"What?" That didn't make sense, but neither did the hitch in Beatrice's voice or the stunned look on Ambrose's face, as if she'd upped and slapped him.

"It's assault and battery," she said. "You knocked him out."

My face began to warm, even though I knew the hotel's air conditioner had run all night. "That man scared me out of my wits. I thought he was a ghost." The nerve of Wyatt to talk about suing anyone. The gall!

"Look, the plantation's attorney said you guys don't have to pay for your stay here," Beatrice said. "Please. We've even booked you some rooms in town. If you leave right now, the attorneys are willing to call it even."

"Even?" I said. "I've been traumatized, and I will not be talked to like a child." I chunked down my napkin and rose, although I had nowhere else to go.

"I'm sorry," Beatrice said. "The attorney told me what to say. He wants you and Ambrose out by noon. I'm so sorry."

"Are you sure you want to do this?" Ambrose calmly entered the fray as the voice of reason. "Missy was acting in self-defense. What she did was perfectly legal."

"I'm afraid so, Ambrose. The hotel can't afford a lawsuit. They said it would put us under."

"But we're doing a fashion show tonight at the church." Unfortunately, my voice came out all wobbly, like maybe I *was* a child and I'd just been told to cross a busy street by myself.

Beatrice's voice softened. "Like I said, we've booked some rooms for you in town. It's at a place called the Sleepy Bye Inn, just down the road. It's not as fancy as this one. Okay, it's a little tacky. But they've set aside the rooms."

The name didn't sound very encouraging. I glanced at Ambrose, but he'd fallen as silent as my discarded napkin. Leave it to him to remain levelheaded while my legs turned to muscadine jelly.

"Fine, Beatrice. If we're not welcome here, we'll go there. C'mon,

Bo." I turned away from the table, forcing my shoulders back. This would surely put a crimp in my plans. How was I ever going to help Ivy if I was no longer staying at the place where her stepdaughter was murdered?

"You're making a big mistake," Ambrose said. "But if that's how you want to play it, we'll leave."

Chapter 12

Fifteen minutes later, Ambrose finished loading the trunk of our car. He even took extra care with my hats, which was sweet of him, since I knew he was only trying to soften the sting of Beatrice's words.

Although it was childish, I refused to look back at the mansion when we pulled away. Why should I? Instead of thanking us for catching Wyatt at his little charade, the plantation had chosen to treat us like common criminals and had tossed us out into the mean streets of Riversbend, Louisiana. Although there were certainly more dangerous places to be.

We could always go home, but I wanted to be near the action and Ambrose had to be close to the venue for the fashion show. What good would it do for us to sit by ourselves in Bleu Bayou?

After a few moments, we drove by the two old broodmares grazing and then the sugarcane field. The parking lot of the Rising Tide Baptist Church appeared next. It was completely full this morning, lined grille to fender with pickup trucks, SUVs, and cars.

Amazing. While most folks spent Monday morning carting around cell phones and laptops to meetings and such, these people swarmed around their church's parking lot with folding chairs, card tables and spools of electric cords.

"Why don't we pull in and say hello?" I asked.

Ambrose nodded and swerved onto the lot. The first person to appear was the lion-like deacon from the day before. Today he wore a purple T-shirt and an old LSU ball cap as he wiped down some folding chairs. It might improve my mood some to help out, so I pointed to an empty parking space.

"Do you mind?" I said. "I might as well introduce you around."

"Not at all. Anything to take our minds off Morningside Plantation."

As soon as Ambrose parked, I swung open the car door. It was too early in the day for humidity, praise the Lord, so the air was cool and dry. The smell of car exhaust and rubber tires drifted over on it.

The man who spoke at church the day before and had pinked up like a rosebush when I spoke to him worked alongside the deacon.

"There's the guy I talked to yesterday. C'mon, Bo."

I walked over to him. He clutched a paper towel and seemed to be struggling with a particularly stubborn crayon mark stretching from one corner of a folding table to another.

"Morning," I said.

Sure enough, he blushed the minute he glanced away from his work and saw me. "You came!"

"Of course we came. I told you yesterday at church that we would." I motioned back to Ambrose. "This is the friend I told you about. Ambrose Jackson."

The man's cheeks reddened even more. Quickly, he brushed his hand on the leg of his trousers and held it out to Ambrose. "It's an honor. A real honor. When Melissa here told us you used to be on a reality television show, I went home and found it on the Internet. Can't believe I'm talking to you."

Ambrose looked genuinely pleased to be recognized. "Glad to be here. Looks like you've got everything under control."

"My mama and me both watched it. She even ran out and bought a new dress for tonight. On a Sunday! Course I told her she should have waited until after the Lord's day, but she was so excited she couldn't help herself."

As usual, seeing someone like Ambrose transformed from pixels on a television screen to actual flesh and blood had flummoxed the man. Something about the transition always made people lose their heads.

"It's all about the cause, right?" Ambrose said. "Here, let me help you clean that."

"Oh, no. I couldn't ask you to do that." The guy looked mortified at the very thought of Ambrose Jackson—television star—cleaning crayon marks from a folding table. "There's coffee in the social hall. Please help yourself."

"Maybe later." I swiped the paper towel from him and began to scrub at the marks. "Here, you need to put your back into it. Is everyone excited for tonight?"

"It's all anyone's talking about."

"Ambrose here has done dozens of these things. You have nothing to worry about." The harder I scrubbed at the mark, the less luck I seemed to have with it. "Here, Bo. Spit on this." I handed over the paper towel.

That gave me a moment to survey the parking lot. A line of men were hard at work next to us. The ones in front held a thick velvet rope, like in movie-theater lobbies, while the men in back toted shiny steel posts that reached waist-high. They were building a barrier to keep people in a straight line. A lot of people.

"Here you go, Missy."

"What?" I tore my eyes away from the men and their work. "Just what kind of a crowd are you expecting here tonight?"

"Hard to say. Course we did an e-mail blast to all the churches, so that'll bring in more people too."

One of the men jerked extra-hard on the rope and a steel post crashed to the ground. By this time the line of poles snaked from the social hall to the middle of the parking lot.

"So, do you think you might get a couple of hundred people tonight?" From what I could see of the social hall, it seemed a tad small for that.

"Pardon me?"

"Some of my best shows have happened in little places like this," Ambrose said. "Makes people want to sit in the front row. I like it because I can read their eyes."

The man with the fallen pole had lifted it back in place.

"We're hoping you get a big turnout. But even if you don't, we'll give it our best shot."

"Excuse me," he said. "But we're not going to have a few hundred people here tonight."

"We told you. It doesn't matter to us," I said. "It'll be amazing just the same."

"No, that's not what I mean. I'm guessing we'll get a thousand."

My jaw dropped. *Of course.* The men with the rope. The trail of posts that snaked from the social hall to the parking lot. A pile of folding chairs ready to be cleaned. "I had no idea."

"Hope that's okay, Mr. Jackson," the man said.

"How in the world can you fit a thousand people in that little social hall?" Ambrose asked.

"We're not. We're opening up the whole parking lot. We'll put big screens everywhere and then put more in the basketball gym."

It took me a moment to recover. That would account for the army of people swarming the parking lot. "I had no idea, Ambrose."

To my surprise, he began to laugh.

"What's so funny?"

"That's fantastic! The more the merrier."

"We were hoping you'd say that," the man said.

Ambrose's eyes danced. "Like I said, the more the merrier."

Lord love him. There was no telling what could happen at the show tonight.

Once we introduced ourselves around, it was time to find our new hotel and dig out the notes for tonight's show. Ambrose and I threaded our way through the parking lot, working our way through a rope that zigged and zagged through most of it.

I didn't speak until we'd driven down the road for a while and a sign appeared for our motel. Our new accommodations had seen better days. The neon sign was missing half its bulbs, and a yellow palm tree leaned against it. The only other vehicle in the parking lot was a Mack truck with silhouettes of naked girls on the mud flaps.

"You still want to stay here?" Ambrose drove us onto the parking lot. "We can always go home, you know."

"I know. But it'll be so much easier to stage the show if we're close by." And so much easier to help Ivy; although I didn't tell him that.

Once Ambrose parked, we both got out of the car and made our way to the manager's office. The room was little more than four cinder-block walls and a roof.

A tinny bell jangled when we opened the plate-glass door.

"Hello there." A redhead stood behind the counter. She'd been reading a copy of *Cosmo,* and she slapped it closed when we approached. "Y'all checking in for a few days?"

"Oh, no." I glanced at Ambrose. "I mean, yes, we're checking in. But not for a few days. Just for one night. Right, Bo?"

"Of course. Two rooms, please. I'm Ambrose Jackson and this is Missy DuBois. The plantation's paying for our stay here."

"Nice to meet you folks." Languidly, the woman reached for a Sharpie lying next to a legal pad on the counter. "You're my first customers today."

Ambrose and I exchanged quick looks, which she must have noticed. "'Cept for old Clyde out there and his truck. But they don't count for much."

"Gotcha." Ambrose took the pen and began to scrawl our names onto the makeshift guest registry.

"Course we'll probably be full up by nighttime. I heard tell there's a big fashion show goin' on around here."

"That's why we're here," Ambrose said. He continued to write, which gave me a moment to look around.

I'd never seen a woman quite as suntanned as the one behind the counter. Her face was the color of wheat berries and her teeth as white as porcelain. When she smiled, tiny wrinkles appeared from her nose to her chin and then disappeared again, like ripples on a pond.

"Do ya want some extra towels?" Maybe it was my imagination, but she seemed to be smiling extra big for Ambrose's sake.

"That would be nice," I said. "Two, please."

Once he finished with the guest book, Ambrose laid the Sharpie on the counter. "We're the ones staging the show at the Rising Tide Baptist Church tonight. You ought to think about going, if you have a chance. Starts at dusk."

That perked the lady up and her face rippled like crazy. "Why, I just might do that. Nice of you to invite me along."

"He invites everyone," I said. "His favorite saying is *the more, the merrier*. That's my Ambrose."

"Oh." That took a little wind out of her sails, but she slid a room key across the counter to me nicely enough. "I'll bring the towels by later. Y'all are upstairs by the Coke machine."

"Thank you." I hadn't meant to be rude, but the day had been so confusing. Who knew we'd be evicted from Morningside Plantation? That we'd be forced to up and leave like common criminals, without even a moment to say good-bye to the staff? It didn't seem fair, or very polite, and I made a mental note *not* to recommend the plantation to my family and friends any time soon.

On top of everything, we learned our fashion show would be seen by a thousand people, instead of the hundred I expected. What a strange and wondrous day, and lunchtime was still hours away.

Once the woman passed Ambrose his room key, we left the office. He went to park the car, while I climbed a flight of chipped concrete steps to the second floor. A laminate door greeted me when I got to my room, along with a rusty air-conditioner vent popping out from the wall like a dirty flower box. A blinking Coke machine flanked the far side of the fly-specked window.

I cautiously opened my room door. It *was* only for one night. If Mary could lay her newborn in a feeding trough, I could put up with cinder-block walls, chipped stairways, and a noisy vending machine.

At least the room wasn't a total pigsty. A poster of a magnolia bush hung over the cheap headboard, and the flower reminded me of my plants back home. Truth be told, I was beginning to feel homesick. But we'd agreed to stay the night and there wasn't much sense in turning back.

Ambrose walked up behind me. "See, this isn't so bad." He began to lay my suitcase on the bedspread.

"You're right." I didn't move. Heaven only knew the carpet was a bit worn, and I didn't plan to walk on it barefoot any time soon. "So, do you want to head back to the church?"

He chuckled. "That didn't take long. Sure, why not."

There wasn't much more to see, though. Every roadside motel seemed the same: a yellowed telephone directory on a wobbly nightstand, a faded plaid bedspread on a thin mattress, and a battered captain's chair by the door. No more, no less, and it would have to do.

We returned to the car and I stared out the window to clear my mind. After several miles, a white police cruiser pulled up alongside us. Darn if the thing didn't need a good scrubbing. Well, pick my peas! It was Lance LaPorte. I lowered my window. "Yoo-hoo!"

He glanced up.

"Pull over," I said to Ambrose. "I need to speak to Lance."

Ambrose did as I asked—bless his heart—and pulled in front of the police cruiser. Then he gently guided the car onto the shoulder of the road.

When Lance saw Ambrose and me, he followed. I bolted from our car as soon as possible and approached his side of the squad car.

"Good morning," I said. "What a coincidence! Didn't expect to see you out on the streets this morning."

"Morning, Missy." He slid a pair of aviator sunglasses down his nose. My, but he looked like his mama when he did that. "Where are you headed so early?"

"Ambrose and I are helping out the Baptists. We're using some of his gowns for a fashion show, and I'm helping to set up shop. And where might you be going?"

Lance pointed to a notebook on the seat beside him. "Got a lab analysis this morning on the Solomon case. Usually it takes 'em weeks, but we put a rush on it. Thought I'd check in with the funeral director and see what's going on with the family."

"*Gah-lee*. That *is* something. And such a coincidence." I eyed the notebook greedily. "Looks like we're going to the same place, since the church is right next door to the funeral home. How about if we meet up? They've probably got a big pot of coffee on and it's too early in the week to be rushing around like a crazy person."

Lance pursed his lips, but I knew he'd play along. It was amazing how much power one could wield on account of knowing someone's mama, and I had every intention of pumping that well until it ran dry.

"Maybe for a little bit," he said. "But I can't stay long. I told headquarters I'd be back soon."

"Now you're talking. You might want to bring along that notebook of yours. Wouldn't want it to get all hot and sticky sitting in the squad car."

The minute I got back to the car, I shared my plan with Ambrose.

"And he agreed to that?" Ambrose asked.

"Of course he did. Why wouldn't he? I've known him forever."

"I know you too. And I know this isn't about getting Lance a cup of coffee and maybe a beignet."

"I have no idea what you're talking about." I turned my head toward the window. "Honestly, you think I'm a busybody, don't you?"

"Your words, not mine."

We'd arrived at the Rising Tide Baptist Church, and Ambrose once more pulled into the parking lot. People milled around the property like dandelions blown about by a headwind. Some, including the elderly deacon in the LSU ball cap, had moved from cleaning chairs to wrangling thick extension cords. Others, like the guy I'd seen in the service the day before, held onto empty spools for the electric lines. Everyone seemed calm, with not a flustered face in the bunch. Which meant I could spend some quality time with Lance and that precious pathologist's report.

"Do you mind if I speak with Lance for a few minutes, Bo? I promise it won't take long, and then I'll run right back to you."

"No problem. Just make it quick, okay?"

I nodded to Ambrose and hopped out of the car. Lance had wrangled a parking space right behind ours. He was tucking his glasses under the car's sun visor when I approached the police cruiser.

"Let's get you some coffee," I said. "I don't have long, though."

"Do I have a choice?"

"Not really. I heard there's a pot of coffee in the social hall."

I waited for Lance, and then we walked through the crowd. I acknowledged some of the people I recognized with a nod, so as not to appear uppity, until we came to the social hall. I didn't see any coffee there, but then I checked a side room tucked next to it.

The room was empty, praise the Lord, except for a clean folding table with an industrial coffeepot, two cartons of nondairy creamer, and a stack of Styrofoam cups. The perfect spot. I pulled a cup from the top and handed it to Lance, since I couldn't pretend to know how he liked his coffee.

"What can I do for you today, Missy?"

"I think you know what I want. Don't make me beg."

"That's the thing." He filled his cup and added a drop of cream. "I can't figure out why this report is so important to you."

"Turns out the Solomons are practically family." Casually, I leaned against the folding table, even though it creaked something awful. Maybe if I acted nonchalant he might be more willing to part with his treasure. "Ivy Solomon is a Girard. You know the Girards out of Bleu Bayou, don't you? They're the most generous people who ever walked God's green earth."

"I didn't know she was a Girard. Wonder if she's Ben's aunt?"

"Probably. You know how big that family is. That would mean she's directly related to sweet Miss Maribelle. How can I turn my back on the Girards—or the Solomons—if I can help them out in their time of need?"

He pursed his lips. "I guess you can't. Family's family. But if I show this to you, you can't tell anyone about it. Okay?" Slowly, he pulled some pages out of his notebook and handed them to me. "It's highly irregular, and I'm sure my sergeant wouldn't be too happy with me."

"You won't be sorry, Lance. Mum's the word." I gently accepted the treasure. I had an excellent reason for asking to see the report, and I'd practically *made* Lance show it to me, so it wasn't his fault. There'd be time later to sort out right and wrong.

The first page listed Trinity's name, age—only twenty-four—and her marital status. Sad to think she'd remain single for all eternity now, and sadder still to consider the baby who would never be born.

The next page was a document from the Riversbend Parish Medical Center, which the pathologist had prepared the night before. It listed the approximate time of death as 23:00, or about 11:00 p.m. A few facts about Trinity followed: date of birth, medications she was taking, that kind of thing. Honestly, I couldn't make heads or tails of a list of numbers and initials that came next. "What's this here: *WNL?*"

"Within normal limits. *This* is the important stuff." Lance leaned over my shoulder and stabbed at a paragraph near the top. "They ran several lab tests since the girl didn't have a history of heart problems. She didn't die of natural causes, Missy. They found traces of cyanide."

"Cyanide? How in the world would cyanide end up in little Riversbend, Louisiana?"

"That's exactly what they found," he said. "Roughly two hundred milligrams of the stuff. Whoever poisoned her knew what they were doing."

"That's horrible. Who would do something like that?"

"We're gonna find out. I'm only thankful they ran the lab analysis so quick. Knowing what killed someone is half the battle."

"But you still don't know *who* did it, or why."

He was about to say more, when darn if someone didn't walk through the door and head our way. It was the lion-like deacon from outside, wearing his LSU ball cap and a determined look.

"There you are! Your friend's been asking about you, Miss DuBois. Said something about needing those notes from the show."

I gritted my teeth.

"Sorry for the interruption."

"That's okay," I said.

Lance quickly took the report back. "I've got to get to work anyway. We're burning daylight."

"Let me know what you find out, you hear?" Not that I wanted to boss him, but I might not get Lance's ear like this for a while.

He nodded and left.

I turned to the deacon. "Okay. Take me to Ambrose." I added a sigh to let him know I was *not* happy about being interrupted, or about being led away like a bull with a ring in its nose.

What really bothered me, though, was knowing whoever killed Trinity was probably going about his or her business at that very moment—maybe even sipping a cup of coffee too—as if nothing had happened. I pondered that as we left the building and walked to the parking lot.

The deacon had mentioned the notes Ambrose needed. No doubt he meant the fashion show we produced for the Ladies' Auxiliary League in Baton Rouge the month before. I'd e-mailed the notes to the league's chair, which meant I could still find them in my computer's in-box. The only problem was that Ambrose would need a hard copy. Although my cell phone was smart, it wasn't smart enough to print out twenty pages of notes on white bond paper.

Speaking of which . . . my skirt's pocket felt unusually light, so I patted the side where I normally stashed my cell phone. Nothing. Oh, shine. I must have left it on the vanity back at the motel. Could this day get any crazier?

"Hold on." I came to a dead stop. "I need a computer to print out some notes. Is there one I can use around here?"

The deacon tilted his head. "Normally I'd say yes. No problem. The men's club donated a fancy Hewlett-Packard with all the bells and whistles a few years back. Only it's been going nonstop since last night and someone said the printer finally gave up the ghost about an hour ago. The pastor's assistant nearly had a heart attack. No telling when they'll get it back online."

Now what? Apparently the day *could* get crazier, after all. I paused to think about my travels over the past few days. When I stayed at Morningside, I'd visited the registration cottage more than once, and on one of those visits, I'd watched Wyatt study his giant Dell computer screen. If I could get to that, I could access my e-mail account and find the right notes for Ambrose. I thought it over as the deacon led me away.

We came upon Ambrose a short time later, standing next to a woman in the parking lot. He must have worked himself into a lather about something or other because he windmilled his arms as he spoke.

"Hey, Ambrose. I heard about the notes." I sidled up behind him.

When he turned, my average mood curdled like milk left too long in the sun. The person standing beside him was none other than the lady from the motel. The one who smiled a bit too much at him.

"Oh."

She froze when she saw me too. "Hello again."

My first thought was to grab Ambrose by the shirt collar and drag him to higher ground, but I had too many other worries at the moment. "Can you take me to the plantation, Bo?"

"Of course," he said. "You remember Vernice here, don't you? She offered to help us out tonight. Turns out she's a whiz with cordless microphones."

I'll bet she is. Of all the things to worry about this morning, why did Ambrose have to be one of them? "Please, Bo. The quickest way to get those notes is to get me back to Morningside."

"I can take you." It was the deacon again, who had the uncanny ability to be in the wrong place at the wrong time.

"We couldn't ask you to do that," Ambrose said.

"Nonsense. You're needed here. I can drop your friend by the plantation in a jiffy. No trouble at all."

"Are you sure?" I asked. "Why don't I just wait for Ambrose to finish up here, and then we can go together."

"I told you . . . it's no trouble." The deacon grabbed my arm and practically dragged me away. "There's only so much time. People will be coming to the show before you know it."

Which was true. I glanced over my shoulder. Ambrose slowly receded into the distance as we scurried away. I had half a mind to peel the deacon's hand off my elbow and bolt right back to Ambrose and Vernice.

But like it or not, we'd arrived at an enormous brown Cadillac.

"Hop in, honey," the deacon said. "And don't forget to buckle up."

I didn't say two words on the drive over to Morningside, which had to be a new record for me. All I could think about was the smile on Vernice's face once I'd been roped into leaving.

My driver made up for the silence by talking nonstop until the Cadillac arrived at the plantation. He was still talking when I climbed out of the massive car.

That was when I heard another voice somewhere over my shoulder.

"Quiet as da graveyard."

That Cajun accent was unmistakable. When I turned, Darryl stood in front of me with a metal garden bench tucked under his left arm. "What in the world are you doing with that heavy thing, Darryl?"

"Deys want it over by da pool." He nodded toward the south side of the plantation. "Not likes we gots da guests ta use it."

"You're moving that by yourself?"

"Not a problem. Nuttin' a child couldn't do."

That was when I remembered how he'd lifted the gravestone the day before. Apparently, those pale aqua eyes masked the will of a much younger man.

"Say, Darryl." I glanced over at my driver, who'd also stepped away from his car but was preoccupied with a pigeon that now hovered over its hood. Just to be sure, I took a step closer to Darryl and lowered my voice. "I talked to the police officer this morning about Trinity."

Did Darryl's eyes narrow when I said that, like the aperture on a camera right before it snapped a picture?

"They say she was poisoned," I said. "With cyanide." I glanced over at the deacon again, but his attention remained glued to the hood of his beloved car and the menacing bird.

"Wat do ya know. Poisoned, huh? Tought she mighta been, since der wern' no blood on da floor."

Darryl had been one of the first people to arrive at the murder scene, right after Laney Babin. He was the one who kept people away from the house until the police could arrive.

"That's what I've been told. Can't imagine someone doing that to a young girl right before her wedding. What do you think happened?" I always said there was no better way to get at the truth than to up and ask for it. Nine times out of ten it wasn't what people told you that mattered; it was how they said it. Sort of like when Ambrose and I first met and I knew he liked me because his voice quivered like muscadine jelly. A wobbly voice, a slight pause, an unintentional flinch, or Darryl's narrowed eyes. All of it meant something. The trick was to find out what.

"Da ya wanna know my toughts, or are you jus' talkin? I tink da general manager knows sometin.' Soon as I met da man, I knew sometin' wern' right."

"You mean Wyatt?"

"Way I see it, dat man was goin' ta lose his job." He shifted the bench under his arm. "Didn' ya know? Mr. Solomon wanted ta buy dis place. Lock, stock, an' barrel."

Darryl stepped back to put some space between me and the chunky garden bench. "Check out da real-estate news, Miz DuBois. Dat's all I'm sayin'."

He began to walk away, his back ramrod straight, even with the heavy cargo under his left arm.

"Wait, Darryl." I didn't want to harass him, or to include the deacon in our conversation about Morningside, but this might be the last time I saw Darryl for a while and his meeting with Lance in the graveyard still bothered me. Fortunately, we could have been speaking in tongues for all my driver cared, because he'd taken a few steps toward the parking lot when he thought his precious car was about to be soiled by the pigeon. "Remember when you were talking to Lance LaPorte yesterday? Out there in the Andrews family graveyard? The acoustics around here are amazing, and I might have overheard you."

"Dat was private. No cause for listin' in."

"I didn't mean to listen in." Okay, I did, but that was neither here nor there at this point. "You said something that didn't make sense. At least not to me."

"Don' know what you're talkin' about, Miz DuBois."

"You said you never knew Mr. Solomon or his daughter, Trinity. I couldn't imagine that to be true, since you worked for the man. He was the one who told you all about the cremation. Surely you must have met him a time or two."

Darryl's face slowly hardened. "Don' recall dat. Never met da man. Only by da phone."

"But Trinity must have spoken to you about the wedding. About the flowers and such."

"Did ya meet her?"

"Well, no."

"But ya made her veil. How can dat be?"

"I worked with the wedding planner—"

"An' ya tink I didn't? I'm tellin' ya, Miz DuBois, I never met da gal. Mostly, I keeps to myself. It's da bes' way."

"Why do you keep saying that?" I asked.

"People git involved when dey shouldn't. Best ting is ta walk away." As if to prove it, he turned his back on me and walked away.

I stared at his retreating form. For one thing, I had no idea the plantation was for sale because no one had ever mentioned it. Then there was Darryl's tone. He knew more than he was telling me; that much was clear.

Too bad Ambrose wasn't with me because he'd know what to make of it all.

Ambrose. By now the overly tanned manager of the Sleepy Bye Inn, Vernice, had probably cornered him and was flirting up a storm, only he'd be too polite to do anything about it. Darn, I wished I had my cell. The only reason I'd discovered it was missing was because of the hullabaloo back at the church with my fashion-show notes and their broken printer.

No use worrying. I'd promised Ambrose I'd retrieve the show notes, so it was time to make good on that promise by hook or by crook.

The best way was to visit the registration cottage and find the wayward notes in my e-mail. There would be time enough to check out Darryl's story about the mansion being for sale and time enough for me to shake off the feeling of gloom he always left behind.

Chapter 13

I told the deacon he might as well have a look around the plantation since we weren't leaving anytime soon. At first he refused. But then I remembered the history museum so few people seemed to know about, with its treasure trove of Civil War artifacts. When I told him about that, he perked right up and trotted away without a fuss. One problem solved, so I headed for the registration cottage on my own.

When I entered the registration building, it was like stepping into a Food Faire at midnight: quiet as a tomb. A hinge creaked when the door closed, but—other than that—nothing stirred.

Even the desk sat empty. Given that it was a Monday morning, I wasn't too surprised. Most hotels stayed busiest over the weekends, with many guests checking out late Sunday afternoon to avoid the traffic on their way home. Either way, whoever was on duty wouldn't leave their post for long, so I needed to hurry.

The Dell computer sat on the desktop as always, along with a pair of walkie-talkies.

I glanced over my shoulder and then ducked around the desk. Someone had been working on the Dell, which meant I wouldn't have to break into the system by trying different passwords. Breaking into the computer would only add to my offenses and land me in the local jail.

I slid into Wyatt's chair and pecked at the keyboard to coax it to life. A familiar blue glow appeared, along with a half-dozen icons on the left-hand side of the screen. One was an icon for the Internet, which would carry me to my precious e-mail account and Ambrose's notes.

Before I did that, though, I studied some of the other icons on the screen. Most of them had boring names like *sales tax, revenue pro-*

jections, and *competitive analysis*, but one was labeled *BigD REIT*. Hadn't Wyatt mentioned something about a real-estate investment trust out of Dallas? Not only mentioned it, but complained about the people who owned it?

I clicked on the icon, which produced a folder labeled *staff letters*. Inside the folder was a letter for each employee. Included were letters for Cat, Beatrice, and Charity, the other tour guide. The first words on each were *draft of termination*. Strange. Darryl had mentioned Mr. Solomon wanted to buy the plantation, which might put Wyatt's job in jeopardy, but he never said anything about the rest of the staff.

The first letter in the lineup belonged to Beatrice. The text said something about a change in ownership, regret to inform you, blah, blah, blah. The letter was dated three days ago. That was right before Laney Babin discovered Trinity in the hotel's bathroom.

The next one was for Charles and it contained the same language. Ditto for Darryl Tibodeaux, whose letter said something about one week's pay, plus the obligatory letter of recommendation. Why hadn't he said anything to me about it? He'd been awful surly, but that struck me as normal by now.

I leaned back to mull my discovery. The only one who didn't seem to have a letter was Wyatt. Then again, if the investment trust had asked him to prepare termination letters in anticipation of the mansion being sold, they couldn't very well ask him to write his own letter. And after his shenanigans the night before, they, no doubt, had more than enough reason to fire him.

Either way, my discovery put a whole new slant on things and expanded the pool of suspects, as they said in those magazines I sometimes read while checking out at the Food Faire. Maybe I should speak again to Beatrice, Darryl, Charles, Cat, and whoever else might be swimming in the suddenly large pool of suspects.

It was something to think about as I tried to refocus my attention on the task at hand. I clicked on the icon for the Internet next and logged into my e-mail account. Within a few minutes I'd forwarded the notes Ambrose needed to his account, where they belonged.

"What are you doing here?"

The voice fell like a sledgehammer. Looking over the screen, Wyatt Burkett stood in the doorway, his face taut.

"But—"

"Be quiet." He stepped up to the registration desk, much larger than I'd remembered and certainly more intimidating. An angry welt appeared near his hairline, and the skin underneath it had purpled like grape jam.

Oh, sugar! And here I'd left my cell phone back at the motel. There was only one other phone within reach and it sat on the desk between us, as close to him as it was to me. If I tried to reach for it, he'd have ample time to grab my wrist.

"Calm down." My voice was surprisingly flat.

"You don't quit, do you? You were supposed to leave. They were supposed to make you and your friend check out."

"Yes, but what about you? I'm surprised you're still here." I couldn't ignore the anger in his eyes or the nasty welt above them.

"They told me I could come back and pick up a few things. Didn't think I'd run into you, though."

"Well, I'll just leave, then."

"Not so fast."

He stood between me and the only way out of the office. If I wanted to run, my words would have to clear-cut a path for me. "I'm so sorry about last night, Wyatt. I swear I didn't know it was you."

"You almost blinded me. Do you know that? The doctor said you were an inch away."

"Really?" My heart sank when I realized he had no intention of letting me leave the office. "It was so black in the hall I couldn't see anything. I'm surprised I hit you at all."

"You shouldn't have done that." He stepped closer, which seemed to suck the air from the room. Funny, I'd never realized how thick his neck was or the way his chest barreled over his waistline. It would be no contest, physically, between the two of us.

"Why did you do it?" I asked. "Play dress up, I mean?"

"Why do you think?"

"My guess is you're mad at the plantation and you wanted to get back at them."

"You're a pretty good little guesser." His hand shot across the desk and he grabbed my shoulder.

Ouch. The man's grip was strong, just like Ivy's when she realized her daughter was missing.

I wasn't about to let him know that, so I gritted my teeth. "Hurting me isn't going to help anything."

Why had I come to the cottage by myself? No one knew I was

there, not even the elderly deacon who drove me over in his huge Cadillac. By now, Ambrose could be heaven-only-knew where, since Vernice obviously meant to monopolize his time at the church. The only other person I'd seen since I arrived at the plantation was Darryl, and he didn't seem happy about Mr. Solomon's plan to purchase the plantation.

Darryl. My eyes darted to the walkie-talkies on the desk, deliciously close to the computer screen. I didn't know the first thing about operating them, but how hard could it be?

Quickly, I grabbed the nearest unit and depressed a button that read *talk*. Wyatt immediately released his grip on my shoulder, which ended the sharp pain at my collarbone. The walkie-talkie crackled into life.

"Darryl!" As the word flew from my mouth, I realized Darryl might not have a walkie-talkie or he might have forgotten to turn it on. I let up on the button to see if anyone responded.

A split-second later, broken air whooshed over the unit.

"Dat you, Miz DuBois?" He sounded confused, or about as confused as I felt.

"I need you at the registration cottage, Darryl!"

"Comin'."

Ah, the man of few words. Before I could breathe, or even blink, a noise sounded at the door. Wyatt had darted for the exit. Oh no, he didn't! If he thought he could threaten me and get away with it, he had another think coming.

I bounded out of the chair and dashed for the door. My fingers touched the cold brass doorknob, which startled me. What was I doing? Wyatt weighed at least eighty pounds more and was ten times stronger. Plus, there would be time enough later to figure out why he'd cornered me like that.

Like it or not, I knew who'd killed Trinity. If Wyatt could hurt me like that—my shoulder still ached—he could no doubt summon the will to poison Trinity.

I reached that conclusion as Darryl appeared in the doorway, his cheeks flushed. It was time for me to call Lance and put away the person who murdered Trinity Solomon.

The sun kissed my face as soon as I emerged from the cottage with Darryl. Across from us sat the enormous brown Cadillac, still moored in its parking space and still without its captain. My driver must have spent the entire time in the plantation's museum, pouring over the artifacts.

No matter. Once Darryl realized I was safe and sound, he left, as well, and I stood by myself on the brick walk in front of the mansion. The place didn't seem nearly as inviting now after everything that'd happened.

It was time to get back to Ambrose and put myself out of harm's way. The quickest way to get to the museum and my driver was by traveling through the garden with the four stone benches and a fountain smack-dab in the middle of it all.

Nothing stirred as I walked. I expected to come upon the soothing sound of water lapping against stone, but something was wrong. Eventually I heard a sound, all right, but it wasn't gurgling water. Two voices came from somewhere in the garden. Angry voices, judging by the tone.

Who would rendezvous in the garden? I peered around the corner.

"You're getting what you deserve," Beatrice said.

"Don't talk like that, Bea."

My view was limited by the boxwood hedge, but I heard every word. Quickly, I stepped backward.

Only two days had passed since Trinity's murder, and Beatrice and Sterling had already found a way to rendezvous twice that I knew of. Shame on them.

"It's not my fault," Sterling said. "At least she was happy before the wedding. I gave her that." Even though he whispered, his tone was confident now. Gone was the whine from the day before in the bar. Somehow he'd grown a spine over the weekend.

"But it was all a lie. You lied to her, Sterling."

Since I knew the speakers' identities, I sank back on my heels. It wasn't fair for me to eavesdrop once again, but I wasn't in the most charitable mood.

"If you'd been honest with her from the beginning, none of this would have happened. Would that have been so hard?"

"But she was pregnant," he said. "What could I do? She told me she couldn't rat out the father and the guy had no idea the baby was his. She couldn't exactly ask her dad for help. You know that guy's a jerk."

"But propose to her? That was a little extreme, even for you. Couldn't you have been her friend instead and maybe helped out with the baby? Did you have to be her husband, of all things?"

"Look, Bea. I'm an actor. By the time we got this far into it, she really thought I was in love with her. What was the problem? I'd give the kid a dad, Trinity would have a husband, and maybe I'd finally have a place of my own."

"Aren't you forgetting something? You didn't love her."

"All bets were off when you told me good-bye," Sterling said. "You wanted me gone, and you got your wish."

"How do you know I didn't change my mind?"

Something rustled in the bushes in front of me—something small and quick and dappled brown—but it could have been the Hope diamond for all I cared. If Beatrice had changed her mind about Sterling . . . if she wanted him back after all . . . who knew what lengths she'd go to in order to make that happen?

Suddenly the thought of Wyatt rushing around the plantation in a borrowed soldier's uniform seemed almost tame compared to the hard edge I heard in Beatrice's voice.

Time was growing short. No matter how much I wanted to hear this conversation, Lance LaPorte needed to be involved. Before Wyatt traveled halfway to Mississippi, or Beatrice destroyed evidence, if it turned out she had something to do with Trinity's murder. I didn't have time to stand in the bright sunshine and listen any longer to this conversation when there was so much work to be done.

I turned my back to the garden. The voices continued, so I knew they wouldn't follow me as I walked on to the museum, where I'd probably find my driver. I ducked low and out of sight until I reached the area by the back of the mansion, just in case.

I was rattled by what I'd heard, and I almost didn't see someone exit the plantation house at the same time. The figure wore a dark blue uniform, just like the ones worn by the Louisiana State Police.

It was Lance, leaving the back door of the mansion with that precious notebook still in his hand.

"Lance, you're a sight for sore eyes!"

He stopped. "Hi, Missy."

"I thought you were going back to headquarters." At least, that's what he'd said when we bid good-bye in the church's social hall.

"I still had a few more things to check out here. What's going on with you? You look a little winded."

"I am. You won't believe what just happened." I proceeded to tell him all about the conversation I'd overheard between Beatrice and Sterling in the secret garden. About Beatrice's wistful tone when she confessed she might have changed her mind about Sterling. "But that's not all." Lance looked shell-shocked after my frantic recitation, but he didn't try to stop me or slow me down, bless his heart. "There's also Wyatt Burkett. I ran into him in the registration cottage. He came at me—right at me, I tell you!"

"Whoa. Slow down, Missy. You're not making sense." He laid his hand on my shoulder—fortunately, the one Wyatt hadn't bruised—to steady me. "What do you mean, Wyatt came at you? And what's all this with Beatrice?"

I inhaled deeply. It was important to get every detail in the right order, even if it sounded insane. "I'm telling you, first Wyatt Burkett—he's the general manager—trapped me in the registration cottage. You know I knocked him out last night, right?"

Lance looked confused, but I didn't have time to explain the minor details. He'd have to take my word for it at this point and play along. There'd be time later to sort out the particulars.

"Anyway, he didn't want to let me go. I think he's the killer." The minute I said that, I realized how absurd I sounded. Hadn't I mentioned Beatrice in the same breath as Wyatt, even though I didn't have any evidence to back it up? At least Wyatt had lunged at me. At least I knew he was strong enough and angry enough to hurt someone.

"There's also Beatrice." My tone had softened. "She has a wonderful motive. Do you know she's in love with Trinity's fiancé? She could have poisoned Trinity as easily as anyone."

Lance was listening, but he shook his head as if he didn't like what he'd heard. "There's only one problem, Missy."

"Problem? What do you mean, *problem*? We need to get arrest warrants right now so you can bring them in for questioning. I'm almost certain one of them is the killer."

"Now I'm sure you believe that," he said.

Why was he shaking his head? And why wasn't he moving? He should have been on the phone by now, calling the station for backup. Instead, he looked ready to pat me on the head and send me inside for a nice glass of sweet tea and a batch of pralines.

"They both have rock-solid alibis," he said. "She was studying for finals at LSU that night. It's on the surveillance tape from the school library. And Wyatt was home with his crippled mother. Had to bring her to the urgent-care center Friday night when she fell and hurt her hip. Didn't get out of there until almost four in the morning, according to the nurse on duty. I'm sorry, but you're wrong." He patted my knee. "Don't take it so hard. I'm wrong a lot of times too. It only means there are two less people to worry about. I'm sure the general manager gave you a terrible fright, but he couldn't have killed Trinity Solomon."

"Who, then?" While neither of my theories had panned out, someone else must be under Lance's microscope. Here I'd spent all day rushing around and I wasn't one step closer to helping Ivy.

"I got the medical examiner's final report back." Lance must have felt really bad for me, because he opened his notebook. He didn't even attempt to put up a fight, which said a lot.

"Look here," he said. "It confirms the victim was poisoned with cyanide. Only takes two teaspoons to put someone under."

"I know . . . you already told me it was cyanide. By the way, whatever happened with the squashed pill capsule we found in the bathroom? Did that have anything to do with it?"

"Definitely." He eyed the grounds around us, although we were the only two people in sight. "Traces of cyanide, all right."

"That's what I thought."

"There's more." Lance glanced over his shoulder again, probably out of habit more than anything else. "It wasn't the type of pill you usually see around here. It was labeled as aspirin, but it was the kind you can pull apart. Those things pretty much disappeared after a cyanide scare hit the country back in 1982."

Who could forget that? Grandma told me all about it when I was old enough to understand. Said something about shop owners having to throw away entire shelves full of Tylenol because someone went around tampering with the capsules and filling them with potassium cyanide. Seven people wound up dead. After that, the capsules pretty much vanished from pharmacy shelves, replaced by tamper-proof gel caplets.

I saw for myself when I snooped in her medicine cabinet. She had three bottles of aspirin and all of them were labeled either *gel capsules* or *tablets*. None of them had been divided in two.

"They also found something interesting in the victim's bathroom." Lance's voice brought me back to the present. "Fingerprints in there that didn't belong to the victim."

"Her name was Trinity." It bothered me that he kept referring to the girl without using her given name.

"Of course. Trinity left prints in the bathroom, but they found someone else's there too. Not Laney Babin's—the housekeeper's—because she was the first person they tested and she came up clean. No, these prints were different."

I leaned toward him, although I knew it would make me look eager.

"Who, then? They could've belonged to anyone, right? Trinity's bridesmaids, her fiancé, her stepmother, even her father. You'd have to haul in a dozen people to get the right match."

"That's the strange thing," he said. "They had a hard time lifting prints, even with a fuming wand, because they were incomplete. Whole sections were missing, or faded away. They couldn't get a clean print even with the fuming glue."

His last words floated around my mind, like wet laundry tumbling in a clothes dryer. So many memories flooded back. Talks I'd had with Darryl, Cat, Charles . . . with all of them, really. But when the tumbling stopped, a single memory clicked into place.

"Oh, shine!" My hand flew to my lips in an automatic effort to keep something worse from spilling out.

"What is it?" Lance looked troubled, either by my words or the way I'd yelled them loud enough to wake the dead in the Andrews family graveyard.

It couldn't be, could it? I finally dropped my hand. There was only one way to find out, and I was pretty sure the answer wasn't going to show up in a shiny gift box while I lounged around at the mansion with Lance.

"I need to check out a hunch. Can you come with me?"

"I'm sorry, but they're expecting me back at the station. Can it wait?"

If the hunch was right, it couldn't. "Not really. But it's okay, I know you need to get back to work."

He eyed me skeptically. "Tell me you're not about to do something foolish."

"Why, Lance. Do you really think I'd run off and do something foolish?"

"Hell, yes." At least he smiled when he said it. "So you need to promise me that you won't go chasing down any suspects while I'm gone. Promise."

I scrunched up my nose before answering him. "I know you have this whole situation under control. I promise not to undermine you in any way, shape or form." Hopefully, my response was vague enough to appease both him and my conscience.

"That doesn't sound right, but I don't have time to argue. Just wait for me to get back before you do anything. That's all I'm saying."

"I'll wait for you to get back before I do anything foolish." There, I said it. And to my way of thinking, what I was about to do next wasn't close to being foolish.

"That's better," he said. "See you soon."

The minute he disappeared around the corner of the house, I took a deep breath for courage and plowed ahead. There was no way I was going to twiddle my thumbs on the back lawn and let the latest clue disappear like a cloud on the horizon.

Chapter 14

Once I said good-bye to Lance, I moved down the curved steps as quickly as the river water that flowed beside me. The fashion show was fast approaching, and there was no telling when my driver would reemerge from the mansion's museum. Once I hit the last step, I sprinted around the eastern corner of the house and headed for the pool out back.

The waning sun hovered on the horizon, threatening to set but not quite there. It still amazed me that someone would murder a girl in such a tranquil place. But after a century of visitors, like me, there was no telling what the walls here had heard or the windows had seen. And now this.

I replayed possible scenarios as I ran. While I had a pretty good idea of who murdered Trinity, the tricky part was to confront the person without getting myself killed. Ambrose always said my feet moved faster than my brain, so I put on the brakes and slowed to a jog.

I rounded the brick wall circling the pool and came upon what I was looking for: a two-story building resembling the main house, only smaller. Same brilliant white paint, same lovingly tended flower beds, same dark storm shutters perfectly kept. The staff's quarters. As I approached them, a painted snake appeared on one of the first doors in the lineup. *Bingo.*

Above the snake trailed a vine of magenta bougainvillea, like something out of a Grimm Brothers' storybook. I knocked on the door and waited. When no one answered, I tried the doorknob, but the door was locked.

Could the unit have a back door, since it was on the ground floor? Best of all would be a sliding glass door. I could sneak right in if the saints and prophets were on my side today. Apparently they weren't, though, because when I jogged around to the back, I found a window and not a door.

No matter. The owner had cracked the window open a foot or so, probably to catch a stray breeze, which was enough for me. I slipped off my sandals and approached the windowsill. It was only three feet up from the ground. Hallelujah. I placed my palms on the sill, pushed the window open more, and hoisted my body through the open space.

Thank goodness my only witness was a marble statue of a mermaid, tucked among the impatiens, and she didn't look like a gossiper. Once I made it through the window in one piece, I was home free.

The room I landed in was small but colorful. Cat's bedroom. An iron headboard sat against the far wall—painted neon orange—and she'd tossed on a fuchsia comforter and some lime green pillows. It was a wonder she could sleep, since the colors fought with each other for attention.

I walked past the psychedelic display to the bathroom, where a light shone. Much like the room outside, the space was tiny and bright and crammed full of shiny things. The sink looked dirty, and she'd littered it with eye-shadow compacts, bottles of Clairol Nice'n Easy, music CDs, and a pill bottle or two. Exactly what I was looking for.

The largest of the two pill bottles wore a baby-blue cap and French words filled the label. She'd told me she studied in France. I twisted open the top and let the contents tumble into my palm, where the capsules twinkled, shiny in the fluorescent lights.

They looked like spores on a honeycomb. Golden, soft to the touch and pliable. Like they'd been spun from amber plastic. Just like the casing I'd found on the floor of the hotel's bathroom.

The minute Lance told me about the unusual cyanide capsules as we met behind the house, plus the disfigured fingerprints, I had my answer. Just yesterday, back there in the kitchen of the main house, I'd cooked up one of my special omelets for Cat after she'd thrown up next to her car. I couldn't exactly let her unborn baby go hungry. When Cat took my steaming offering and scooped it up like it had come straight from the refrigerator, my eyes widened to the size of saucers. But she didn't feel a thing, she told me, even though I worried that besides being pregnant, the girl would have burned fingertips too. Apparently her fingers had been burned so many times—not to mention her tongue and the roof of her mouth—that she'd lost the feeling in them. And apparently the prints on her fingers too.

"You found 'em, huh?"

Someone had walked up behind me, as unexpected as a rear-end collision. I didn't turn, although I desperately wanted to. I was frozen in place, the capsules still winking in my palm. Surprisingly, and to my credit, I didn't gasp, but when I glanced in the mirror, Cat's reflection appeared behind mine.

"What are they?" As if I didn't know.

"Why, Missy. Those are the vitamins I take for my baby."

The bathroom counter slowly spun away. It wasn't that Cat had caught me red-handed in her bathroom. I was more surprised by the look on her face. Her eyes were so dull and black they reminded me of the skillet I'd used to cook up her omelet.

"I saw you take your vitamins in the kitchen, Cat." I closed my fingers around the contraband. "You took some regular vitamins. From a bottle in the pantry."

My calm recitation snapped her back to reality. She grabbed my arm hard, which jarred the medicine free and sent it tumbling into the sink. When she twisted me around, I came face to face with the tattooed snake on her neck. It grew larger and thicker as her body tensed.

"You shouldn't have come here." The snake writhed when she jerked her head like that. "What made you think you could break into my room?"

"I didn't break in." Which wasn't a total lie. Nothing had been broken, although I knew exactly what she meant.

"Come with me." She tightened her grasp and pushed me out of the bathroom.

Pain radiated up my arm. "Ouch." I tried to shake her off. "You're hurting me."

She shoved me to the bed when we were back in the room, and I tumbled face-first onto the fuchsia comforter. No one knew where I was, did they? I tried to remember what I'd told Lance, but I had trouble focusing on anything but the sharp ache at my side.

"You're not going to get away with this." I twisted around to face her. Pink and green pillows fell away like blooms from the bougainvillea outside. "They're going to know it was you."

"Funny you should say that, considering you're the one who doesn't belong here. Me, I just came back to my apartment to change clothes, and there you were." Cat inched closer as she spoke, her tattooed snake zeroing in on its prey. "That's it. That's what I'll tell the police. How could I know it was you?"

She glanced at a bedside table, probably looking for a weapon. Odds were good she'd turn me facedown and strike me with a heavy lamp or something even worse.

"You didn't know Trinity Solomon," I said. "What did she do to you?"

"Do? To me?" Cat's breath brushed my cheek and her tattooed snakeskin glistened with sweat. "Everything. Everything."

She was so strong, my only hope was to stall. The more Cat talked, the less time she had to find a weapon.

"Think about your baby," I said. "What will happen to your baby if you hurt me? Sooner or later they're going to figure out it was you."

She screwed up her face, as if she'd swallowed a mouthful of bleach. "You don't get it, do you? Wyatt said we'd get this place closed down by scaring everyone away. But that could take months. When I found out the Solomons were here, I knew what I had to do." She snorted. "Told the stupid daughter the pills were a cure for morning sickness. Brilliant, right?"

I slowly understood. And if Cat could murder Trinity in cold blood, she could do it again . . . with me.

She closed her eyes. "The baby's kicking," she whispered. "He knows this is right."

Now was my chance. I remembered something when Cat leaned over me on the bed and her tattoo drew closer. Every scale on the snake telescoped larger and larger. Where had I seen a tattoo like that? It'd been a year or so, but the tattoo definitely looked familiar.

And then I remembered. I had just opened my shop and was having lunch with my next- door neighbor, a handsome guy named Ambrose. My new friend was worried about a string of burglaries in our building. He told me about a self-defense class at the local Y and even offered to pay for my tuition, since I was broke.

I decided to go—for his sake, more than mine—and gamely watched a young guy in a karate jacket and slacks enter the Y. After spending half an hour in the overheated studio, the instructor stripped down to a T-shirt and exposed an enormous tattoo on his arm. A snake slithering down to his elbow and then on to his fingertips. I remembered thinking the tattoo would make a good story for Ambrose, because I didn't expect much else from the class.

But darn if I didn't learn something. That night I learned a sure-fire way to escape a kidnapper. The teacher pointed to the heel of his hand and then pretended to smash it against his chin, which didn't seem too complicated. He made us practice the move over and over on a row of punching bags until sweat streamed down our cheeks.

I felt ridiculous, of course, but I practiced it anyway until my hand purpled like ripe eggplant.

The snake on Cat's neck eyed me now as I mumbled a quick prayer for forgiveness, since I was about to strike a pregnant woman. Then I shoved the heel of my hand into her chin for all I was worth. The crunch of bone hitting bone rang out and her head snapped back like it'd been ripped clean from her spine.

As she fell, her head crashed against the iron headboard with a sickening thud. Only then did I feel pain radiate through my hand.

I had no time to think. I rolled off the bed and scuttled crablike toward the kitchen. Halfway there, the sound of a doorknob being turned reached me and I froze. When the door didn't budge, something crashed against it—hard—and the panel flew open, raining wood splinters onto the carpet. It was Lance, his leg still poised in the air as if he might kick the panel again for good measure. Cat must have locked the door behind her when she entered, which sent a chill down my spine.

"Lance!" I shouted. Across the room, Cat lay as still as an iceberg marooned in the sea of pink. Hallelujah for that punching bag in the Y's basement and for Ambrose's worrisome nature.

"Missy?" Lance peered at me. "You okay?"

I lay on the ground and clutched my throbbing hand. "I think so. It's Cat, Lance. She's the one who poisoned Trinity. She's in the bedroom."

Quickly, Lance strode through the doorway and headed for the back bedroom. When he returned, he held Cat in his arms, her head bobbing against his shoulder.

"You did this?" Lance squinted, as if there must be another explanation for the unconscious girl in his arms.

"Sure did. And I found a bottle of doctored pills in the bathroom. She gave them to Trinity and said they were a cure for morning sickness."

"Why?" Lance looked wary, as if he couldn't quite trust his eyes.

"Her daddy died at Mr. Solomon's refinery, and she wanted to get back at him. Guess she didn't much care how she did it." I shrugged, since nothing Cat had said would ever justify murder.

"You're okay, right?" Lance asked.

"Fine. A little shook up, but I'll be fine." My hand still hurt like the dickens, but it was nothing compared to what could have happened. "Guess I should have waited for you, after all."

He grinned as he walked around me, the lump in his arms as silent as the stone mermaid outside. "Let me put this one in the squad car and then I'll come back for you. We need to get your statement when you feel up to it."

I nodded and watched him walk through the jagged doorframe. Someone else arrived a few seconds later, but this person wore the most wonderful pair of pressed khakis and Sperry Top-Siders.

I finally rose to my feet. "Hi, Bo."

"Oh, Missy. I'm so glad you're okay." Ambrose rushed to me and enveloped me in a hug so strong I couldn't help but squeak.

"How'd you know where to find me?"

"Lance called the church and they tracked me down. Said something about how he was going to look for you."

"Y'all worry about me too much." I looked into those beautiful blue eyes and smiled. "But I'm glad you do."

I didn't ask—or care—how he knew where to find me. All that mattered was that we stayed in each other's arms for way too long. Neither of us could think of another thing to say—but, then again, conversation could be highly overrated.

"Thank you," I said.

"Whatever for?" Gently, Ambrose brushed aside some hair that'd fallen in my eyes.

"For making me take that silly self-defense class back at the Y. Turns out it wasn't so silly, after all."

Chapter 15

The first person to greet us when we arrived at the church social hall that night was the elderly deacon from before. We'd rushed back to the motel to change after spending hours at the church organizing this and setting up that, and now it was time to watch our hard work pay off. Like before, the deacon flanked the open doors, like an alabaster lion, and he gave us each one of the colorful flyers the church's staff had whipped up with the help of the local print shop.

Fortunately, we were able to borrow most of the ideas and the talent from the fashion show we'd staged in Baton Rouge the month before. Heaven knows the days of a sedate show, with pretty girls on plywood runways, is long gone. Today's fashion shows had omnidirectional lights, digital sound, and theatrical outfits that—truth be told—looked more like costumes than clothes.

The only difference between tonight's show and the affair for the Ladies' Auxiliary League was the music. Tonight we paired each gown with a hymn instead of a popular song, since the proceeds would buy new choir robes.

The first girl would wear a gown Ambrose designed that looked like Grace Kelly's dress when she posed for the cover of *Life*. As the model walked the runway, the organist would play "Amazing Grace." We booked the second outfit as an all-white sheath with seed pearls paired with a rousing rendition of "When We All Get to Heaven." We even decided to borrow some angel wings from the choir's Christmas show and add them to the dress for special effect.

There was a fine line between clever and sacrilegious, though, so we'd combed through every detail before we finalized the plans.

Hallelujah—we had tons of connections in the fashion industry, because we were able to book the same models we'd used in the

Baton Rouge show. We pulled in every favor our friend Natasha, who owns Southern Model Management, ever owed us, and she lured back the same six models with the promise of walking the Lanvin trunk show the following week. Working with the organist and the church's choir wouldn't be a problem, either, since we'd chosen only well-known hymns with which everyone was familiar. As for Ambrose, he knew his gowns better than most of us know our birth date, so he wouldn't need to memorize anything, either. Odds were good he'd teach the audience more about hemlines, bias cuts, and beaded appliqués than they ever thought possible.

Our final stroke of luck involved Ambrose's assistant. Although I'd complained about her earlier, she was able to pull the twenty-four dresses we needed on only a moment's notice. Plus, she went to the trouble of pulling the same trilbies, fascinators, and veils from my shop we'd used earlier and then lugged everything to the church in her minivan. Thank goodness I'd given her a key earlier for special emergencies, because in my book this show surely qualified.

I even offered to give his assistant one of my hats if she agreed to work with me as a dresser during the show.

When she quickly said yes, I knew she'd never actually done the job before. Although fashion shows looked easy from the outside, it was the dressers who did the yeoman's work from behind the scenes.

Dressers were the ones who chased after the models backstage with safety pins to stitch clothes together a split second before a show. They improvised with rubber bands to bind a shoe to a model's foot when her gown was extra-long and her heels were extra high.

The most challenging trick was dressing a model in a black gown. Even a speck of lint could attach itself to a hemline and look like a white stain under a stage light. Whenever I dressed a model in black, I draped the gown's skirt over my arm for as long as possible, even if it meant the girl had to wobble around with me while I worked backstage.

It was a small price to pay to watch seed pearls sparkle under stage lights like tiny starbursts and to touch silk so smooth it was like running water. Dressing a model was the closest most of us would ever come to owning a ten-thousand-dollar gown, which was fine by me.

I smiled at the deacon as we walked into the social hall, which had been transformed. Workers had hidden the plain white walls behind yards of tulle sparkling like the underbelly of a cloud. They'd also gathered the material together in the middle of the room and tied it into a rosette.

Even Darryl surprised me. His towering arrangements of Eremurus in hammered steel vases were like sculptures against the velvet curtain. I'd definitely use him again whenever I needed flowers.

By now, some ten minutes had passed, and we still had another thirty to go until the lights dimmed. A few people headed into the social hall, their eyes darting back and forth like pinballs as they scoped out the best place to sit. The crowd was mixed, with matrons in nude hose and sensible heels, teenagers in ripped jeans and too much eyeliner, and a few token males thrown in. The women all dashed for the front, but the men strolled behind nonchalantly, as if they couldn't understand what the fuss was about.

Finally, it was show time. I retreated through a back door and ended up in the parking lot, where a canvas canopy served as the staging area. Hallelujah! A long rolling rack awaited me with twenty-four bulging garment bags lined up like soldiers. My models trickled in, one by one, each holding a makeup box; although they'd already applied their own cosmetics at home. The boxes held everything they might need for touch-ups between gowns. Normally a show like this might employ six makeup artists and at least four or five dressers, but we didn't have the money for that.

From that moment on, I heard nothing but the sound of my own breath. I rushed around zipping up this and fluffing out that and stabbing safety pins into fabric and sometimes my own fingers. I was so startled when someone spoke into the microphone that I actually stabbed a model's skin for once, instead of my own.

The preacher introduced himself and welcomed everyone to the show. I heard only snatches: *world-famous designer, honor to have him, please hold your applause.* Next was Ambrose's voice, deeper than when he and I spoke, but every bit as warm. Did someone actually wolf whistle when he took to the stage, or did I imagine that?

My eyes never once peeked above a model's head for the next hour. By the end of the show, I felt as if I'd lived two lifetimes.

Ambrose found me in the tent afterward, slumped over a card table strewn with safety pins, double-stick tape, and Dr. Scholl's shoe insoles.

"Hi, darling," he said.

"Hi, yourself." My head was too heavy to lift, so I waved a safety pin at him instead. "How was the show?"

"Perfect. Not one wardrobe malfunction, and the crowd seemed to like it. How you holding up?"

Only then did I lift my head. *My, he looks good in a tuxedo.* "I've been better."

"Have I ever told you you're the best dresser I've ever worked with?"

"No, but go ahead. I need the validation."

He smiled and began to stroke the back of my head, smoothing down what I imagined to be a rat's nest by now. "We make a great team, Missy. By the way, there's someone here to see you."

"Me?" I dragged myself upright. Apparently a girl had walked in behind Ambrose and she wore an intriguing, yet familiar, hat. It was Beatrice, of all people, wearing her pretty cloche from the hat competition, which seemed a million years ago.

"Missy!"

I worked up a smile. "Hey, Beatrice."

"You two did a wonderful job tonight," she said.

"We did, didn't we? I almost forgot you go to this church. Charles told me that." The memory of Charles and me back at the restaurant, all alone, resurrected so many others. "Here. Have a seat."

I dusted some talcum powder off the folding chair next to me and motioned for her to sit. I also gave Ambrose the high sign.

He took my cue and pretended to study his watch. "Wow. It's getting late. There's a reporter here from the *Times-Picayune,* so I'd better get going. But don't you fall asleep on me, Missy. Come find me in a few minutes and we'll go back together."

"Sounds good. See you in a minute." I turned to Beatrice again. "Did you come alone?"

"Sure did."

I took a deep breath. "You know, I never told you this, but I overheard some interesting things when I was at Morningside." At the top of my list was the conversation with Sterling Brice I'd heard from behind the bar. Not to mention her little spat with him in the garden.

"Like what?" She seemed genuinely curious and not the least bit alarmed.

"You and Sterling were talking about Trinity. About how she died.

And you were mad at him for proposing to her. Do you remember that?"

I didn't want to intrude—well, maybe just a little—but her conversations left me confused and concerned me enough that, at one point, I thought Beatrice was the murderer. It seemed far-fetched now, but I still had a few questions.

"I didn't know anyone was listening to us," she said. "You see, Sterling and I go way back. I won't bore you with the details, but he never should have asked Trinity to marry him."

"That's what I got from your conversation." I began to brush some pins into a pile to give my hands something to do. "But why?"

"Last year, before Trinity or the Solomons ever came along, Sterling asked me to marry him."

I wasn't the least bit surprised. I'd suspected she and Sterling were a couple. No one argued like that unless strong feelings flowed underneath and, even though he'd moved on, it sounded like Beatrice might not have.

She sighed. "I always thought one day we'd work it out. One day we'd stop arguing and get back together. But I realized something this weekend. I was mad at him, but I wasn't devastated. Does that make sense?"

My hand stalled over the pile of pins. "Can't say that it does."

"See, if I really loved Sterling, his proposal to Trinity should have crushed me. But it didn't. Not really. It was the *idea* of him getting married that bothered me more than anything else."

"Let me get this straight: You didn't want him to marry you, but you didn't want him to marry anyone else, either?" The story didn't make much sense because I'd heard how exasperated she sounded back at the plantation.

"Exactly. Let's face it—Sterling's gorgeous, but he's pretty shallow."

"Maybe you didn't give him enough credit." I didn't want to argue with her, since I didn't particularly like Sterling, either, but I'd overheard him say he wanted to give Trinity's baby a father, and that didn't seem so shallow to me.

"He always needed someone to take care of him," she said. "Before now, it was me. But then Trinity came along with all that money. That was one thing I couldn't give him."

I added a few more clips to the wayward pile. "So you weren't jealous he was going to marry Trinity?"

"No, I *was* jealous, but for the wrong reasons. Even though I didn't want to be with him, I didn't want him to be with anyone else, either. Guess that makes me selfish."

I chuckled. "No, it makes you human. You can't help how you feel. Sometimes feelings have a life of their own." Thank goodness again for those psychology textbooks back at Vanderbilt, which taught me about something called *validation*. It was important to recognize someone's feelings even if you didn't agree with them.

"I'm glad you understand," she said. "I've been thinking about it all day. Guess I should grow up and stop worrying about myself all the time."

"Sounds to me like you're no different from most people."

She rolled her eyes. "I liked being seen with Sterling. Now *that's* shallow."

"Yeah, but it's perfectly normal. And he *is* good-looking. But there are lots more important things than how a person looks." The moment I spoke those words, I wanted to reel them back in. I'd done the very same thing. I'd judged Vernice back at the Sleepy Bye Inn by the suntan on her face and her extra-bright teeth. Wasn't that hypocritical of me? "We all do it. Sometimes we pay more attention to the package than the gift inside." Which reminded me of one other thing. "And don't forget, there are wonderful people all around us. Though, we don't always realize it at the time."

"What do you mean?" She must have sensed I wasn't pulling my words from the clear blue.

I added a final pin to the pile. "Well, there's Charles, to begin with." The way he'd looked at her, back there on the porch at Morningside, was hard to forget. She'd sent him right over the moon with only one smile.

"Charles?"

Oh, my. I did have my work cut out for me. "Don't tell me you've never noticed him. Haven't you heard that still waters run deepest? He seems to have a lot to say to you, if only you'll give him half a chance."

"Charles?"

"He's in college too. You even go to the same school."

She paused. "Well, he does seem really nice."

"He *is* nice. And he's a hard worker. Something that may not mean a lot to you now, but it will one day. Trust me. There's a lot more to Charles than meets the eye. You need to give him a chance." Sitting with her, watching volunteers trickle past, I remembered one last thing I needed to do before I could say good-bye. "There's something else. It looks like you're married, by the way you're wearing your hat."

"Me? Married?"

To be honest, I'd noticed her mistake right away. "Women wear a knot on their cloche to tell the world they're married. If you're single, then you'd use a bow. The bigger, the better."

"All this time I've been wearing my hat wrong?"

"It's not a big deal. Here, this will just take a second." I gently untied the knot while she waited patiently, like a show dog being fitted with a new collar. In a few seconds, I whipped up a respectable bow and smoothed it back down again. "There, that's much better."

"Thank you, Missy. For everything."

I patted her hand as I rose. "No problem. Tell me, what are your plans now the plantation's been sold?"

"Well, the best part of my job was helping brides plan their weddings. I'm good at it. I can pick out the decorations, choose the menus, that kind of thing."

"Are you saying what I think you're saying?" I hoped I was right, because she'd make an excellent wedding planner.

She nodded happily. "Yep. I think I'm going to go freelance. Work as a wedding consultant all up and down the Great River Road. I know there's a market for it because I've seen how busy it gets here during the wedding season."

"That's wonderful!"

"Maybe I'll even work with you and Ambrose sometime. Looks like any woman would be lucky to own your hats and his clothes."

Ambrose. He was still waiting for me back in the social hall. "I couldn't agree more." I nodded toward the building. "I've got to go. Take care of yourself, Beatrice. I'm sure we'll run into each other real soon."

"You too. And I'll think about what you said. About Charles, I mean."

I grinned all the way back to the social hall. Ambrose stood near the rear entrance, next to an elderly lady in a flowered dress. He seemed energetic as he listened and nodded his head every once in a while.

But I knew the truth: although exhausted, my Ambrose would never shortchange a fan. I'd find him in the same spot come morning if he had his way. I only knew because I'd seen him emcee dozens of events and make dozens of exits afterward. Why, he'd still be there when the sun came up.

"There you are, Ambrose. I'm sure you don't want to leave, but I'm about ready to drop." I smiled sweetly at his companion, hoping my acting skills were up to par.

"Of course." He turned to his companion. "I'm afraid I need to go, but tell your husband you're not too old to wear red. You'd look fabulous."

The lady beamed, and I knew she'd recite those words to her husband when she got home. Then Ambrose draped his arm around my shoulders and guided me back to the social hall.

Volunteers swarmed over the space. People on ladders ripped the fabric from the walls, a line of workers scooped up folding chairs, while others dismantled our makeshift stage. Amazing how quickly the illusion of glamour disappeared when faced by an army of eager volunteers.

"That was one of your best shows, Bo," I said as we walked out to the parking lot. "They'll be talking about it for years to come."

Our path was brightened by the moon, which had grown fat over the past two days. I paused when someone emerged from the shadows.

"Evenin', Missy. Ambrose."

"Why, Lance! You scared me half to death." I almost didn't recognize him without his police uniform.

"Sorry about that," he said. "I wanted to say good-bye and tell y'all how wonderful the show turned out. But I also had some police business to discuss."

"Do tell." What a nice surprise. And an even nicer one: He wanted to include me in his police work. What a difference from that first day, when he shooed me away from the restroom and made me promise never to tell another living soul I'd been there.

"We took Wyatt in for questioning today," he said. "Even though he couldn't have killed Trinity because of his alibi, we knew he was involved in some way. Especially after he threatened you like that."

"That's good," I said. "I was afraid for my life, to tell you the truth. Wyatt looked mad enough to hurt me."

"He had good reason to."

"What did he tell you?" I asked.

Lance clasped his hands together. "He confessed."

"Confessed to what? I thought Cat was the one who poisoned Trinity Solomon."

"She was. But she had an accomplice. Turns out she and Wyatt were a couple."

But, of course. Once again, a puzzle piece fell into place. I'd watched Wyatt tenderly stroke Cat's cheek in the garden and I'd wondered why a boss would touch his employee like that.

I tilted my head. "Let me guess ... Wyatt's the father of Cat's baby."

"Bingo. He thought he'd help her get back at Mr. Solomon by ruining the plantation's business. So he dressed up in a uniform and pretended to haunt the place." He let his hands drop. "But Cat wasn't so patient. She wanted revenge right away, and that's when she heard Trinity was coming to town to get married."

"They're both excellent actors," I said. "I overheard Cat and Wyatt in the garden, and I'd be happy to give you my statement."

"We'll talk tomorrow." He offered me his hand. "Good night, Missy."

"Why, Lance. Don't be so formal." I ignored the handshake and gave him a great big bear hug instead. "I'm just down the road, you know, not that far away."

Standing there in the faint light of the moon, with Ambrose on one side and someone from my childhood on the other, I almost hated to see the evening end. Almost.

Chapter 16

We arrived at the parking lot of the Sleepy Bye Inn soon after, both of us exhausted beyond measure. Between the hoopla back at the church—and then speaking with Beatrice and Lance afterward—I didn't have one ounce of energy left.

Ambrose parked his car and shuffled over to my side, where he slowly swung open the door. *Bless his poor little heart.* We made a fine pair as he struggled to help me out of the car, and I tottered around like I'd just had a fifth of vodka. *Oh, well.* We were the only ones in the parking lot, so even Clyde must have left for the open road again and wouldn't be able to see our pitiful return.

Before I got very far, though, I noticed a light in the manager's office, giving off a dull blue fluorescent glow.

Vernice had come to our show, after all, even though I'd been so uppity to her earlier. She slunk through the staging area a few minutes before it began. She apparently didn't know anyone, because she ducked through the social hall's back door without acknowledging a single person.

Now a pale blue light spilled out from the office window to the concrete. Poor thing must get lonely in there with no one for company but the telephone, and that didn't seem to ring too much. "You go on ahead, Ambrose. I want to say good night to Vernice."

His forehead wrinkled in surprise. "I thought you didn't like her much. Seems funny you'd pick now to be sociable."

"I never said I didn't like her." Heaven only knew I hadn't said more than a dozen words to her. "You don't have to come. Go on up. I'll follow you in a second."

He started to protest, but his exhaustion seemed to win out. "Okay.

Give her your best and then come upstairs." When he turned, I marshaled my last ounce of energy and began to trudge toward the office.

Vernice sat on the other side of the streaked window. She gripped the guest registry in both hands and didn't seem to notice me until I opened the noisy plate-glass door.

"Hi, Miss DuBois. Need more towels?"

"No, I'm fine. I came to say good night. Thought you could use a little company in here." It was time to make up for my rudeness earlier. No wonder she preferred to speak to Ambrose. "Did you like the show?" I asked.

"It was nice. I've never been to that church before."

I stepped closer to the counter. "Really?" That didn't seem possible, since she seemed to be a local gal. From what I knew about small towns like this—or Bleu Bayou, even—almost everything happened at the local church. Weddings, funerals, bingo games . . . even special fashion shows, like ours.

"Clyde doesn't like me to go."

"Who?" It took a moment for me to realize she was talking about the trucker. Probably because I'd been on my feet forever and my brain was mush.

"Clyde," she repeated. "My husband. He trucks for Louisiana Foods."

"Oh, the rig." The one with naked girls on the mud flaps.

"Yeah, but I'm thinking maybe he's wrong about the church. The people seemed real nice."

I leaned against the countertop. If it was possible to feel pleased and guilty at the same time, then that was how I felt. Happy other people had welcomed Vernice to their church, but sad I hadn't done the same. "You should make a habit of going."

"I think I'll do that. At least we got some guests tonight. Tell you the truth, I was worried I'd be fired if things didn't pick up." Her face darkened. "Most of the month was slower than Methuselah."

"But don't you get a lot of traffic from the interstate?" Seemed to me truckers like Clyde would set this place up with a steady stream of business.

"No. Nowadays teams of people truck and they don't stay anywhere but on their rigs," she said. "That's what Clyde and I will have to do if things go back to normal and business drops off again."

"That wouldn't be too bad, would it? Sounds like fun. You could cruise around the country with your husband and see all sorts of things. Or am I talking out of turn?" I didn't have the slightest idea how truckers made a living and, for all I knew, this woman would *not* be happy to spend that much time on the open road.

She glanced at the registry again. "It's not that. I like hotel work. Being in one place, meeting people . . . when they come in, that is. Don't know how long they can keep me employed here, though, even with the extra guests tonight. Clyde told me the minute they let me go I'll have to start trucking with him and then we can take on more routes."

My eyes widened. "I have a great idea." Maybe it was because I wanted to make up for my grumpiness earlier, or because I loved to put people and situations together, but I remembered my conversation with Beatrice. "Apply at Morningside. They'll have to hire a whole new staff."

She blinked. "They wouldn't hire me. That's a fancy place full of fancy people. I don't belong there."

"Yes, you do. They'd be lucky to have you. As a matter of fact, I happen to know they need a general manager. If I were you, I'd head on down there tomorrow morning."

She looked wary, as if she were waiting for a punch line. "Why are you telling me this? I thought you didn't like me much when we met yesterday."

"Sorry. That was my misplaced aggression. I'd tell you all about it, but I'm so tired I can barely see straight. I'll bend your ear about it in the morning if you want to join me for a cup of coffee."

She grinned. "That sounds nice. I'll see you in the morning. And sleep well."

"I will. Thank you." I turned to leave, so tired the room wobbled, when Vernice suddenly called out.

"Miss DuBois, I forgot something. You got a package." She ducked under the counter and reappeared with a cardboard box. It couldn't have weighed much, because she easily hoisted it onto the counter. "Someone left this for you."

"Me?" Who'd leave anything for me? I barely knew a soul in Riversbend. Could it be a thank-you from the church? That seemed a little soon, since the fashion show had barely ended.

Vernice handed over some scissors so I could slice through the duct tape holding the box together. A layer of crumpled newsprint came first, which I whisked away, like a little girl on Christmas morning.

"What in the world?" I said.

Underneath the newsprint was a hunk of rounded wood, as smooth as a butcher's block. I pulled it out and set it on the counter. The curved wood looked like a ball chopped in half. If I didn't know better, I'd have sworn it was a doorstop or something similar. But I knew better.

"What do you know?" I flipped the dome over and found a small cross etched into the grain and another one across from it.

Vernice leaned forward to get a better look. "What is it?"

"Watch." I tilted the block toward her so she could see underneath. "See those marks?" I waited for her to nod. "Those marks tell hat makers where to find the center front and center back on a block like this. When they lay fabric over a block—we call the stuff we use *buckram*—they know where to place it."

She pursed her lips. "Hmm, I thought it was something for a cook. Maybe to make pie crusts or something."

"Oh, no. These antique hat blocks are very expensive and they're hard to find. They cost thousands of dollars. Usually people walk right by them in antique stores because they don't know what they are." I held the dome up to the bluish light to admire its size and shape. The craftsman had lovingly worked it over with a lathe until the grain was as smooth as ice.

Vernice peered into the box again. "Wait, I think there's more."

I joined her and saw two more bulges. It was like finding several toys in a Christmas present when I expected only one.

"Oh, my." Carefully, I withdrew the second one, which was half the size of the first and cut straight across its top. "Look. This one's for a porkpie hat."

She took a step back. "Okay, now you've totally lost me."

"These are different hat blocks. The first was used to make a hat with a domed crown. Try to imagine those old-time pictures of ladies riding sidesaddle and wearing black felt hats. That's how a milliner would shape it. And this one would be used to make something called a *porkpie*. See how it's cut straight across and shaped like a fat pie? Ladies wore porkpies in daytime because they weren't as fancy."

Laying the second treasure by the first, I knew what I'd find at the bottom of the box. I reached in again. "All that's missing is a brim block to shape a huge brim on a sunbonnet." I smiled when I saw it. The final block was shaped like a large salad bowl turned upside down. "I was right!"

"How did you do that?"

I waved away her awe. "Don't be too impressed. They only had a few hat styles back then. Women couldn't get new hats during the Civil War, since the Union put up blockades."

"But who sent them? They arrived before I got back from the church."

I shrugged. "That's a good question. Who around here knows I make hats, and who would give me something so expensive?"

"Maybe this will tell us." Vernice withdrew a single sheet of stationery from the box and held it up for me. It was cream, with a beveled edge and the monogram *IS* engraved at the bottom. "Do you want me to read it?"

"Of course. Hurry up. The suspense is killing me."

She cleared her throat. "*Please accept this gift. It's the only way I knew to thank you. For everything. They belonged to Belle Boyd, a lady who did brave things like you. Your friend forever, Ivy.*"

She stared at the card when she finished.

"That's so nice," I said. "I'll put them in my shop so everyone can see them. I don't quite know who that Boyd person is, but I'm sure there's a story there."

Vernice held onto the card delicately, as if it were made of gold. "Oh, my. Belle Boyd was a spy during the Civil War. A hero around here. She almost died several times. Women didn't do things like that back then."

"What do you know?" I studied the three wooden forms on the counter. They seemed even more beautiful now and the wood glowed under the fluorescent lights. "That's about the nicest thing anyone's ever done for me."

The day had been so surprising. Too bad I couldn't accept such a special gift. "Let's pack them up again. You can take the box with you when you go to Morningside tomorrow."

Vernice's mouth had fallen open. "Why? You said yourself these things cost thousands of dollars. You could sell them on eBay or take them to an antique store. Think about it."

"No way. They belong in a museum, not in my shop. I love the gesture, but I can't keep something that means so much to the people around here."

"You sure?"

"Definitely. I'll write Ivy a nice, long letter and explain, but treasures like this belong in a museum. They're part of the history of this place." I began to tuck the forms back in the box.

Ivy's gesture had warmed my heart, and the treasures looked radiant by the time I closed the lid.

Chapter 17

My room at the Sleepy Bye Inn didn't seem nearly as dingy the next morning when I awoke. Rays of sunlight splayed across the brown bedspread and softened everything to beige.

I'd slept like a rock. Even better than my nights in the Eugenia Andrews room at Morningside, because now we all knew who killed Trinity.

I rolled over. The carpet on either side of me looked cleaner with sunshine to brighten the shadows and chase away thoughts of bedbugs underfoot. My skirt and top lay at the foot of the bed, where I'd tossed them last night. A program rested next to the door, and the buzz from the Coke machine outside seeped through the walls.

A moment later someone was knocking on my door.

"Who is it?" I yelled.

"Santa Claus."

"Hilarious, Ambrose. What are you doing at my door at this ungodly hour? Go away, please."

"C'mon, Missy. Open up. I brought you a gift and everything."

I smiled and then rolled off the bed and padded over to the door. "I shouldn't let you in. Not before I've had a chance to change and run a comb through my hair."

"Will it make a difference?"

"Ha, ha." That was what I loved about Ambrose. No matter how much grief I gave him—and heaven knows I tried—he served it right back to me.

"All right," I said. "But don't say I didn't warn you."

I opened the door. Ambrose was standing on the stoop with a steaming cup of coffee.

This man knows me too well.

"You look a fright."

"And that coffee looks wonderful. Just what I need. You can come in since you're bearing gifts."

"That's my Missy." He stepped into the room and offered me the cup. I didn't know which of the two I was happier to see: my sweet Ambrose or the coffee.

"Careful, now. It's hot."

"Ambrose, you spoil me." I took the cup.

"We've had a time this weekend, haven't we?" He settled onto the edge of the bed. "Never thought we'd walk into a murder scene this weekend."

"Agreed." Funny, but the sight of Ambrose lounging on a corner of my bedspread seemed about as natural as the sunbeams that danced across it. More natural, in fact. "To be honest, I thought the most exciting thing I'd do was get a facial or maybe swim a few laps in the pool."

"You still can, you know. I got a call from Morningside while you were asleep. Beatrice invited us to come back for breakfast if we want."

"That so?" I took a hearty drink from the cup. Hang the chances of another caffeine overload, like the night I overindulged and ran into Wyatt Burkett in the hall. "Let me finish this and we can hop to it. I need to stop by the office too and write Vernice a note, so she knows I didn't forget about her this morning."

Once I finished the coffee, Ambrose left the room so I could dress. By all rights, I should have been dead tired, but the thought of sitting down to breakfast with Ambrose in the elegant restaurant gave me energy I didn't know I had.

We left the motel soon after—after dropping a note by the manager's office and scooping up the gift I wanted to return to Ivy—and drove to Morningside. The mansion seemed as grand as ever and not the least bit ominous now.

But, for some reason, I no longer wanted to be the lady of the house with a parasol as we climbed the staircase. Maybe because it was true what they said about the grass being greener. Right now I only wanted my little apartment back in Bleu Bayou, with its one bedroom and tiny kitchen, not to mention neighbors next door.

We walked down the hall to the dining room, where someone else stood at the maître d' stand. Charles had probably returned to LSU for his morning classes. Amazing to think that soon Mr. Solomon would buy the hotel and everyone would be replaced. I couldn't imagine Morningside without Beatrice to lead tours through the golden ballroom, or Darryl to sneak up on people in the gardens or Charles to roll up silverware all nice and tight in the dining room. Would it even be the same place without the people who made up its heart and soul?

The new person seemed capable enough, though, as she briskly led us to my favorite table by the picture window.

"Care for some water?" The girl lifted a pewter pitcher from the table next to ours.

"Yes, please," I said. "So, is Charles back at school?"

"I don't know." She began to pour without missing a beat.

"Charles waited on us this weekend. The nicest guy you ever did meet."

"Someone told me all the waiters who were here before planned to go into business together. Think they want to start a waitstaff service to work at the banquets around here. They even have a contract with the Hollyhock Plantation down the road."

"A group of banquet servers for hire? That's a great idea."

She returned the pitcher to the other table. "They're supposed to work at weddings and parties. Maybe funerals too. Do you both want the breakfast buffet this morning?"

"That depends." Ambrose had finally shifted his attention away from the magnificent view. "What's on it?"

"Fresh fruit, country breads, and pastries for the cold offerings. For the hot, we have quiche Lorraine, scrambled eggs, and low-country steak."

"That sounds fine to me," he said. "Missy?"

"Me too. By the way, I'm Melissa DuBois. What's your name?"

The girl flinched. "You can call me Cynthia." She retreated from us so stiffly she reminded me of a toy soldier wound too tight.

"She didn't seem very friendly," I said. "What's the harm in sharing your name?"

"Maybe she doesn't like it. Let's go get some breakfast while there's still some to be had."

I rose and followed him to a long table filled with chafing dishes, ewers of orange juice prettied up with some fresh-cut fruit slices and whatnot. Once we'd taken a bit of this and a bit of that, we returned to our table to find our waitress had gotten there ahead of us.

"Can I get you two anything else?" she asked.

"Got any ketchup for the steak?" Ambrose asked.

"Oh, Bo!" Of all the things to ask for in a fancy restaurant. I almost pinched him on the arm, but I didn't want him to drop his plate. Our waitress didn't seem to mind, because she whooshed away from our table to hunt down some sauce from the kitchen.

"Hope you haven't insulted the chef," I said.

"I'm sure they don't mind. You know it's how I like my steak."

Luckily, no one ran out of the kitchen hollering for Ambrose's head on a platter, and I went back to eating my quiche in delicate bites. When the waitress returned, the water pitcher was gone, replaced by a brand-new bottle of Heinz.

"Here you go, sir." She dropped the bottle on our table as if it were hot to the touch. "And how's your quiche?"

"Couldn't be better. Thank you, Cynth—" I stopped short, remembering her hesitation earlier. "As a matter of fact . . . I'd love to get the recipe if you have a chance."

"I can do better than that. Let me get the chef out here for you."

"Oh, no. I don't think she'll want to be disturbed." And I didn't want the chef to see a dripping bottle of ketchup on our table.

"Nonsense," Cynthia said. "She's only filling in here. Normally she works as a caterer."

Before I could stop her, she stalked away, determined to drag the poor chef out of the kitchen. At least it gave me time to swipe the bottle of ketchup and tuck it under my chair.

"Imagine that!" I said. "The chef owns a catering company, so she must work at all of the fancy shindigs around here."

A moment later the girl returned. She led someone in a chef's toque as tall as a wedding cake. When she stepped aside, I almost fell out of my chair backward.

"Why, Odilia LaPorte! Shut my mouth and call me Shirley."

"How was your meal, ma'am?" Mrs. LaPorte grinned like the cat that up and swallowed the canary.

"What in the world are you doing here?" I asked.

"Didn't I tell you? The hotel asked me to work part-time until they hire someone. Must'a heard about my catering business. Just hope I can live up to my reputation."

I decided to play along, since everything she'd said made perfect sense to me. "Well, ma'am, in that case . . . our meal was wonderful. Perfect, as a matter of fact."

"Perfect." She repeated the word, obviously pleased. "And how was yours, sir?"

"Real good. Just the way I like it."

"I like ketchup on my steak too." She winked at me.

I'd completely forgotten about that! No doubt Ambrose would tease me all the way home, but it was a small price to pay to see Odilia LaPorte wearing a chef's toque, a professional apron, and a big grin.

"Mr. Jackson?" The prickly waitress—Cynthia—had disappeared once we began to talk, but now she reappeared.

"Yes?" Ambrose asked.

"The night shift took a message for you. It's waiting for you at the front desk."

"Lord only knows what it could be." He sighed and pushed his chair away from the table. "What's that saying of yours, Missy? It's never nothin', always somethin'? Guess that pretty much says it all."

The minute Ambrose left, Odilia began to tell me about her catering business. So many people had booked weddings, funerals, birthday parties, and whatnot at the old mansions in the area, which only opened for special events, that she was completely booked until fall. Which pleased me to no end; although I hoped she'd set aside a little time for us now we'd gotten reacquainted.

"Are you headed back to town?" she asked.

"'Fraid so. We've only been gone since Friday and already Ambrose's assistant has called him more times than I can count."

"No matter what, let's book a time for us to get together. I might even give you my recipe for quiche Lorraine, if you say *please*." She turned away reluctantly, since we both knew it was time for her to go. "You stay in touch, now. Don't make me wait for my son to tell me you're here."

We hugged and the smell of sifted flour, cinnamon cloves, and clean cotton wafted from her apron. The minute she left, Ambrose reappeared. He wore a sly smile I couldn't quite place.

"Missy, you are *not* gonna believe this."

"Try me." After everything that had happened, nothing he said could surprise me now.

"It was the Hollyhock Plantation down the road. Someone decided to renew their vows next weekend and they forgot all about the clothes until now. They saw our web sites on the Internet, and my assistant told them we were staying here. Course I said no."

Nothing could surprise me, except for that. "Why in the world would you say *no*?"

"Let's see." Ambrose waggled his fingers, prepared to count down at least ten reasons. "First of all, it's a miracle you didn't faint when you ran into Wyatt in the hall." Down went his thumb. "Then, we all know you could've gotten yourself killed when you hunted down Cat like that." Sure enough, his index finger folded next. "Third—"

"Okay, okay. I get it." As a matter of fact, I had some numbers of my own to recite. "How about this?" I pointed my index finger straight at him. "Maybe—just maybe—we could finally have a relaxing weekend. That's all I ever wanted. And here you go and turn down a perfectly good invitation. All on account of one or two little hiccups."

He chuckled. "You sure about this?"

"Of course I'm sure. The way I see it, what could possibly go wrong if we come back to the Great River Road?"

Please turn the page for an exciting sneak peek at

Sandra Bretting's next Missy DuBois mystery

SOMETHING FOUL AT SWEETWATER

coming in December 2016!

Chapter 1

Heaven only knows I should have brought back a tote sack full of beignets that day like I'd planned, and *not* a sales flyer for the old Sweetwater mansion down the road.

But how could I resist something so full up on Southern charm first thing in the morning? Especially when I rounded the last curve before Dippin' Donuts and saw a *For Sale* sign waving at me from the property's front lawn like a friendly neighbor saying *hey*.

I swerved off the road, my tires spitting pea gravel and chalk dust, for a better look. Ever since I moved to Louisiana to open a hat shop, about a year and a half ago now, I'd been mesmerized by the antebellum mansions that seemed to sprout from the soil here every so often, like elegant daylilies planted in the sugarcane fields by mistake.

This particular mansion sat high on a hill. Two regiments of live oaks lined the front walk, their limbs bearded in wispy Spanish moss and their branches arching until the boughs touched. Beyond this leafy keyhole sat the mansion, which was held aloft by at least half-a-dozen alabaster columns. Bright August sun glanced off a column to the east, as if God had wanted to shine a spotlight there, while the rest of the pillars patiently awaited their turns.

Best of all, a Plexiglas box full of flyers rested against the *For Sale* sign. My granddaddy always did say it didn't cost nuthin' to look, so I scrambled out of my VW and retrieved a flyer, which was written in fancy cursive type: *Historic mansion for sale. Built in 1850. Jewel in the rough!*

This was all well and good, but not the most important thing. I found *that* two paragraphs later: *Owners willing to finance. Asking price: $250,000.*

Well, that can't be right. A house this grand—surely on the National Register of Historic Places and surely as pretty inside as out—should go for double or triple that amount. A builder would kill for the columns alone, not to mention the expensive iron railing that curled along a widow's walk on high.

Between all that and a wide plank veranda that circled the ground floor like a hoop skirt, I figured the flyer must be lying.

Ambrose needed to see this. Given my best friend was already at his design studio and waiting for me to bring him some beignets, though, I'd have to choose my words carefully and not go running off at the mouth. I dialed his cell and patiently waited through a few rings.

"Hi, Missy. What's wrong?"

Unfortunately, that's the greeting you got when you've called your best friend so early on a Monday morning. "Nothing's wrong. Any chance you're up for a little drive?"

"Why?" A suspicious pause. "You didn't run out of gas again, did you?"

"No, nothing like that. I was driving along, minding my p's and q's, when I saw that old mansion on the road to the doughnut store. You remember the one? Only now it's got a *For Sale* sign in the front yard, and I'm pretty sure it's a sign from heaven."

His sigh said more than any words could. "Missy, everyone knows those old houses eat money. Best thing you can do is walk away."

That was my Ambrose—practical to a T. Whereas, I believed that more was more and never less, Ambrose was of a different mind. Bless his heart.

In Bo's defense, he couldn't see the forest-green shutters that bookended perfectly spaced windows or the attic dormers that gazed over the manicured lawn with obvious approval or how the whole shebang culminated in an actual widow's walk. Breathtaking, it was. Simply breathtaking.

"That's the thing." I added my own pause for special effect. "The price is right here on the flyer. Could be a typo, but it's a sight less than what they charge for new houses around here."

"Missy." Out came the voice he used when he tried to protect me from myself. "Think about it. Do you know how much it'd cost to cool a place like that all summer?"

"No." I hadn't even considered the more practical matters, like air-conditioning or heaters or keeping the grass green. "Wait a minute. Someone walked out on the front porch. Wonder if they'll let me in?"

"Missy—"

"Gotta run. Meet me back at the rent house," I said.

Ambrose and I shared what the locals called a "rent house" down the road, although one day I hoped we'd share a whole lot more. I tucked the cell into my skirt pocket and hurried up the lawn. "You-hoo! You there."

The stranger froze. Judging by the crook of her pale neck and the wispy ponytail she'd feathered over one shoulder—which happened to remind me of the silvered moss—the old gal was about eighty or so.

"Are you the owner?" My voice boomed in the morning quiet, but I didn't want the stranger to hightail it back inside before we could speak. "I see it's for sale. I'm renting a house down the road with my best friend, and I've driven by your property a thousand times."

I was rambling, but by this time, it'd be plum rude of her not to acknowledge me. That was why what happened next startled me so. Instead of giving me a proper greeting and ushering me inside the house, like any good Southerner would do, this old gal turned tail and ran back through the door lickety-split, as if I'd waved a Smith & Wesson high in the air and not a real-estate flyer.

Well, I never. Southern hospitality, my foot!

I stalked to the front door and began to knock, since I never did truck with bad manners. It swung open after a moment, but only because it was manned by someone new. This woman looked to be about my age, or as I liked to say, on the north side of thirty, and she wore a frothy green business suit with matching shoes. Her face seemed vaguely familiar.

"I'm sorry about Ruby," she said.

"I should hope so." It wasn't this woman's fault I'd run into the rudest person I'd yet to meet in Louisiana, but the old gal had wounded my pride. "I only want to peek inside."

"Of course you do. Come on in."

The stranger waved me in, which caused a tangle of bracelets on her wrist to jingle like wind chimes. "Sorry again about Ruby."

The sting of the slight faded, though, the minute I walked through the front door. Hardwood floors glimmered beneath my feet like still water on a bayou and the walls wore rich panels of striated mahogany. A needlepoint tapestry of herons two-stepping somewhere in the Gulf covered an entire wall, the gentle S curve of the birds' necks like a wavy line of sea foam.

"It's so beautiful!" I said.

"The house was built in 1850. That's before the Civil War."

Slowly, my eyes adjusted to the dim light. "I know all about these old mansions."

I'd been hired to work for a bride at one of them some six months back. Unfortunately, I ended up smack-dab in the middle of a crime-scene investigation before everything got put to rights again, but I ended up loving the mansion even so.

Now small details began to emerge from the furnishings around me. Bits of silk dangled from the tapestry's hem like marsh grass, the baseboards beneath it wore decades of scuff marks, and even the front door didn't quite meet up with its frame. *No matter.*

"A wedding planner hired me for a ceremony at Morningside Plantation," I said. "Course this mansion's a lot smaller, but that's just as well. I never thought people actually sold these old houses."

"Well, you're lucky. This one's owned by a trust and they're in a hurry to get rid of it. Are you interested? I'm the Realtor here. Name's Mellette. Mellette Babineaux."

She thrust out her hand, which set off the bracelets again and also called up the smell of menthol cigarettes.

"Why . . . I know you." I shook her hand, amazed to meet some-one from my past right here in Louisiana. "I'm Missy DuBois. You went to Vanderbilt, right?"

"I did indeed. Thank goodness for those academic scholarships."

"But you were in a sorority too," I said. "Weren't you the chapter president of Pi Phi? I was a coupla years behind you."

She seemed pleased to be recognized. "Ain't that the berries! We're sorority sisters. My godmother paid for that, hallelujah."

"Do you ever get back to Nashville?" I asked.

"'Fraid not. Work keeps me too busy. You?"

"The same. I still have T-shirts from the parties, though. Boxes and boxes of them. Can't quite make myself toss 'em in the garbage."

She smiled wistfully. "I only bought a few. What did you say your name is again?"

"Missy. Missy DuBois. I moved to town about a year and a half ago."

Her eyes widened. "Are you the gal who opened a hat shop in

town? People told me that store wouldn't last more than six months, but look at you! It's been a sight longer and it seems to be going great guns. Amazing we haven't met up before now."

"Well, not to brag, but Crowning Glory turned a year old at Christmas." Which felt wonderful to be able to say. When I found out Southern plantations all along the Great River Road attracted brides like flies to honey, I set myself up making hats, veils, and whatnot for wedding parties. Ambrose owned a shop next to mine, only he made custom gowns for brides and their maids.

"You're gonna make us all proud," she said. "Maybe you could speak to our alumnae group sometime. We meet once a month at the Junior League."

I was about to respond when the older woman who'd been so rude to me earlier emerged from the shadows.

"There you are," Mellette said. "Ruby here is the caretaker. Unfortunately, today's Monday. You know what that means, don't you?"

I racked my brain, but came up empty. "Can't say that I do."

"It's bad luck to be visited by a woman first thing on Monday morning," she said. "In some parts of the bayou, that is. Silly superstition, if you ask me. As if that would make a difference."

Ruby quickly cut her eyes at Mellette. "Ya bes' not be sayin' dat, madam."

Why, I'd know a Cajun accent anywhere. I'd met a gardener at that wedding a few months back who stretched out his vowels like this old gal.

"You must be Cajun," I said. "French Creole, right?"

"Born in des parish."

Before I could speak again, Mellette turned.

"Where are my manners? Ruby, go get our guest some sweet tea. This humidity is going to be the death of us all. Guess we should expect as much come August."

When Ruby didn't hop to it, Mellette's smile hardened. "Today, preferably."

That made the old woman finally back away, but not before she scowled at the Realtor.

"That one's a pill," Mellette said, once Ruby was gone. "Wouldn't be surprised if she's got a voodoo doll back at her house that looks exactly like me. Bless her heart. Now, let's start in the drawing room and we'll work our way up."

I followed along as the Realtor led me from one room to the next. The rooms were small by today's standards and desperate for some fresh paint and spackle, but other than that, I couldn't see any major flaws. And thick crown molding covered the walls, not to mention cut-crystal wall sconces reflected light onto them like dusty diamonds.

"I have to ask." I couldn't hold my tongue any longer. "Why the low price? It should go for double or triple that amount."

"There's a bit of work to be done." Mellette shrugged. "And there's been some talk about voodoo ceremonies or some such. Not that this particular mansion had slaves, mind you, because it didn't."

Funny she felt the need to answer a question I hadn't even asked. After a bit, we wandered back to the staircase, where Ruby stood with a tumbler of sweet tea.

"That voodoo's all nonsense. Right, Ruby?" she asked.

"If'n ya say so." Ruby handed me the sweating tumbler. "Nobody be doin' dat stuff 'round here no more."

"Well, that's good." I accepted the tumbler and took a sip. Just the way I liked it . . . sweet as honeysuckle. "Although it's hard to imagine why they'd pick somewhere so pretty to do it in the first place."

"Da place don' much matter, missus. It's all in da charms. Wot ya can do wit' da amulets an such."

"Ruby, you know that's a bunch of hooey," Mellette said. "Let's not give Missy here any crazy ideas, okay?"

It's a little too late for that. "So, when's the last time they had one of those voodoo things around here?" I asked.

"Years. Decades." Mellette tried to sound nonchalant, but her pinched face gave her away. "The house has been vacant for many years now. That's why the trust is selling it. They know it needs work, but the heirs don't want to keep it, so it's ripe for the picking. Did I mention there's even a studio out back?"

"You don't say." I followed her gaze to the window. "What kind of studio?"

"Look." She pointed to a whitewashed cottage that lay just beyond the glass. Pink swamp roses ambled over a pitched roofline and purple verbena ran wild through an abandoned vegetable bed meant to hold carrots or cabbage. I fully expected seven dwarfs to emerge from the bottom of the Dutch door with pickaxes slung over their shoulders.

"It's a great place for someone to work on projects," Mellette said. "There are sweet little hidey-holes like that all over this place."

My heavenly days. The cottage would be perfect for a design studio! Even though the roof sagged some and the door was all catawampus, I could block and stitch and steam hats out there to my heart's content.

"Yep, imagine all the privacy you'd have," she added.

"You can say that again! But I need to talk to my best friend first. Maybe bring him out here for a tour. I trust his opinion on everything."

"Fine by me," she said. "But I suggest you get a move on if you want this place. Someone's bound to come along and scoop it up."

No doubt she was right. Places like this only came along but once in a blue moon. Maybe I could convince Ambrose to come over and tour the house with me and then I could bend his ear about all the wonderful ways we'd renovate it.

Although the morning had gotten off to a sour start, something great might come of it yet.

Chapter 2

If the way to a man's heart was through his stomach, then everything I needed were in a greasy bag of beignets I'd placed on the car seat next to me. One taste of that powdered sugar and *choux* paste and Ambrose would say *yes* to anything I proposed. Even to buying a derelict mansion so we could renovate it side by side.

My VW pitched and rumbled on the journey home, the sack of beignets bouncing along. Compared to Sweetwater, the little rent house we shared up ahead looked tiny.

Tiny, but quaint. It had bubblegum-pink walls and a used brick fireplace, and it reminded me of something Barbie would own if she and Ken ever settled in the deep South. Best of all, I'd planted bee balm next to the front gate when we first moved in, and now hummingbirds and butterflies flitted around the place in abundance. I passed several as I made my way through the gate and into the house.

I slowed as I approached the kitchen. Here sunshine warmed the buttercream yellow walls and splashed across a farmhouse table that went back two generations. That was where I found Ambrose, hunched over a plate of scrambled eggs and Jimmy Dean sausage.

"Look at you," I said. "And here I thought you'd starve to death."

His knife clattered onto the plate. "Hey, there. Where've you been? I thought we'd meet up an hour ago."

Today he wore my favorite polo; the lapis one that brought out his eyes. As we said down South, "I can't-never-could resist a man with long eyelashes," and his reminded me of Bambi's.

"Here's the thing," I said. Our farmhouse table had benches instead of chairs, so I plopped down next to him and laid the beignets between us. "I got to tour the Sweetwater mansion with a Realtor. Boy, did I learn a thing or two."

"That so?" To be honest, his beautiful eyes kept leaving my face to scope out the oily sack on the table.

"It goes all the way back before the Civil War," I said. "Turns out a trust owns it, and they're looking to sell cheap. Do you know they only want two hundred and fifty thousand dollars for it? Never in my life did I think a house like that could be so inexpensive."

"Does it have a roof?"

I shot him a look. "Of course it has a roof. You've seen it. And real hardwood floors on the inside. Looked like mahogany to me. Point is, someone could fix up that place like nobody's business if they had half a mind to do it."

"So it's falling down, right? Maybe that's why they don't want very much for it. Sounds like a lot of maintenance to me."

If there was one thing my Ambrose was allergic to, it was maintenance. Didn't much matter if it involved our shops back in town, this old rent house, or his brand-new Audi Quattro. He had a hard time looking beyond the elbow grease. Whereas I was the exact opposite. Give me a paint brush, a rotary sander, and a crescent wrench, and I was happier than a dead pig in the sunshine.

"But you've always told me it's good to have a hobby," I said. "This is something we can do together, now that our businesses have taken off."

What a relief to be able to say that. Ambrose and I had both arrived in Bleu Bayou with nothing more than our designer look-books and our desire to bring high fashion down to the South. Course, Ambrose also needed a fresh start, since his college sweetheart, a pretty catalogue model, had passed away from breast cancer a few years before.

Now we owned side-by-side design studios, where a stream of brides kept us up to our elbows in netting, silk flowers and, thankfully, sales receipts.

"Yeah," he said, "but I was thinking maybe we could try line dancing or fly-fishing. Or go off-roading in the bayous. Not renovate an old mansion. I thought those stayed in families, anyway. Why'd this one come up on the market?"

"Beats me. But it's owned by a trust and they want to sell it right quick. That's what the Realtor told me. We could do it together. C'mon, Bo."

He didn't look convinced, so I reached into the sack and pulled out a doughnut. "Beignet?"

He finally smiled. "Now, don't think I'm gonna agree with you because you brought home-fried fritters." He accepted the powdery offering. "I have half a mind to tell you no."

Hallelujah. That meant the other half was as good as mine. "It couldn't hurt to look around the place," I said. "I even know the Realtor. Turns out she went to Vanderbilt too. We can head on over there, poke around, and maybe test the plumbing. Aren't you curious to see what it looks like on the inside?"

"Well, now that you mention it—"

He never could tell me *no.* I planted a big, wet kiss on his cheek to show my gratitude. "I'll grab the car keys while you finish up here. You're gonna love it. I know you will."

The road to Sweetwater seemed busier now. Contractor pickups, windowless work vans, and Marathon Oil tanker trucks cruised alongside us. Once I spied the old Sweetwater mansion, I pulled over nice and easy, so as not to scatter the pea gravel.

Ambrose's eyes widened when he realized where we were.

"This is the place you're talking about?" he asked. "It's enormous! But I have to hand it to you, it's a good-looking house."

"I knew you'd think that. And it's not so big when you get inside. It's the columns make it look that way. C'mon."

I hopped out of the VW. Now that we'd hit August, humidity settled over me like a wet bedsheet, so I twisted my long hair into a bun and poked the stray ends in nice and tight.

My plan had been to march straightaway up the lawn and rap on the door—hang the chances of running into that Ruby again—but something looked different.

An expensive sedan sat near the kitchen now. The car's enormous hood fanned across the space and a gleaming chrome bumper shielded its tires. Oddly enough, I'd seen it somewhere before.

"Wonder who's here?" Ambrose asked. "The owner?"

"I told you, it's owned by a trust, and I don't think the heirs live here. But I've seen that car before." A pair of interlocking R's on the hood jogged my memory. "Why, it's Mr. Solomon's Rolls-Royce. Wonder what he's doing here?"

Herbert Solomon had hired Ambrose and me back in May to design his daughter's wedding apparel. He'd booked Morningside Plantation down the road—now a gorgeous hotel—and even commissioned the Baton Rouge Symphony Orchestra to play "Here Comes the Bride" on the front lawn.

Unfortunately, his daughter was murdered right before the big event. People still bragged on me for helping the Louisiana State Police solve that crime, although any law-abiding citizen would have done the same.

"C'mon, Bo. Let's go say hello to him."

The front door blew open the minute we started up the lawn. Herbert Solomon barreled through the entry, looking the same as always: a deep scowl, a bulging briefcase, and an expensive business suit, even on a warm day like today.

I panicked and hopped in front of the *For Sale* sign. The last thing I needed was to enter a bidding war with Herbert Solomon over this property. He'd already bought Morningside Plantation and everyone knew he could afford to buy this place with his pocket change.

He began to trek down the lawn, the designer briefcase slapping his leg with each step, until he reached me. "Well, well. This is a surprise, Miss DuBois." He nodded at Ambrose. "Mr. Jackson."

"I could say the same." Although I hadn't seen him since his daughter's wedding, I'd often thought about his wife, Ivy. While Herbert Solomon was brash and overbearing, Ivy was sweeter than the tea I'd had earlier. Shame on me for not paying her a visit before this. "How's Ivy doing?"

"She's holding up," he said. "Some weeks are better than others."

"Please tell her I'm thinking about her. I'll have to pay her a visit soon."

He grimaced. "It might not be easy. She spends all of her time at the Mall of Louisiana, I'm afraid. But I'll tell her. Hello, Ambrose."

"Nice to see you, Mr. Solomon."

"Whatever brings you out here this morning?" I asked. The briefcase in his hand seemed obvious enough, but I hoped I was wrong.

"Business, same as always."

"You're not thinking of buying this dinky place, are you?" My heart stilled at the very thought.

"Haven't decided," he said. "My other property's working out pretty good. It's booked all summer, as a matter of fact. Thought I might be able to work out a deal here."

"But this one's so much smaller than Morningside." I tried to keep my voice level. "And not nearly as grand. Don't those brides expect the world these days?"

He shot me a funny look. "I guess so. What are *you* doing here?"

"Nothing. Curious, more than anything else."

"You're wasting your time," he said. "I couldn't find the Realtor. That person should be fired, if you ask me."

"That's too bad. But I think we'll poke around anyway. Ambrose has never seen the inside."

"I told you, you're wasting your time. But suit yourself." He gave a brusque wave. "Good day, Miss DuBois. Mr. Jackson."

He strode over to the Rolls while I hovered protectively by the *For Sale* sign. I stayed there until he fired up the car and drove off the property.

"That's not good," Ambrose said, once he'd left.

"Tell me about it. If he wants to turn this place into another hotel, we're doomed."

"Don't jump the gun, Missy. I haven't even seen the inside of it yet."

Which was true enough. I finally abandoned my post and headed for the front door. Apparently, Mr. Solomon hadn't bothered to shut the thing properly, and it stood open a half inch.

I shouldn't, should I? Somehow I never could resist the lure of an open door, and my eyes widened at the thought of all those secrets begging to be discovered. Begging, I tell you. My hand reached for the doorknob.

"Why don't we knock?" It was Ambrose, standing behind me.

Leave it to him to always do the right thing. "You heard him . . . the Realtor's gone. We could always peek around a little before she comes back. Doesn't cost nuthin' to look."

"Seems to me—"

I gave in to temptation before Ambrose could finish his sentence and pushed open the door. Like before, sunlight glanced off the hardwoods and made them shine like that still water on a bayou.

Ambrose whistled. "Look at that. Mahogany."

"That's nothin'. Follow me."

I tiptoed into the foyer as quiet as a church mouse. I didn't mean to intrude, but I wanted to gauge Ambrose's reaction to all of that glorious wood paneling.

"Wow!" He turned round and round like a little boy in a funhouse. "This is something."

"I knew you'd like it."

"Look at that crown molding. That's at least four inches thick."

"You haven't seen anything yet. C'mon." Since Ruby could emerge from the shadows at any minute and cut her eyes at me, I hustled Ambrose through the foyer and into the dining room. Here the wallpaper bloomed with fading magnolias, and chipped dinner plates adorned an antique dining table.

"See what I mean?" I said. "All it needs is a little work to put it right again. And look out there." I pointed to the kitchen garden, like Mellette had done.

"What's that?"

"A studio," I said. "Can you imagine me out there working on my hats? Think about it, Bo. I could turn it into a showroom, and you could have this dining room. We wouldn't have to write rent checks anymore."

"It's something to think about." He glanced nervously toward the foyer. "Maybe we should come back later. I have lots of questions for the Realtor. And then she can show us the second floor."

"Okay, if you say so." He was right, although I hated to admit it. "Let's take a peek at the studio on our way out, though."

We retraced our steps through the foyer, Ambrose's head still swiveling around like a child in a fun house. I let him walk ahead of me and made sure to close the front door extra tight on the way out. Wouldn't want someone to wander in off the street and traipse through the house all willy-nilly now, would we?

A pea-gravel path led around the house to the garden. By this time, sunshine kissed the Doric columns out back, and a chorus of cicadas practiced trills from inside an overgrown rosebush. We followed the path until it ended at the shed's Dutch door.

"This is where you'd work, huh?" Ambrose said.

The door's top half stood open, so I peeked over his shoulder to get a glimpse inside.

On the opposite wall sat a rusty metal shelf filled with broken pots, a few trowels, and leftover bags of fertilizer. A pile of towels or rags lay beneath a small window. The room seemed just large enough for a sturdy worktable and my collection of antique hat blocks; not to mention a display rack or two for my finished creations.

"It's perfect," I said. Tiny motes of dust swooped and swirled through the light of the window like drips falling from a garden hose.

"Looks to be about the right size." Ambrose inched open the door's lower half. "We could even put an awning between this cottage and the house for people to walk back and forth between our two studios."

I quickly moved around him and stepped into the cottage. The minute I entered, though, I noticed something unusual: the smell. Not a normal garden smell like mold or compost or rotting leaves . . . the room smelled like mint. A chemically mint odor, like the kind they used in menthol cigarettes.

I glanced around for the source. The pile I'd spied beneath the window turned out to be a rumpled green business suit and matching shoes.

It was Mellette Babineaux. Her feet splayed out at unnatural angles and her unseeing eyes stared straight ahead. My scream tore through the small space.

"Missy!" Ambrose rushed forward. "Call nine-one-one. Quick!"

But I couldn't move. My feet had become rooted to the ground. Several seconds—or were they minutes?—passed.

"Now!" he said.

That woke me. I whipped out my cell and dialed 911.

A voice answered before the second ring. "This is nine-one-one. What's your emergency?"

"There's been an accident at the old Sweetwater mansion. Not inside, but outside. We're in a shed. Come quick!"

"Slow down, ma'am." The woman sounded much too calm. "What's the address?"

"I don't know." A flash of memory brought me back to my conversation with Herbert Solomon, though. We'd stood on the front lawn not more than half an hour ago. "It's down the road from Morningside Plantation. That's the one they turned into a big hotel."

The dispatcher was silent, and then she rattled off an address for me to verify.

"That sounds about right," I said.

"And just who are you?"

"Missy DuBois. The gal is the Realtor here."

"Is she breathing?"

"I don't think so."

"Are you with the victim right now?"

Victim? I hadn't really thought about her as a victim. All I knew was that Mellette Babineaux—the one who'd toured me around the house not more than an hour ago—now lay puddled in a heap on a dirty cement floor. "Yes."

"I'm sending help. Keep your phone on you, you hear? Someone may call you back." With that, the line went dead.

I spun around. "They're coming."

"Good," Ambrose said. "Wait for them in the main house. It'll make it easier for them to find us."

I rushed to the Dutch door, anxious to put the sight of the limp body behind me. Quickly, I stumbled over the threshold and hurried down the gravel path.

All sound had disappeared. A cicada probably called to me from its rosebush as I ran by, and my heels no doubt churned through the pea gravel, but I heard none of it. The back door quietly swept open, my shoes floated over the hardwood floor, and I landed in the kitchen.

I paused to catch my breath. Truth be told, I was happy to leave the cottage. At least here I didn't have to look at Mellette and her ashen face. The legs splayed at unnatural angles. And dear Ambrose trying to keep his composure while my screams woke the dead two states away.

Since I still couldn't breathe, I began to look around. Above my head hung a pendant light with a hammered copper shade, its soft light illuminating a soapstone counter. Next to that was a farmhouse sink surrounded by a backsplash with dozens of tiny rose-colored tiles. Maybe if I focused on something else, I could catch my breath. I began to count the tiles from top to bottom. On the thirty-fifth tile, or thereabouts, a siren finally wailed in the distance.

Twelve more tiles and a police car arrived. Staccato bursts of light popped through the kitchen window in candy-cane colors when the cruiser pulled into the driveway. Someone opened and closed a car door before footsteps sounded on the stoop outside.

"In here," I yelled at the top of my lungs.

A man in a navy uniform appeared on the other side of the screen door. Short and Hispanic, he wore a crewcut and mirrored sunglasses. "Did you call?"

He looked like a teenager—all chubby caramel cheeks and black hair. Too young to be a police officer, let alone to carry a sidearm. "Yes, it was me." I pulled the cell out of my pocket and laid it on the counter. "I used my cell phone."

The officer entered the kitchen and whisked off his sunglasses. "Officer Hernandez. Second district. What's up?"

"My friend and I found someone in the shed outside not more than five minutes ago."

The officer pulled a notepad from his pocket, where I fully expected to see race cars doodled on the cover but, thankfully, it was blank. "Did you know the person?"

I nodded. "Yes. We went to college together a long time ago. Her name's Mellette Babineaux, and she's the Realtor for the property."

When he didn't react, I could tell he didn't know Mellette. Instead, he continued to jot notes while he carefully studied my face.

Someone explained to me once why policemen watch their witnesses so carefully while they speak. Apparently, if a witness glances left the officer knows she's relying on memory. The witness looks right, and it means she is lying. I purposefully stared straight ahead, since I had nothing to worry about.

"I wanted to show my friend the studio out back," I said. "That's where we found her."

More writing on his part. "I see. My partner is out there now. We'll start with that area and establish the chain of custody."

I nodded again. That was a term I was very familiar with, since I'd taken a couple of classes in police procedure as an undergrad at Vanderbilt. At one time I actually toyed with the idea of law school, until I took those classes and realized I'd rather spend my time with sketch pads than cops' notebooks or legal briefs.

"Did you see anything else unusual?" He finally lowered his eyes from my face.

"Now that you mention it, I did." Hadn't I been surprised to see Herbert Solomon's Rolls-Royce hulking outside the house earlier? The man lived in Baton Rouge, after all, which was almost two hours away. He didn't say anything about having an appointment with a Realtor, and that seemed a little strange.

"We ran into Herbert Solomon when we got here," I said. Even though he'd never met Mellette, odds were good he'd know about Louisiana's most famous billionaire.

"I've heard of 'im. So he was here too. Coming or going?"

"Going," I said. "Told me he couldn't find the Realtor here. Didn't even know if it was a guy or a gal."

"Did he seem upset?"

I thought back to our meeting on the lawn. "More mad than upset. I assumed he wanted to buy this place, only he couldn't find anyone to talk to."

"Anyone with him?"

"No, that was it. But I did meet someone on my first visit."

He squinted up at me. "First visit?"

"I'm interested in buying this place too. But I had to drag my friend along so he could see it for himself."

"So you met someone else, then?"

"Sure enough . . . a caretaker by the name of Ruby," I said. "Don't think she liked me, though."

"Why's that?"

I shrugged. "Apparently, it's bad voodoo to visit someone around here first thing on a Monday morning. If you're a woman, anyway. I'd never heard that before."

"You're not from around here, are you?" Officer Hernandez seemed surprised—or was he amused?—by my ignorance.

"No, I moved to town about a year and a half ago," I said. "I live down the road. Didn't even know the mansion was for sale until this morning."

"Tell me more about the caretaker."

"There's not a whole lot to say. She seemed to think they did voodoo ceremonies around here a while ago, or some-such thing. Said something about amulets and charms. Does that mean anything?"

Now it was his turn to shrug. "It could. We get strange stuff out here. Think that's enough for now. You'll be free to go in a minute."

"But aren't you going to ask me to come back with you to the station so you can write up my statement?" That's how they explained it back in those classes at Vanderbilt.

"Definitely. But we have to wrap up things here first. Get our report to Investigative Support Services. You can go, though. Do you have a ride home?"

"I drove over with my friend." That's when I remembered Ambrose. Poor thing was still trapped in the shed with Mellette's limp body and a police officer. "I'd better go find him."

I hastily said good-bye to the officer and stepped through the kitchen door. Somehow the sky seemed darker now than when we'd first arrived. I tiptoed along the garden path and met up with Ambrose about halfway down.

"Hi, Bo. Did they ask you a lot of questions too?"

"Sure did." Ambrose looked drained. "The guy seemed surprised I didn't know the lady lying on the floor right next to me. Once he got past that, though, he said I could go. Said something about you and me heading over to the police station later."

I nodded. "I know. By the way, was she—"

"Yes," he said. "She's dead." Ambrose stopped in the middle of the path, his eyes haunted. "But there's something else, Missy."

"What is it?"

"I saw something, back there in the shed. Something strange."

I laid my hand on his shoulder. "We found a dead body, Bo. Of course you saw something strange."

"No, it's not that." He shrugged my hand away. Whatever he'd seen, it'd shaken him to the core.

"Tell me. What's wrong?"

"Somebody left a cross back there. A black cross."

"Why would they do that?"

"I don't know. But there's more."

How could there be more? Already my legs felt like muscadine jelly and I longed to sit on a garden bench or a backyard swing or even an overturned bucket.

"There was something on the cross," he said. "Looked like blood to me. Fresh blood too."

"But that would mean . . ." I couldn't finish the sentence.

"Yeah," he said. "They must have killed her right before we got here."

I sagged forward, suddenly winded. Thankfully, Ambrose caught me and steadied me against his chest. Why, oh why, did we ever come back to Sweetwater Plantation?

We remained like that for several minutes, each of us lost in thought. Finally, some feeling returned to my legs, and I straightened.

"Whatever we do, Bo, we've got to find out what happened. Mellette Babineaux and I went to college together. Same sorority and everything."

"Okay." His eyes narrowed. "But only if we do it together. Promise me you won't go running off by yourself. I don't want you to get hurt."

"I promise." I raised my hand in the Boy Scout salute to prove it.

"The only question is . . . where do we start?" he asked.

"My granddaddy always said it's best to start at the beginning and keep going 'til you get to the end."

Of course, my dear granddaddy stole that line from a famous book about a girl and a White Rabbit, but that was neither here nor there at this point. Somehow, Ambrose and I had landed smack-dab in the middle of another crime scene. Time would only tell if we'd stumbled down a rabbit hole of our own.

Sandra Bretting has served as a freelance feature writer for the *Houston Chronicle* since moving to Texas in 1996. She received a journalism degree from the University of Missouri School of Journalism, and spent her early career in health-care public relations. She's also written for the *Los Angeles Times* and *Orange Coast Magazine*.

Bretting's previous mysteries include *Unholy Lies* (2012, Five Star Publishing) and *Bless the Dying* (2014, Five Star Publishing). Her short stories have appeared in *BorderSenses Literary Journal* (a publication of the University of Texas at El Paso) and several anthologies.

Readers can visit her website at www.sandrabretting.com